THE CEDARS OF LEBANON

A Novel

D. C. Zook

Published by Shantiwala Books
Cover design by James at GoOnWrite.com
ISBN: 1947609068
ISBN-13 (print): 9781947609068
ISBN-13 (E-book): 9781947609044

To R & S —Garantie à vie

ACTORS

1

In the distance I could see the mountains. Later, after everything I'm about to tell you was done and over, I would learn they were the Organ Mountains. But in that first moment I was too entranced by the play of reflected light on the etched and angular rock faces to care. The mountains seemed to embellish their own presence, to be something other than what they were, to hint at something they were not, as fire that was not fire, atop a desert reflecting water that was not water. This was an act of deception, a landscape that offered up a vision that was not itself, illuminated by colors that were not what they seemed.

In one moment, the play of color and light could only invoke the kind of faith that makes a person believe in things they will never understand. In the next, it betrays and erodes their most inspired convictions. Hope and wistfulness merged, and I felt nostalgia for things I had only once imagined. The whole scene professed an extravagance that would embarrass the humble of heart. It was a landscape that effortlessly seduced many a mythmaker and taleteller, driving them to madness in the search for words to describe what they already knew to be indescribable.

The rough, red-rock landscape was like a new planet after what seemed like an eternal drive across Texas. As I crossed into New Mexico, I felt something change. I had a sense of something different—a premonition perhaps, but I was also the sort of person who knew, or believed I knew, never to trust my feelings. I had a long history of getting into all sorts of trouble and coming to all sorts of grief for believing in things and trusting in signs that in the end proved to be nothing but sleight of hand tricks created out of coincidence, circumstance, and wanton chicanery.

I had always wanted to believe that things happen for a reason, but they don't. They just happen. Yet there I was in New Mexico, mesmerized by the shifting light on the mountains, and once again I felt the stirrings of hope and anticipation. I glanced in the rear view mirror, and had the intense suspicion that I was deceiving myself.

At the time, I was several days into a very long road trip that had started in New York City. Truth be told, it started in New Jersey, but I had a habit of telling people that I was from New York City because that was where I worked and for some reason I always sensed that people hesitated slightly whenever I said I lived in New Jersey. *You're from Jersey?* No one ever asked that of New Yorkers.

I had been working as a journalist and was slowly building what I thought was a career, at least something that had the appearance of one, when I got called out for certain inaccuracies—I prefer to call them enhancements—in a number of my stories. I had no idea that there were people who cared about whether a fire was five-alarm or two-alarm. The fire was hot, things got burned, and those details remained true, regardless of how many alarms had actually been sounded. And really, I said to my editor, how many stories appeared every day that didn't have a detail or two that had been stretched, distorted, manipulated, or otherwise invented? That didn't matter, said my editor. It didn't matter if the readers knew there was artifice in the stories. What they didn't want was to be made aware of it. There was a tacit agreement between the writer and the reader that turned fiction into fact: if readers had good reason to believe that something was true, then in their lives, it was true. People need to believe in things, they need to believe that certain things are true. It's what gives order to their lives—whether it's an illusion or not is irrelevant. But once you call attention to the illusion, faith is gone and it can rarely if ever be restored. What separates truth from fiction is that with fiction, the lie has been unveiled.

And so I left my job. Well, actually, I was fired. I think—I'm not really sure. I never said I quit and no one ever told me I was fired. One day I left and no one stopped me. I was neither here nor there, in my own private purgatory. Sitting in the moment I am in right now, as I write out these words, what happened next seems in my mind more like a movie I once saw about someone else's life than an actual moment of my own. I left the office, went home, and started packing things. Then, for reasons I only now understand, I was on the road for parts unknown, though in actuality they did not remain unknown for all that long.

I wanted to reinvent myself, to be born again into the person I had hoped to be the first time around. I could only think of one place where a person could do that—Los Angeles. Yes, I decided to head for the City of Angels, to leave Babylon behind and head to the Promised Land, based purely on my idea of what I thought California was, an idea based purely on what I had seen in movies or heard in stories that others had told me. The euphoria of heading to my new homeland stayed with me, as it does on almost all road trips, for about an hour. After that, I became acutely aware of just how much driving I had to do, and euphoria quickly gave way to ennui. All journeys are great when they start and great when they end. Everything in between is the struggle to come to terms with doubt, fear, and tedium.

Consider, for instance, the situation in which I found myself several days into my trip, as I was driving across Texas. Sure, when you first cross the state line you feel like you have arrived in the great vast land of the cowboy. You can feel, or you think you can feel, your dreams grow just a little as they expand to fill the space around you. Yet ten hours later, I found myself cursing Texas for going on much longer than a state should be allowed to go. A state really had no right to be that big. I yelled profanity out the window of my car, with no particular target other than the open space, of which there was simply far too much.

After the anger dissipates, of course, there is time for thoughtful reflection. I found myself drifting into imaginary conversations with people, such as my editor. Sure I enhanced the truth, I would explain, but a good truth always needs an even better story. All truths are embellished to some extent, and many truths are better truths for it. Why does a handsome man wear a well-tailored suit? Why does a beautiful woman wear make-up? You take something that is already fine as it is, and you make it a little better. In these imaginary conversations, I did not let me editor respond.

My father was a carpenter who wore nothing but overalls and strangely stained shirts six days of the week, and yet my mother always said she fell in love with him all over again every Sunday when he put on a tie to go to church. She used to call him *dreamy* when he dressed like that. Of course, my father did not go quietly into this transformation—he wore that tie for my mother, not for God. *God doesn't care what you wear but what you bear,* my father would say. To this day I have no idea what that means—not even the generous time afforded by the endless expanse of Texas could help with that—but something about it sounded like the sort of thing you should take to heart. I sometimes repeat my father's words to others, and they usually nod in approval, as if it must mean something profound. I found myself grinning on a long stretch of interstate under a bright blue Texas sky over the thought that there were at least a few people in the world who knew the words of my father, had believed them and committed them to memory, and yet like me still had no idea what they meant, even as they pretended they did.

It didn't help matters that the car I was driving, a 1963 Mercury Monterey, turned out to be a rather poorly informed choice for a cross-country expedition. In New York or New Jersey (or wherever you think I'm from), it made perfect sense—it was an accessory to my image, a projection of who I was, a part of my act, so to speak. The lack of any effective heating and a rather lethargic air conditioner only added to the allure, as did the retractable rear windshield that at some point stopped working, leaving a permanent one-inch gap that siphoned out most of the comfort and left in most of the misery.

In New York, that car was my image, my act—cool, cavalier, retro. Now it just felt sad. By the time I hit

Austin, I could tell that the Mercury was ailing. I found myself talking to the car and whispering little prayers for her to no one in particular, as if divine forces in the universe had an interest in the fate of my car's engine. *Come on, baby, just make it to Los Angeles,* I would say. After Austin, I said it more frequently, and with more urgency. The Mercury was trying to tell me something, but I was in no mood to hear its truth.

At the last place in Texas where I stopped to get gas, I could tell the Mercury was suffering. The car sputtered when I turned off the ignition, gasping for a full minute before it finally collapsed into exhaustion. After I filled up the gas tank, it took even longer for the car to come back to life. I cranked the engine several times, and for a moment it seemed like all was over. At one point I put my hand on the dashboard, as if to comfort the car and assure her that I needed this to happen, that it wasn't yet her time. The mechanic at the station stared at me in a way that gave the impression that he knew something I didn't, that he could see my fate and yet had no interest in telling me what it was. He was going to just let it all happen. It was very unsettling. Rude, in fact. If you know someone's fate you should tell them. And yet, in that moment, miracle of miracles, the Mercury came back to life, not without an enormous cloud of smoke that shot out the back like its own private thunderstorm, but it was resurrected nevertheless. If I could just make it out of Texas, I thought, everything would be fine. I convinced myself of this, and it was something that in that moment I came to believe. Or maybe it was something I had to believe. Either way, I felt a sense of comfort in believing it.

I made it out of Texas and entered the gates of the land of enchantment, New Mexico. I didn't think of it as particularly enchanting when I crossed the state line, but every license plate told me that this was indeed the land of enchantment, and I had no good reason not to believe it was so. This was certainly a strange, new land. Parched and arid tracts of desert gave way to lush, green valleys, with the unexpected appearance of apple orchards showing off their fruit in the relentlessly bright sun. The mountains seemed to recede a mile for every mile I drove, as if I were never getting any closer, as if space and time had suddenly stood still. Rock walls appeared here and there, like strange forms of writing across the vast textual landscape. The walls were old and dilapidated, stuck in some eternal moment between structure and ruin. None of them appeared to be more than knee-high. Even when I couldn't see them, I knew they were there, I just didn't know what they meant. Walls always have a reason.

Over the radio came the voice of Peter Gabriel. It was an unfamiliar song, so it must have been from the beginning, the early days when he was with Genesis. I wasn't sure. I remember thinking at first that everything around me was just one color—mouse brown, like an old overcoat. But perhaps out of a sense of relief, or perhaps out of a sense of some rediscovered hope, I noticed the colors seeping back into the world around me. Everywhere I looked I noticed a new color, one I had not seen just the moment before. I could see them, but I could not name them. There were too many of them and too many variations. As my eyes adjusted to the new landscape, and as the sun moved across the shamelessly blue sky, I felt rejuvenated. I felt like I reached a new starting point, like my journey was starting again for a second time. I had a strange desire to look at a map.

I knew enough to know that Las Cruces was my next stop, my imminent goal and destination. Once I got there, I thought, I could rest, resuscitate, relax, and above all else look at that map. I wanted to understand where I was and where I was going. I had a destination, I reminded myself.

Las Cruces felt more like a staged scene than a random moment. It's hard to explain—not déjà vu, but a feeling like I had been there before when I was quite sure I hadn't. Three crosses stood at the entrance of town, beckoning one and all. Across the low-lying wall in front of the crosses, someone had written as an act of protest, *I am atheist.* Just next to it was another bit of spray-painted monologue—perhaps a reply, perhaps a counter-protest, perhaps a graffiti-laden act of wry mischief. *I am a theist too,* it said. Two actors, two lines, one irreconcilable conflict: a short but perfect play. I mouthed both lines as I drove past. To me, this short dramatic work had to be a comedy—I could not see it as a tragedy.

What happened next was a series of events I would later describe to others as strange, by which I mean I could not explain them, only narrate them. Just after I passed into Las Cruces the Mercury decided to give up the ghost and I coasted to a slow stop just off the main road into town. I didn't have a cell phone, mostly because I didn't want to be attached to anything. I wanted to float freely. Some Samaritan must have called for me because a tow-truck appeared quite miraculously out of nowhere. I rode in the truck alongside the mechanic while the Mercury was towed into town. I explained to the mechanic that I really needed to have my car back as soon as possible, since I had a long trip ahead of me, to Los Angeles, to the City of Angels, and was anxious to reach my destination. The mechanic drove on quite laconically, occasionally glancing in my direction, as I explained my sense of urgency to him over and over again, perhaps overemphasizing certain things and perhaps gesticulating a bit more than a person should when talking to a stranger. He said nothing, but I had that feeling he knew I was exaggerating. He acted as if he already had his own idea of how things would play out and my suggestions and efforts to push things in a different direction were futile. He had his vision, I had mine. It was only when we got back to the garage, after one more round of me trying to find the magic words that would get my silent interlocutor to understand that I really wanted to be on the move, that I was on my way to the City of Angels, that he spoke his first words to me.

—Maybe your car is trying to tell you something, he said.

What an odd thing it was to say. I was annoyed. Angry, in fact, though I only let myself show my annoyance. The anger I kept for myself. But since he wasn't even going to look at my car until the next day—I still think to this day he only did that to enhance the sense that I was powerless as to the direction of the events in my life—I now found myself in a strange town with unrequited time on my hands. And so off I went.

I was near the university, that temple of higher learning that makes many a smaller town put on many a larger air. Knowledge makes people act out. They pontificate. Or worse, they talk of things with authority and confidence, even when they know nothing. They learn how to act like they know. It's a confidence game at best. They control the knowledge, and we hapless souls who enter the vaunted halls of learning as acolytes, hoping that we too may learn the secrets that the great ones possess—we find ourselves frustrated. The secrets the great ones possess are incomprehensible, but then we slowly come to learn not the secrets themselves—no, what we learn is their incomprehensibility. It is as close as we get to any real knowledge. We act as if we have learned, but all the while we are wrecked by a nagging suspicion that we have learned nothing at all and never will. Others appear to us so sure in their knowledge, but really, what do they know? They must have doubts like we have doubts. That much I know.

I came upon an odd museum and wandered inside. It was dedicated to a small community set up in the area around Las Cruces over a century ago, a community that called themselves Faithists and, like me, came from New York. Apparently they wanted to set up a community of believers, united by their faith, and so sure of their choices that they gave up everything to live together in a perfect community, or at least one they believed to be perfect. Sometimes I wish I had that kind of faith in something. But truth be told, it scared me to have that kind of faith in anything. I find a lack of faith comforting, reassuring. It means I'm still searching.

I lost track of time. When I emerged from the museum, the light had changed. The shadows were strange and opaque. Things had shifted. The great blue sky had given way to a grey and agitated array of billowing clouds. The wind blew from directions that made no sense and gave no bearing. I heard thunder, and saw lightning. I walked back in the direction of the garage, for some reason thinking it would be the safest place to be, but then the sky opened up and the rain came down hard and fast. I was drenched in no time, and only in the unexpected rain did I realize how much grime and grit had accumulated on my body in the course of the day. I felt a thin layer of dust and ash being washed from me, I could see it drip gently off the ends of my fingers. My lips tasted salty. The rain was relentless and it was fierce, and I knew I had to find shelter. The thunder got more articulate and the lightning more dramatic. I entered the first doorway I could find. Soaked, cold, weary, and strangely thirsty, I found myself staring through the open doorway, gazing into the immaculate face of the Virgin Mary.

2

I stared into the eyes of the Virgin Mary, transfixed by an unexpected vision. It's not every day you see the Virgin Mary, especially when She is encased in a large glass box, but on this day, there She was. And there I was, wet with water, standing at the threshold. It was in the midst of this unexpected vision that I heard an unexpected voice.

—Are you searching for someone? said the voice.

I turned to see a bearded man with long brown hair, the details of his face unclear. He appeared only as a silhouette in the dimly lit interior. Standing in front of the rows of bright lights behind him, the man appeared to have an aura.

—No, I said. I've only come in to get out of the rain.

Instinctively, I walked toward the man. He stood rather authoritatively behind a long structure of dark wood, and as I came near, the man pushed what I perceived to be an old document of some sort in front of me. At the top of the document, which turned out not to be the antediluvian relic it at first appeared to be, but merely paper made to appear antique without actually being so, there was written only one word—Church. This was followed by a list of various cocktails and libations, and at the very bottom of the page, written in quotation marks, was this: "As if you needed a reason to go to Church." I remember thinking how unnecessary those quotation marks were, because really, would anyone challenge the truth of the quote without the quotation marks? Quotation marks make me suspicious—they suggest doubt rather than truth. But alas, the plague of unnecessary quotation marks is only one of the minor apocalypses of the world, so I let the matter rest. I looked up from the faux but not false document and then looked around. This was a bar. The man in front of me was a bartender. The bright lights behind him were bar lights showcasing the lines of bottles. The aura of the man had vanished. Yet why was the Virgin Mary standing just inside the front door, as if She were the Holiest of Hostesses to welcome patrons in search of spirits to Church?

Later I would learn the story. At one point in time, this place was indeed a church, but the number of faithful in the congregation of Our Lady of Grace had steadily grown and so the church sold the property and relocated to a new and larger building on the outskirts of Las Cruces. The present proprietor reopened the place as a bar, exchanging one set of spirits for another, and for some reason settled on the impressively unoriginal name of Church for the new watering hole. The decision to open a bar where once there was a church was not without controversy, of course, and the result was two rather peculiar remnants of the former architecture of the church, now Church. One was that the cross that had been decoratively embedded as a mosaic on one of the walls would not be dismantled, defaced, or painted over, and the other was that the Virgin Mary would stay put right where she was. The new congregation had collected funds to have a new virgin created, from local materials and by a local artist, and so had no more use of the old one. The owner of the bar had the Virgin Mary encased in glass, lest She be damaged or defiled in any way by the more profane congregation She now watched over, or by the errant fist of an over-spirited patron defending his worldly honor in a Church brawl. The cross on the wall became the symbol of the new bar. The Virgin Mary, its protector.

Then there was the fact that, even if the new patron had wanted to remove the Virgin Mary from the premises, there wasn't a worker between Las Cruces and California that would have done the deed. And it wasn't just the workers. Everyone was afraid to remove the Virgin. Even those who had no faith wanted Her there. It seemed the right thing to do, or at least, not having Her there somehow seemed wrong. In this matter at least, all were in agreement, and one could not tell the difference between the faithful and the faithless, as both acted the same when it came to the Virgin. To the faithful She was a holy presence, to the faithless She was a local symbol, but in the end, having the Virgin Mary watch over the bar and its patrons, positioned as She was just inside the front door, seemed to comfort all the thirsty souls—some troubled, some not—who walked through that front door. Many residents in the town affectionately refer to Church as Our Lady, perhaps as a sign of respect for the Virgin, or perhaps as a subtle act of protest against the insipidly-named bar and its brash misuse of quotation marks.

—I'm thirsty, I said to the bartender.

I asked for a glass of water, and pondered briefly the oddness of asking for water while dripping the very same onto the floor of Church, my clothes still quite wet from the rain. The laconic bartender was lording over the bar as if it were his own personal fiefdom. Behind him stood the symbols of his authority: the bottles that contained the various spirits he could invoke and evoke through the strange rituals of his mixological craft. He even had the tattoos and the appropriate vestments to prove his powers. His hair was brown and long, his boots were black and thick, his jeans were blue and torn, and his shirt was white and worn. His face was stoic and unmoving, though in the changing light his beard veered between holy and unholy in appearance. In one moment he looked demonic, in another he looked cherubic, if a cherub could somehow ride a Harley and craft an excellent Manhattan.

The bartender pulled out a bar gun and shot water into a glass, then placed the glass in front of me, all without a word.

—Cheers, I said.

—No cheers with a glass of water, he said. It's bad karma.

I stared at the glass of water with that ponderous, unfocused stare that people always have when they drink alone at a bar. Strange liquid, that. Not enough of it, we desiccate and die. Too much of it, we sink and drown. And even when we have it in just the right amount, what we need from it to live we can neither see nor taste. The water, too, has its own unseen spirit, the water of life, so perhaps all water is holy water in its own watery way. I thought I might share this insight with the bartender to show I was not in complete agreement with his insistence that a toast made with water was an empty, inauspicious toast. I also thought to dispute his understanding of karma, but I found myself distracted and so let the unsettled matter remain unsettled. Off to the right there was the dull but comforting glow of an old jukebox, and around it, the ambient murmur of voices. I could not discern any meaning in their words, not because their words had no meaning, but rather because the hum and din of voices in quieted conversation is always elusively out of range. Huddled whispers are seductive. We are always drawn toward them, never away from them.

I approached and saw five people—one woman and four men—all acting rather strangely. The ambient voices became clearer, and I heard both English and Spanish. They appeared to be repeating what they said to one another several times, and also kept going through the same motions, walking to the same places and then walking back, over and over again. I stood there and watched this little drama, and realized that it was in fact exactly that—a little drama. These were actors rehearsing their lines for some sort of performance, of what sort and for what purpose I did not then know. None of them noticed me standing there, at least not at first, and it was only after a few minutes that the woman caught sight of me. She stopped the drama, looked at me, then walked directly towards me, never once taking her eyes off of me.

—I am Maria, she said simply, and held out her hand.

I put my hand in hers, and I felt something I had not felt in a very long time, something I cannot fully fathom, not even now. As she held my hand, she never took her eyes off of me. She had eyes that were both unsettling and comforting, and she had a warm intensity about her that is difficult to describe now but was easy to feel then. Only now do I reflect on that moment and realize that she never asked my name, and that I never told her.

She released my hand and turned to her companions. It was clear even then that the others followed her lead. She didn't ask them to. She didn't need to. One at a time she introduced me to her fellow actors. First there was Jim—a tall, lean, youngish-looking man with a sun-weathered face, whose voice came with a slow earnestness that could only be from Texas. Then there was Joe, who was part Native American—not sure which part, he liked to say—and who had local roots in Albuquerque. His dusty boots, frayed jeans, and Western-style shirt were well-worn, and he seemed the type of man for whom the costume fit the part, unlike the many others I would subsequently see in these parts who wore them merely to act local when everyone knew they weren't. Joe had an earthiness about him, if that makes sense, an earthiness broken only by the bright turquoise ring he wore on his right hand. Next came Simon, who immediately asked that I call him Si, though at the time I wasn't sure how to spell that, thinking maybe Psy or perhaps the Greek letter Psi. Turns out it was just Si.

—Si? I asked.

—Yes, he said.

Si was from California, from the central valley farmlands just inland from Monterey. I would never have guessed he was from California, yet after he told me, I could not think of any other place from which he might have come. He had come to New Mexico less because he wanted to leave California and more because, as he put it, he just wanted to wander. Finally there was Jesus. Yes, Jesus. Well, actually Jesús, with the Spanish pronunciation, since Jesús originally came from El Salvador. Odd how you can be Jesús in Spanish and no one cares, but if you want to be Jesus in English, suddenly it's an act of sacrilege or dementia. Jesús, I would shortly learn, was in the country illegally. He didn't like the word *undocumented*, since as he pointed out, he had documents—they were just the wrong ones. He refused to call himself a refugee, largely because he didn't like the pity the word invoked. He was proud only in his humbleness, which if you knew him would make perfect sense, and he was honest to a fault. He was the kind of person who would seem like a local everywhere he went.

—I'm sorry I interrupted your rehearsal, I said.

—Not at all, said Maria. We try not to rehearse too much.

—Aren't you supposed to rehearse? I asked. As actors?

—Well-rehearsed lines never sound right, said Maria. They never sound natural. They sound only like well-rehearsed lines.

—How can you tell the difference? I asked.

—If anyone spoke like that in real life, you would never believe them, she replied.

Maria walked over to the jukebox, a retro accouterment that displayed vinyl but played digital, and made a selection. Moments later *Hey Jude* came flowing out of the decidedly inadequate speakers.

—We should talk, said Maria directly to me.

I had no idea why we should talk, but I didn't think to question her. This was the first time I saw Maria's way of acting. We all crowded into a poorly-lit booth near a window, one with more shadow than light, and sat on wooden seats that seemed every bit as stern and punitive as church pews. My glass of water, which I had just set on the table, was taken away by Maria, who then returned with five glasses and a bottle of wine. Wine was poured, and words were spoken. Maria spoke first.

She said she was born in Asunción. Her full name was Eva Maria, but she found that too presumptuous so she went simply by Maria. Her family had fled Paraguay when she was still a child, and she remembered her parents always being close to the church. The church, they would always tell her, had protected them in Paraguay and sheltered them in America. Now, older and on her own, she wanted to repay that kindness—pay all things forward, as she liked to say.

She remembered as a child the street-theater groups in Paraguay that would spring up out of nowhere, break into a performance on this sidewalk or that corner, offering words of rebellion and hope to anyone who stopped to listen. They would vanish before the authorities would arrive, timing their performances perfectly to flee in a timely manner. She remembered also the passion plays and other performances at the church, all of them with their subtle messages of resistance and redemption woven in between the rote rites and rituals. She was too young then to grasp the meaning of those performances, those little dramatic acts of a few spirited individuals, but now that she had a bit of age and experience, she knew there was meaning in all of it. This is why she formed the theater group in whose company I now found myself. They say that in New York, half of the city consists of actors, either actual or aspirational, though there have been moments when I thought perhaps all New Yorkers were actors of one sort or other, but only half of them were aware of it.

The members of the troupe had abandoned whatever lives they thought they had before to come together for the sole purpose of becoming the actors they now were. None of them knew quite how that happened, but now that it had happened, none of them could see their lives being anything other than what they now were. And what a peculiar sort of acting troupe this was. The one thing they all agreed upon was that an audience didn't matter. The meaning, they explained, was in the act itself. Even if no one watched the performance, the acts still had meaning. If an audience formed, then it was an act of good fortune, a blessing of sorts.

The troupe seemed close, though I admit it is hard to tell the difference between moments when people are truly close and when they only act that way. Actors are fiendishly liable to such antics. But I would soon learn that my first impressions were right and they were not acting at all. They performed religious plays for churches in exchange for food and shelter, and lived their lives solely on the charity of others. In their spare time, they wrote their own plays—well, mostly Maria did the writing—usually on religious issues or scenes drawn from scripture, and performed them at any venue that would have them. This is how they ended up at Church, which they were using as a rehearsal space before they went to church to perform their rehearsal for real.

As the red wine began to work its magic, the words they were speaking began again to recede into ambient babble, and I was overcome with sadness and trepidation. Already, as they were telling me their stories, narrating the events and circumstances that led them to this point and to this moment, I began to fall into my old habits, the same literary sins that put me on this personal exodus in the first place. The journalist in me wanted to write all of this down, and yet as I imagined myself writing it down, I would also start to imagine the story I would tell. I also knew that the story I would tell would be different from the story that was told to me. I would imagine it differently. I always did. I drifted into my own space, my own internal refuge, and suddenly I was in my own good story. When you are a writer, you see everything as a good story.

I was no longer talking to people. I was talking to characters in a book I had yet to write. I was inventing them as characters in my head, telling myself different stories about them than they were telling me. I was imagining the story I would write about them, and I was imagining me writing that story and I was imagining the movie that someone else would make from the story I wrote. And yet these weren't characters at all. These were real people with their own real stories. I still couldn't see the world for what it is. I could only see it as a story. All I could see were words on a page. It didn't matter that I had been told before I left on this journey that I couldn't trust my own words, and no one else could either. The word was all I had to believe in. The word was the only thing I had to make sense of the world and the story it told to me. And now my faith in the word had unraveled. The font of life had bled to scribble.

When I was young and my parents would read me stories to send me to sleep, I would fall asleep in the hope of dreaming the story all through the night. When I was old enough to read stories on my own, I would always feel a sense of anxiety as a story approached its end. The last page would fill me with sadness—I wanted more pages, more words. I felt confused by the real emotions generated by an unreal story. Sometimes I felt betrayed, even angry. I wanted my life to match that story, and while something in me always knew it never would and never could, another part of me continued to believe it might.

—What about you?

It took me a moment to realize that someone was speaking to me. I shook my head slightly and looked into the red pool of wine sitting at the bottom of my glass.

—What about you?

It was Maria, asking me about my story, about how I got to this place and this moment in my life. It was all I could do to chase out the phantoms in my head and try to tell her the answer, or at least an answer, but it was really no use. I had already listened to them, and I had mixed their stories with mine. Of what use was it to make my story theirs? I had been sent into exile for doing this, for telling a story better than the story was originally told, for *embellishing the truth*, as the charge stood. I was told that I was wrong. I was deceptive, even mendacious, at least in the words of one overly judgmental editor. Only the grit and substance of the world around me, only what was visible and verifiable—that was the domain to which I was told to confine myself, that was the truth I was told to learn before I could be trusted with pen and paper again. So what about me? My story was the story of someone who liked to tell stories, and when my stories got better and better, I was then told I should no longer tell stories. No one could believe me, they said. I had told an incredible story, and for that, I was sent away. Who would believe that? Who would want to believe that?

I drank the last of the wine in my glass, and looked at the faces of those who had just shared their stories with me. Were their words true? That was the thing—it didn't seem to matter to me. They seemed like good people, and I did not want to deceive them. I knew that if I stayed, I would do something to betray their trust and undermine their faith. I knew I could not stay, that I had to keep moving.

—I have to go, I said to Maria.

—I know, she replied.

This was her only response, which for some reason did not seem strange to me. I bid my farewell to these actors and wished them all the best with their performances. I then walked past the Virgin Mary, through the open door, and into the dusky street. The rain had stopped, and all that remained of the storm was the subtle fragrance of damp clay and soil and the resonant heat that was slowly reclaiming what was left of the evening.

3

I don't understand anything about what makes a car run. The great machine under the hood remains for me an impenetrable mystery, full of secrets known only to those mechanical wizards who practice their craft in the greasy cathedral that nonbelievers refer to as the garage. Sure, when it comes to car craft there are those who will try to pass themselves off as wizards, those who go through the charade of wizardry—these are your standard tricksters and charlatans, the confidence men who imitate the wizard but possess none of the knowledge and substance of the craft. They'll take your money of course, but beyond that, they are as bereft of hieratic knowledge as the rest of us poor souls. Fortunately my beloved Mercury was in the hands of a true priest, whose oil-anointed vestments and rough-calloused hands convinced those of little faith that miracles could still be performed here. The grease-priest's name was Pedro, and when he handed me the key and opened the gate of the garage, I turned over the ignition and the spark of mechanical life flowed through her body once again. He had brought the Mercury back to life. I did not understand how, though he certainly tried to explain it to me, and so I simply had to take it for the act that it was. No doubt for Pedro, there was far less mystery involved. For him, there were various alternatives he could draw on to explain how the car had been revived—science, mechanics, physics, or even blind luck. But for me it was a miracle, or perhaps a feat of wizardry and magic, and it didn't much matter to me that I didn't understand how the engine came back to life. All that mattered is that it did.

I felt a tremendous sense of relief as I pulled through the gate and turned onto the road. I followed the signs that would put me on the path to the West, a path that some called by the number 10, as in Interstate 10, and as soon as concrete gave way to creosote, I knew I had once again found the open road that led through the desert. The heat was precocious for this time of the morning, and the cactus already seemed to shimmer in the glimmering mirages the desert offers up to its pilgrims to lure them away from the journey they thought they knew. The faint fragrance of yucca and granite lingered listlessly in the morning air, but by the afternoon, the merciless heat would suppress even the most recalcitrant of rebel plants and creatures to acquiesce into a somatic stillness.

I drove in the direction of Deming, unaware that I was driving faster than usual. I exceeded the speed limit over and over again, each time feeling that sudden guilt of having done something wrong, then glancing in the rear view mirror and enjoying the subtle giddiness of having gotten away with it. I was troubled by the feeling that I was fleeing—but from what? The whole conversation in Church from the day before, with Maria and the troupe of actors, seemed frustratingly opaque. They hadn't asked me to write their story, or had they? Now I couldn't remember. Maybe I merely assumed that it was something I was expected to do. Maybe I was actually trying to flee from myself, which in any case would be impossible, even if desirable. My mind was disquieted by continuous bouts of doubt and guilt. I noticed I was speeding again.

By the time I reached Deming, the heat of the day had made things palpably uncomfortable. I was hungry and thirsty, and stopped to rest and rejuvenate at the Roadside Café, which sat unsurprisingly at the side of the road. When I walked in, I could see that I was the only stranger in the place. Or maybe I just felt that way. It wasn't clear. I sat at the counter and ordered something to eat—I don't remember what. What I do remember was the conversation I had with the man sitting next to me.

—Where're you from?

—New York. No, New Jersey.

—Well, which is it, New York or New Jersey?

—New Jersey. Definitely New Jersey.

—Then just say so.

There was a brief pause as the man sipped his coffee. He turned on his stool and looked out the window at my car. He looked back at me, then again at my car, then again back at me. He looked at me for longer than I thought necessary.

—Where're you headed?

—Los Angeles.

The man took out a long and worn wallet that seemed inexplicably thick with all sorts of papers and cards, took out some cash, studied the bill on the counter, and carefully laid the cash beside it. He reached into his pocket and methodically counted out some coins. After this little ritual, which struck me as something he did habitually, he turned around and stared distantly out the window.

—You're not gonna make it.

The man left without so much as a glance at me. I was flummoxed. Why would he say that to me? Was he trying to scare me? To annoy me? To warn me? Was this some kind of game he played with strangers? Or was he some kind of coffee shop prophet, dispensing his prophetic insights as carefully as he dispensed with his metallic coinage? It was unnerving, to say the least. I wanted to laugh it off, and yet I couldn't. The idea was already there, the seed was already planted. To believe it would be to indulge the oracle of a man whom I had met by pure coincidence, a random juxtaposition of two people at a café counter. That would involve the reckless and feckless abandonment of anything resembling reasoned thought. Yet not to believe it would be to engage in a strain of arrogant bravado that encouraged me to disregard and dismiss the possibility that there was more to the visible world than I could comprehend. It would be equally irresponsible to ignore what might have been a message or a sign or a premonition. Just because it happened at the counter of a café rather than at the altar of a temple, and just because it was uttered by a gruff man who lacked the initiative to clean his wallet rather than a soothsayer or sadhu who lacked any wallet to clean—would I really reject the message because the messenger did not fit the role or dress the part I expected?

I was in a state of agitation and decided the best thing to do would be to drive on to the next town. Driving for me was a time to reflect and to meditate on things. Besides, if I drove on to the next town, I was reclaiming my fate from the man at the café. At least that's what I told myself. I also knew that I was really just hedging my bets—believing and not believing at the same time, a sort of purgatory in which I waited to see which direction the faith winds would carry me. I might have resolved that line of thought were it not for the fact that I faced an unexpected interruption. I had forgotten my newly-acquired habit of driving faster than I should have, faster than I was aware of, only this time around when I snapped out of my trance and glanced in the rear-view mirror, I found that my luck had changed.

The flashing blue and red lights filled me with a sense of dread and helplessness. There's always a brief moment when you think or hope they are meant for someone else—even non-believers have been known to seek divine intervention in such moments—but when you finally have no choice but to accept that you are the chosen one, there is a transformative moment when you acquiesce to the elective preference of authority. There was a tangible presence of anger, regret, and inevitability in my car, and I stared with fateful resignation in the side mirror as I watched the reflection of a person in blue cloth, gold metal, and black boots walk slowly to the side of my car and ask me for proof of who I was and what I owned. There was chatter over the radio, a strange blend of voices and static that I could not understand. The voice of authority—a woman's voice, I remember—then spoke to me.

—Nice car, she said.

—Thanks.

—I was being sarcastic.

—I see.

A few more minutes of the strange static-laden and coded language ensued, while I uttered the choicest of profane words under my breath in the hot car, sprinkled in between with a few requests for divine intercession. The combination of prayer and profanity seemed inappropriate and offensive, not brazenly blasphemous but not particularly pious either, and so I interspersed both with an additional layer of apology.

—Where're you headed? asked the female voice behind the golden shield.

—Los Angeles.

—Really?

—Yes, really.

—Well, watch that foot. Ain't no need to speed through these parts.

—Thank you. Will do.

A brief moment of silence hung in the air.

—You really headin' to Los Angeles?

—Yes, really.

—Good luck with that.

—Thanks.

—No, really. You're gonna need it.

Jesus, why was everyone in this parched parcel of desert so concerned with my fate and future? Had I stumbled into some sort of holy land where everyone was a sage or a soothsayer or a sadhu or a mystic or a prophet? Granted it is probably unfair to characterize a whole region of a country based on the actions of two of its people, but it was discomfiting to get the feeling that other people knew more about my fate and future than I did. It was *my* fate and *my* future after all, so shouldn't I be the one who knows them best? Didn't I have any say in the matter?

I drove on to the next town, the town of Lordsburg, as it were. I was physically tired and emotionally weary, and so I decided to stop there for the night. I pulled into a motel, a standard one-story road-side American-style motel—clean sheets, plastic cups, white soap, rough towels, no character. The woman at the reception desk, whom I guessed to be about eighteen years of age, was exceptionally chatty, a bit of charm for which I was not particularly appreciative, given my haggard state. As I registered my information, I noticed a small plastic stand on the counter with a handwritten notice that said—*Things to do in Lordsburg!* I had no idea why there was an exclamation point, but there it was. The stand was empty. I assumed it had once held brochures and was now temporarily empty, but looking around, the thought crossed my mind that perhaps there was absolutely nothing to do in Lordsburg. Maybe the emptiness of the stand was exactly as it should be. Or maybe irony was something one did in Lordsburg.

The woman looked at my registration card and as was apparently the custom of the country felt obligated to make commentary on my life's path.

—You're really from New Jersey?

—Yes.

—Did you drive all the way here in one day?

—No.

—Where'd you drive from, then?

—I drove from Las Cruces.

—Ah, the big city.

—It's not that big.

—There's a great bar there called Church.

—I've been there.

—Did you see the Virgin Mary?

—Yes.

Pause.

—Do you like chilies?

—Why?

She then related a story to me, whether I was interested or not was not her concern, about something that happened a few years ago in her hometown, the city of Hatch, which as everyone knows is famous for its chilies. A few years ago a local farmer was harvesting his chilies when he noticed that one of them had what looked like the image of the Virgin Mary on it. It made it to the local news and soon people were coming from all around to see it for themselves. Some people even said it was a miracle, a sign from heaven. But then an art professor from the university noticed something strange, something familiar about the image, and said it looked uncannily like the style of a local artist who had been trying to make a name for himself in New Mexico's vastly overcrowded art scene. An investigation of sorts ensued and sure enough the artist confessed to the whole thing. It was meant as a publicity stunt for his upcoming show at an art gallery in Santa Fe.

At first some had prayed for the chile, now they prayed for the artist. Others cursed him. The artist was ostracized by his community and excommunicated by his fellow artists, but the big question was what to do with the chile. It seemed wrong to eat it or roast it. Sure, the whole thing turned out to be a fraud, but the image of the Virgin Mary was real, and that part had to be respected and revered, regardless of its fraudulent origins. Eventually a small ceremony was held at a local church to bless the chile, and a photograph was taken that still to this day hangs in a local church. As for the chile itself, the farmer was told to put it back in his field and let nature take its course, and now that same farmer believes that the spirit of the Virgin Mary lives in each and every one of his chilies. Local people claim his chilies are now blessed with just the right amount of sweetness and heat—no other field in all of New Mexico produces chilies like that. Or so they believe.

Did I care? Not particularly, but I still couldn't let myself invoke the cynicism necessary to write the whole thing off as a bit of local folklore and superstition. People are always inclined to dismiss these things, and there are all sorts of people who relish the opportunity to point out to others that the whole basis of their belief is nothing but fakery and quackery. *Just a bunch of nonsense*, they say with smiley contempt. What these people don't understand is that it isn't the basis of the belief that needs to be real—it's the belief itself that needs to be real. It doesn't really matter that the image on the chile was a fake and a forgery, and pointing that out is irrelevant to those for whom the belief is itself already real. Even if someone could prove beyond a shadow of doubt that Jesus never existed, or that the Virgin Mary was not a virgin, or that the Wise Men weren't wise, or that any one of a number of stories in the Bible could never have happened in the way they were told—that wouldn't change a thing. Come Sunday, the churches would be full and the beliefs would be as real as they ever were.

The woman handed me a key. I felt a weariness I had not felt in a long time.

—Where're you headed? she asked.

—Los Angeles.

—Really?

This was the third time in the same day that someone had doubted my destination.

—Yes, really.

The woman let out a long sigh.

—People say you can drive it in one day if you leave early enough.

I walked out of the reception office with the key held tightly in my hand, as if it were an amulet of some sort. There was a reddish and amber glow beginning to settle on the horizon. Evening in the desert is something of an uprising. All of the creatures of the earth that had been cowed into submission by the oppressive heat of the day now stage their own defiant rebellion and spring back to life. As for me, I had no rebellion left in me against the day, and no spirit of defiance for the night for that matter. I went through my usual rituals of brushing my teeth and so forth and then eased myself into the unnaturally crisp white sheets of the motel bed. I took great comfort in the words of the woman at the reception desk, and faded to sleep with a surprisingly untroubled mind. I was only one day from my destination. Only one day, I said aloud to no one there.

4

At first, there was only a hint of light, a brief flitter and flash that intruded on my inner world, which had until then been quite at peace with itself. But the nearly imperceptible flicker that danced gently across my eyelids shortly gave way to a seductive pale yellow, then an ingratiating amber, and finally a rude orange that adamantly and petulantly demanded a response. I opened my eyes. What time was it? I was still under the crisp and irksomely abrasive white sheets, but the curtains of the room were drawn shut. The light that entered the room could only hint at its true intensity, sneaking in as it did around the edges. The orangey hue intimated that it was far later than I wanted it to be. I had an anxious, uneasy feeling. When I went to sleep, I had imagined leaving just before the first visual whisper of daybreak, out the door and onto the open road. By the end of the day I would be in the City of Angels. But what had happened? What was the time? The room had no clock in it, so I grabbed my pants and pulled out my watch—a hand-wound pocket model. Eleven a.m. How did it get to be so far into the day? *If you leave early enough you can make it in one day.* But it was no longer early. The cosmic plan was undone. I felt lost.

I got out of bed slowly and then methodically went through my morning rituals, which were pretty much my evening rituals in reverse. I went down to the reception office and discovered that the donuts and pastries that were promised as a free breakfast were now only crumbs on a plate, though I did not see any other guests at the motel. I was suspicious. There was hot coffee, which I poured into a cup, along with three packets of sugar and some white substance that looked like milk but wasn't—ah, this world of illusion—and then tried to stir it all together with a red plastic stick that for some reason is called a stirrer though it remains tenaciously unable to do the one thing for which it was created. I took a sip of the coffee, which I would describe as something in between diabolical and unholy, and so left it on the counter, as an offering to the trash gods.

—G'morning, said a voice.

It was the same receptionist from the night before. I looked for pastry crumbs or donut residue around her mouth, but couldn't see anything I would call firm evidence. I was about to return the greeting, but was interrupted.

—Check out time is noon. Just so you know.

I looked at the clock on the wall. It was 11:45 am. I was perturbed and disoriented. The receptionist's comment sounded like an ultimatum. I had to leave or stay and I had to make my decision on a fifteen-minute deadline. Just then I noticed the *Things to do in Lordsburg!* stand, the one that had been quite empty the night before, now had a flyer in it. One flyer. I looked at it. It was a rather poorly printed advertisement for something called Shakespeare Ghost Town.

—Did you put this here? I asked.

—No.

—Who put this here? Have you been here all night?

—I don't know, and no.

A brief pause.

—You wanna go?

—Do I wanna go where?

—To the ghost town.

—Why is it named after Shakespeare?

—I don't know.

Another pause.

—If you wanna go, you can tell me. It's on private land but I know the guy who owns it and I can get him to let you in.

In my reporter days, I would have jumped at the chance to go. I would have called it a local angle story, or a bit of Americana, or even a travel feature, and it would have been an easy sell. But now, what with the anxiety of having to decide whether I would stay or go in just under fifteen minutes, coupled with the new challenge of having to decide on an outing to Shakespeare Ghost Town, I didn't know what to do. The receptionist could see I was troubled.

—You may as well go to the ghost town. It's too late to drive to Los Angeles anyway. What's one more day?

I took a deep breath, and let it out slowly, something I often did to focus my thoughts.

—Alright, I said. Just one more day.

Only one more day.

Another pause.

—You may as well point me in the direction of that ghost town.

She gave me directions on how to get there—basically drive down the highway and it's there. I opened the door of the office to head out.

—Don't forget your coffee.

—It's not my coffee.

—Yes it is.

I walked toward my car, coffee in hand, and when I was just out of view of reception office I poured the coffee onto a bush, apologizing to the bush as I did so, and set out in the direction of this Shakespeare Ghost Town. It was a short drive and when I got there the gate was open, though no one was around. As soon as I got out of my car I could see that it was the type of thing you do because you think you should do it, and then you spend the rest of the day wondering why you did it. The whole ghost town was about a hundred yards from end to end, and looked exactly like you would think a ghost town would look. I'm not even sure why they call it a ghost town. Do any ghosts actually live there? Do ghosts really need shelter? And if they do, why would they stay in a place like this? Are they in some sort of jam? When it comes to the material world, we always insist on all mod cons for ourselves, but when it comes to the spirit world, we easily think any hovel will do. Maybe ghosts don't actually haunt us—they're just pissed about the accommodations and keep trying to register a complaint with the corporeal management. I think the whole thing was an act, some way of luring hapless souls like me to Shakespeare, just to see this so-called ghost town. Would anyone really visit this place if it were called Shakespeare Ghost Slum? Probably not. So instead we call it a town, and a strange one at that. That's entertainment, I guess.

When I was done wandering around—boredom set in quickly—I got back in my car and drove to the gate, which for some reason was now closed. Next to the gate was a man in a truck, whom I took to be a rancher because he drove a truck and looked as much like a rancher as Shakespeare looked like a ghost town. Not sure why he closed the gate—it wasn't like there was an influx of visitors, ghostly or otherwise, that required crowd control—but in any case he seemed friendly enough and tipped the brow of his hat to me.

—Had a look around?

—Yes, thanks.

He looked at my car and rolled a toothpick in his mouth a bit. Then he opened the gate for me to drive through. I stopped on the other side of gate.

—Where're you headed? he asked.

—Los Angeles.

He looked at my car, then he looked at me.

—I doubt that.

He closed the gate without another word, got in his truck, and drove off. The dust trailed from his truck and covered my car in a thin brown dry veneer, something I took to be partly intentional.

I was agitated and edgy. I started to get angry but then got angry that I was angry. I drove fast, this time because I wanted to, and I wanted to drive all the way to the state border and cross over, just to prove everyone wrong. Who were these people who thought they knew my fate? Was I was not the master of my own destiny? Did I not have free will? I drove faster and faster still, not as if in a rush but more as if I were guided by some celestial voice. I passed a highway sign that said *Dust Storms May Exist*, which struck me as oddly existential, or hypothetical, or both. Or perhaps it was a little Zen koan unintentionally inscribed by the authorities of the Transportation Department. I turned on the radio, and heard the voice of Peter Gabriel again—this time I felt I had to listen, had no choice.

I set my mind on crossing the state line just to show everyone and everything that I could do it all on my own, that I could make my own future, that I could write my own story, that I could pull my own puppet strings, if I even had any puppet strings left to pull. I was my own man. This was a personal mission. I drove into a town called Road Forks—seriously, who names these places?—and knew I was close. I saw a sign for a rest stop—Last Stop in New Mexico—and I'll be damned if at the last minute I didn't jerk the wheel and pull into the rest stop. To this day I don't know why I did that. But I did. I shut my car off and I looked to the horizon. I could see the state line and knew I could make it there and make it across if I wanted. But I sat there in a little plot of shade and started to think. And I thought for a long, long time.

Twilight is the time of day when a person is most vulnerable. Something about the indeterminate moment when it is no longer day and not yet night makes us wistful, makes us want to believe in things, no matter how improbable they might be. What would I have proved if I had crossed that state line? I was still under the control of those minor prophecies and predictions, since any action taken to disprove something is as much under the spell and power of the belief as taking action to prove it. I had mistaken an act of free will for free will itself, and acting out the act is always nothing more than just that—an act. I had become an actor. I remembered my ancient Greek lessons from high school. The Greek word for actor was *hypokrites*—a hypocrite. The ability to convince people you were something or someone else was highly valued on the stage, but it was despised in public life. I was acting, and I was not on a stage. Who was I?

I never crossed that state line. The only thing I crossed was the center median—an illegal act, I know—to get to the other side of the highway and drive directly in the opposite direction. I knew I had to go back. For the first time in a long time, I felt like I was no longer running away from something, but running toward it. I felt tremendous peace with that. In the passing moment of twilight, the world seemed very still.

I drove back to the motel, where I had one more conversation with the woman at the reception desk.

—I'm leaving tomorrow.

—Did you visit the ghost town?

—Yes.

—How was it?

—It was small.

—Do you believe in ghosts?

—How do you mean?

—I mean, do you believe in ghosts?

—You mean, do I believe in them the way people believe in unicorns, or the way people believe in God?

—God ain't no ghost.

—Then what of the Father, Son, and Holy Ghost?

—Well, He ain't no scary ghost.

—Then why are people God-fearing?

—You're just mixing words, mister.

A moment passes in which she eyes me up.

—Do you believe in ghosts or not? I mean, do you believe they exist?

—I have no reason to believe they don't exist.

I left first thing in the morning, at the break of day. I wanted to take a different route back, either to tempt fate or to let fate tempt me. Or maybe fate can't be tempted—it always is as it should be, and if tempted, the temptation is itself fate. There were clouds in the sky and as the morning sun climbed its gentle and inevitable path upward from the jagged horizon, a ray of light burst through the clouds to illuminate and awaken the desert below. At a different time in my life, I would have found something meaningful, even ominous, in that sight. In the moment, however, I only found it distracting.

I reached for my sunglasses. I knew what I was thinking. I was thinking of the photograph I should take, the visual story that it would tell. I wanted to capture a brief moment, and show it to others as if it were eternal. It would only be another embellishment of another moment of my life. I had to stop doing that. I had to learn to see things for what they were. In three hours it would be a cloudless and miserably hot afternoon. No one takes a picture of that. I could not see it for what it was. Not yet—though I wanted to. I saw it only for all the other things it could be. But at least I knew that, and that was a start.

I drove Route 90 to Silver City. In Silver City, a woman served me coffee and a chocolate brownie with cayenne and told me not to buy any blankets at the roadside stalls. The blankets were sold to unsuspecting tourists as Native American blankets, an authentic souvenir of the southwest, but the blankets weren't really Native American blankets. They were fake. I wondered why she told me that, and I wondered why it mattered if the blankets were fake. If tourists buy them and they truly believe they are Native American blankets, then where is the harm done? What purpose does it serve to make them question their belief, and who by right should do so? I had a friend in New Jersey who loved to point out to Christians that Christmas was not actually the birthday of Jesus, that it was all just an act of historical artifice to conform to the Roman calendar. He was always upset when Christians didn't seem to care. To believe in what is fake is still to have belief, and maybe that's the important thing—not the object of belief, but the belief itself. Still, I didn't buy a blanket.

I drove the route known as the Trail of Mountain Spirits. I wondered if it was also a ghost town, only without a town. Did the spirits wander the trail? Or would the trail take me to the spirits? And why did the Trail of Mountain Spirits seem evocatively spiritual while the Shakespeare Ghost Town seemed depressingly contrived? I thought the Trail would be a good place to cast off some demons, but then realized I would be more inclined to pick up a few new ones instead. All in all, my spirit count would probably remain the same. I imagined I was on a pilgrimage, though at the time I did not know what meaning it held.

I followed the road through to Kingston, then turned right for no good reason and ended up following Route to 27 to Route 26, where I found the town of Nutt. The town of Nutt claimed to be a ghost town, but people lived there still and they didn't look much like ghosts. There was also the Middle of Nowhere Bar, which was meant to be amusing but was in fact disingenuous and deceptive. It was here in front of me, so it had to be somewhere, so it might be the middle of somewhere but definitely not the middle of nowhere, in which case no one would be able to find it, except perhaps for some lost ghosts in search of spirits.

I drove to Hatch, and knew that somewhere out there, there was a whole crop of chilies imbued with the blessings of the Virgin Mary, or at least an artist's depiction of Her. I came to an intersection that told me to go left for the *Jornada del Muerto*, which struck me as odd because in some ways all *jornadas* eventually lead to *muerto*, just at different speeds. There was also a sign for the road to Truth or Consequences, which I later learned was a town that renamed itself entirely as a publicity stunt—a town of actors hoping to attract other actors. Actors and ghosts, actors and ghosts.

Often I wondered if this place were some sort of holy land, or simply a caricature of one. I also wondered if I would be able to tell the difference.

The arrow that pointed to the right told me it was the way to Las Cruces, where everything about this whole story began. I turned right to head back to the beginning, as if it were all one big karmic circle paved in asphalt and gravel. I hit Las Cruces and went straight to Church—and I had a reason to go to Church, which was the bartender. I asked him if he knew where Maria and the other actors had gone. He said they were headed east, toward La Luz. It seemed somehow appropriate that now I had to head toward La Luz. And drive that way I did. After six long tumultuous days, on the morning of the seventh I pulled into the parking lot of the only church I could find, Our Lady of the Light.

I walked into the church, and there sat Maria surrounded by the others in the troupe. She did not seem surprised, and appeared almost to be waiting.

—I came back, I said.

—I knew you would.

She got up and walked toward an open door.

—*Vámanos.*

I and the others followed.

5

In New Mexico, it is impossible to separate earth from sky. Only people who have been to New Mexico will understand that. That's not to say that other skies in other parts of the great wide world don't have their individual charms. But in these parts, no matter where you look, your eyes are always drawn upwards. You can look at the tallest mountain, and as soon as you look at the peak, you notice the sky above it. In the day, it's got a million shades of blue, and in the night, a million brilliant stars. Every day is different—it's never the same sky. It's as clear blue straight up as the clearest blue water is straight down. You can see forever, and some say you can hear forever, too. The whole town of Ruidoso is named after the noise of a creek that echoes off the canyon walls so that you can hear it no matter where you are. In a New Mexico sky, the bells ring more clearly, and the birds sing more sweetly, than in any other sky.

I stared into that big deep blue and pondered. A week had gone by and I had resolved to create my world anew, but what was I doing here? I left my car in the parking lot of Our Lady of the Light. When I kept checking each door and the trunk to make sure they were locked, Maria stopped me. *It will be safe,* she said. *Trust me.* The troupe went from town to town in an old school bus they had been given by a church where they had once performed. It was the short style, not one of the long unwieldy ones. The inside had been changed a bit, but the outside—marked as it was with the name of St. Mary's Catholic school—was left untouched. As Joe explained to me, no one would ever think to bother a school bus from a Catholic school. Maria was at the wheel, and the rest of us were sitting, each by a window, each with our own view, each in our own thoughts.

—Are you a religious man? Maria asked me out of the blue.

—How do you mean?

—There's only one way to mean it.

—I don't know. Yes, I suppose.

—Do you believe in God?

—Isn't that the same thing?

—No, it's different.

—I don't know. I have a hard time with the origin. It's hard to fathom.

—When you see a river, do you not trust that it's made of water until you see the source?

By now the others had stopped facing outward and began to face inward. I turned to Jim, who was in the seat next to me.

—Does she talk like this all the time? I asked.

—Yes, all the time, said Maria before Jim had a chance to answer.

I felt embarrassed since I did not think Maria had heard me. I did not think she could hear me.

—Dude, she does this, Si said to me with an accepting shrug.

It seemed to me that the group acted more like a family than a troupe. Jim, Joe, Si, and Jesús acted like brothers, but Maria was something different—neither sister nor mother. Maybe a caretaker, or caregiver, as she watched over the others with her own sense of compassion and concern. I wondered if Maria had her own vulnerabilities. I couldn't see them, but I thought they had to be there—somewhere. Everyone is vulnerable to something, even if it is only the fear of being vulnerable. No one in the troupe called each other *brother* or *sister*, though Si did have a very consistent habit of addressing everyone as *dude*.

What was I doing here? Where did I fit into this group, this troupe? A few days ago I turned back from the state line and followed a new clarity. Now I was doing what I felt was right and yet still felt haunted with doubt. With every new mile, with every new step further from my car, I felt pangs of anxiety. Who were these people? I felt like I knew them in one moment, and then did not know them at all in the next. And what was this strange landscape around me? Now, of course, I know it well, but then, the *cholla* and yucca and brushy mesquite seemed like an alien landscape to me. It was all so strangely out of character for me, and yet at the same time it seemed like there was nothing else I could have done.

—This is Mescalero Apache land, said Joe.

Joe had a habit of adjusting the turquoise ring on his finger. I don't know if he was actually adjusting it, but he did seem to touch it with a rhythmic frequency. I don't think he was aware of it. Somehow watching the rituals of someone else made me feel more at ease. Not sure why. There is something about rituals that creates a comforting predictability. When I was young, I remembered with distaste the rituality of religious services. People mumbling the words to chants and hymns they neither knew nor understood, people offering a collective amen to prayers they did not follow. Those rituals seemed empty. To be fair, there's no way a person could tell if a ritual were meaningful or meaningless, at least not from the outside. Maybe that's what separates actors from hypocrites. Rituals directed inward have to have meaning, for what is the point of trying to fool oneself with meaningless ritual? Rituals directed outward need not have any meaning whatsoever—it's the difference between being pious and acting pious. My father used to say that only fools believed in heaven. But perhaps it is equally true that heaven is full of those who have never been fools.

The bus stopped outside a wooden building, in a place not far off the highway. The others tumbled out, so I tumbled out too, without knowing why. An old man came out of the wooden building and approached us, with a certainty of demeanor that told me he knew everyone—except me, of course. He wore a thin taupe hat with a feather tucked into the brown rim band, and had a bolo tie cinched with a turquoise pendant reminiscent of Joe's ring. Joe spoke first.

—Elan, we are passing through the lands of your people and seek your blessing.

—May you move gently across the land, said the old man.

The old man noticed me.

—I don't know you, he said.

He walked toward me—Jim and Si stepped aside to let him pass. He held out his hand, as if to shake mine, but when I put my hand in his he grasped it firmly with both of his hands and then looked into my eyes, as if looking for something. I was nervous. Several moments passed.

—You are a kind soul, he said to me with conviction. You are welcomed as a friend among friends.

He continued to grasp my hand. I grew less nervous. He kept staring at my face. No, he kept staring into my face.

—You did the right thing, he said to me. Do not ever doubt that.

He let go of my hand and the intensity went out of his eyes. Everyone gave their thanks to the old man, calling him Elan, which I took to be his name. I followed suit and did as the others did. We all climbed back into the bus—I climbed in last, feeling like an apprentice or a novice. Jim took the driver's seat this time, and we all found our places as if we knew the right place to sit. We drove off as Elan waved farewell with his feathered hat. I felt a sense of relief in the words that Elan had said to me, but still, I was confused. Did I really believe his words, or did I really want to believe them? Was it what he said, or the way he said it, that I found so comforting? I had a long-standing habit of keeping the fortunes from fortune cookies—had quite a stack of them, actually. I would laugh them off in restaurants and share them with friends, but quietly—especially the ones that I wanted to be true—I would slip them into my pocket to save. I knew they were placed in the cookie by a machine, or perhaps by a bored or mischievous baker, but I felt that to throw the fortune away was to disrespect the possibility that life could be something other than a random and uncontrollable series of events. I didn't want to act like life had meaning. I wanted to believe truly that it did.

—You think too much, said Maria.

Si then told me a story about one of their early efforts to be, as he put it, artsy. They decided to experiment with puppet shows, and not just for children. They quickly learned how to master pulling and manipulating the strings. Of course at some point, the idea of playing God came up, especially given the fact that many of their projects had a religious theme to them, and so they decided to embrace the idea and stir it up a bit, and tried to create a puppet theater where one set of puppets were puppeteers who controlled the strings of another set of puppets.

—Dude, it was a total mess, he said.

—What happened? I asked.

What happened was the brief experiment was dismantled, or disentangled, not only because it was too artistic for its own good, but also because it never overcame the puppet problem. Puppets and puppeteers live in separate worlds, and must do so by definition. Where the string ends is the point that separates the world of the puppets from the world of the puppeteers. It's a point you cannot cross without becoming something other than what you are.

—Is this what you call string theory? I asked.

Maria smiled gently. That was the first time I really saw her smile. I felt more at ease.

We passed by a place called the Inn of the Mountain Gods.

—That's an Apache hotel, said Joe.

—How can you tell? I asked.

—You can't, he said. I know the owner.

Joe smiled with a subtly sarcastic grin.

—We all know the owner, Jim said. Sometimes they let us stay there for free if they have room. They're good folks.

—Are we staying there tonight? I asked.

—Nah, said Joe. We got a little further to go.

I realized that I had never bothered to ask where we were going, and so at that point, I asked.

—The fact that you ask only now says something about you, said Maria.

I didn't know Maria well then, but I already knew enough to know that she wasn't going to tell me what that something was. I thought she might at least tell me where we were going, but before she could, and I didn't know for sure that she would, Jim chimed in.

—We're going to an alien place, he said.

—An alien place? I asked.

—Roswell. It's just a bit further up on Route 70.

I had never been to Roswell, but I knew the name. Everyone knows that name. It's an artifact of popular culture, a launching point for alien cults and conspiracy theories, a pilgrimage site for true believers. There's even a link between the Apaches and UFOs, at least according to some Apaches and according to Joe. There's also a whole industry of people trying to disprove and debunk every claim made about aliens, UFOs, and other paranormal events that occurred in or near Roswell, but what those perennial skeptics never understand is that, for those who want to believe, nothing can be disproven or debunked. The city of Roswell, I would soon discover, put a space alien right on its official crest, not because they officially believe anything—authorities are rather agnostic on the possibility of alien life in Roswell—but because they officially want to draw in tourists. Like the town of Truth or Consequences, officials here figure if you put on a good enough show, an audience of tourists will show up to watch.

Whether they believe in angels or aliens, people always look to the exact same place—the sky. In Roswell there are a number of people who believe that angels and aliens are the same thing, so they look to the sky with a special sort of conviction. Others aren't so sure. Sometimes it seemed like the entire population of New Mexico was always looking to the sky, perhaps searching for answers, or perhaps simply seduced by its alluring azure. The space industry—the private version, that is—decided this was the best place to send people skyward to the heavens, and there's even a spaceport under construction near the Jornada del Muerto as it happens. Area 51 can be found, or perhaps not found, near here as well. And if going to outer space to greet aliens or angels isn't convenient, then New Mexico also sports Trinity Site, where the powers of the universe were brought to earth by science wizards, packed into a metal container, and blown up like an atomic sun. One of those wizards, a certain Robert Oppenheimer, even quoted Hindu scripture at the sight and site of that blast, thus bringing even more divine figures into the already heady mix of gods and spirits and ghosts and aliens that seems to spring from the New Mexico landscape as easily as tiny kangaroo mice spring from the tufts of the skunk-bush sumac that prevails in these parts.

—Have you ever been to White Sands? Jim asked.

—I drove by it, I replied.

—You should go there. Nothing but pure white gypsum on flat dusty earth.

—So it's white? I asked.

—It's not that. You can walk for miles and think you've never gone an inch.

—You can walk in circles and swear you've been moving in a straight line, said Joe.

—No way to know which way is which, added Jim.

—I imagine it's like that in outer space, I remarked. Except that it's not white.

Jesús had been quiet for so long a time. I was surprised to hear him join as if he had been part of the conversation all along.

—In Carlsbad there are these deep, dark caves, he began. You can walk into them and you have no idea which way is out. The darkness is unimaginable. You can hold your hand in front of your face like this and not even see a faint trace of it. And the caves are full of bats.

—Humans are helpless inside, but the bats seem right at home, said Jim. They come out of the caves in a mass exodus at exactly the same time of day, though they cannot see outside to know if it is day or night.

—Some of them migrate to Mexico when the seasons change, said Jesús almost philosophically. No one knows how or why they do it. It is a great mystery.

—The bats know, said Maria. For them, it is not a mystery.

Roswell loomed and my first impression was of an unexceptional town with wide, straight streets. One couldn't wander in circles even if one wanted to, and no one in history every wandered in squares. That's another mystery, one even the bats don't know. This would be my first outing with the troupe, though I did not yet know my place. Was I an actor, or merely an observer? Would I be an insider, or an outsider? How would I know, and when would I know? Driving in the strangely straight Roswell streets, we passed image after image of alien creatures. Aliens on billboards using vacuum cleaners, aliens as statues outside of schools, even aliens on advertisements for legal help to more earthly aliens crossing more terrestrial borders. I imagine if space aliens actually arrived in Roswell they would think everyone saw them as gods, responsible for everything from vacuums to education and perhaps even to the legal codes that brought order to the gentle people of this unremarkable but well-ordered town.

We pulled through the gates of what turned out to be St. Peter's church. I was relieved to see no aliens at the gates, but there were plenty of angels to be found, though they were all made of cement. It was late and we were all tired. A man came out to welcome us and we followed him into an attached building that had a few rooms, a bathroom and a shower, and a small kitchen. Maria spoke with the man for a few minutes. He walked off, and she came back.

—We can stay here.

I helped unpack a few things from the bus, including my own small bag—the one thing I had taken from my car before we left. The beds had sheets on them, folded into neat little squares, alongside a towel, a washcloth, and inexplicably, a small packet of goldfish-shaped crackers.

—It's a Christian thing, said Joe.

We made up our beds, and I noticed that the blankets that had been brought in from the bus were the very blankets I had been warned against buying when I was in Silver City.

—You know those blankets are fake, right? I said.

—I don't care that they are fake, said Maria. I only care that they are warm.

And that was the end of the first day.

6

The story of Jesús is a long and sorrowful tale—
there is really no other way to put it, and so I
won't put it any other way. I hadn't really had
a chance to sit with Jesús or to talk with him in detail about his life—and Jesús struck me as the sort of
person who did not openly talk about the details of
his life—but on the next day, in the morning, in the
flower garden behind the church, we had one of those
moments that open up every once in a while, where
different people come together and realize they are
not different people. Talking with Jesús reminded me
of the wistful fact that we will forever remain ignorant
of most of the families to which we might have otherwise belonged, and will at the same time become dis-
enchanted with most of those that we do.

I did not ask Jesús to tell me of his life. I did not ask
Jesús to tell me anything. But that morning, I walked

outside, into the garden where Jesús was already standing, drinking his coffee and staring contemplatively at the flowers. When I entered the garden, he turned to me and began to narrate a series of events which then, as now, I never had any reason to doubt. Jesús tends toward silence, and there were long, silent gaps in his story, but the gist is there, and it is every bit as truthful as Jesús intended.

Jesús came from a small town in western El Salvador, more of a village, really, as he described it, with the name of Santa Cruz. Before I continue with the story of Jesús, I would like to point out that there seems to be a Santa Cruz in every part of the world. *Holy Cross.* Again with the names. It's like the whole surface of the earth is named as a reminder that we need to believe in something, as if people throughout history lived in constant fear of forgetting.

—A friend of mine went to school in Santa Cruz, I said. In California.

—Was it a religious school? asked Jesús.

—No. But there was a cult there devoted to the banana slug.

I then felt an awkward regret in sharing information that seemed utterly irrelevant to the conversation, and Jesús showed a politely affective certainty that he wished to know nothing further of this strange Santa Cruz in California and its sluggishly cultish ways, confirming that it was indeed, as I correctly surmised, irrelevant. After an appropriate moment of silence to allow the spirit of awkwardness to dissipate, Jesús returned to his narrative.

Santa Cruz, the one in El Salvador, that is, was an impoverished place, one where every new day was a day of new struggle.

—I have heard people say that you don't know you are poor until you see what it is like not to be poor, Jesús said ruefully. But this isn't true.

Jesús thought in silence.

—When you are poor, poor like we were in Santa Cruz, you know you are poor. No one has to tell you, no one has to show you. You feel it.

Once a year, in September, his mother would take what little money she had set aside to take Jesús and his younger brother to the big city of Ahuachapán, for the festival in honor of the birth of the Virgin Mary. Mind you, Ahuachapán was not really a big city at all, at least according to Jesús. But compared to Santa Cruz, it was a place that seemed indescribably endless and endlessly indescribable, especially in the eyes of a child from a village named Santa Cruz.

—The bus ride was awful, he said. The road was full of holes, and the bus was full of people.

You would think that people heading to a town for a religious celebration would be in a religious state of mind, but according to Jesús, no one on the bus seemed to be in any particular hurry to be holy, let alone considerate. The only hurry was to get to Ahuachapán, and only then, after disembarking from the hot and crowded bus, was everyone in a hurry to act as holy as possible as quickly as possible.

—My mother would grab our hands. We would always walk the same route, the same little pilgrimage. First we would go to the Iglesia Nuestra Señora de La Asunción, where we jostled with people to get the chance to light a candle for the Virgin. Then we would jostle again for a good view of the procession through the town to celebrate the Virgin. After that, we would go back to the bus station and jostle again, to get on the bus that would jostle us home. I hated it.

—If you hated it, why didn't you just tell your mother? I asked.

—Even as a child, I could tell how important this was for my mother. I still remember her face, how serious and devout she looked, and how she wanted my brother and me to understand the meaning of what we were doing. She wanted us to believe.

—Did you believe?

—Whether I believed or not was not important. What was important was that my mother believed that we believed. She was trying to show us how to believe, and what to believe. My brother and I were really too young to understand religious things, but we both knew that this desire of our mother to make us understand, to make us believe, was born out of her love for us. The love was real, we believed in her love, and you could say that was our true faith. We learned to believe because we knew how to love.

After that, Jesús told how he had come to New Mexico. His father, a mediocre carpenter and expert drinker, had abandoned the family right after Jesús was born. His younger brother had been killed in an accident, hit by a speeding car one morning in Santa Cruz as he walked home from school. The car never stopped and the driver was never found.

—People say that over time you get over things like that, he said.

Another ponderous silence.

—But you don't. You never do. When my brother was killed, I felt for the first time that there was true evil in the world.

Jesús was angry—angry that his brother was gone, angry that he was poor, angry that his mother's life was so difficult—angry at everything. It was that anger that drove him to leave Santa Cruz, vowing, as so many others have before him, and no doubt so many more will do long after, never to return until he could set things right and make things better.

—I never expected to come to the United States. Santa Cruz is just across the border with Mexico, and I thought I would simply go into Mexico and do something, try to find work. But Mexico was rough. Rougher than I ever imagined. I didn't want to go back to Santa Cruz, and the situation in Mexico kept pushing me further and further north. One day, I don't remember when, I crossed into America.

The last part of the story told of how Jesús came to be with Maria, with the troupe of actors, with me, there and then, in the garden.

—When I came to America, I met so many others who had crossed. At first I thought, this is good, these are my friends. But then I began to feel that I was being used. I was expected to play the part of a victim, to profess innocence, to tell a story that was not my own. It's like there is some strange cult of the innocent refugee in this country, and as I was expected to join that cult and know my role. I had played so many roles in my life just to survive. I was tired of playing those roles, and I wanted to do more than just survive. I wanted to live.

Jesús went his own way and met Maria a short while later.

—She never asked me to join. But here I am.

The reason?

—Maria expected nothing of me, nothing from me. For the first time, I felt I no longer had to act, to play a role that someone else expected of me. With her, with this group, everything felt genuine to me. It felt like it was supposed to. When I found Maria, I was no longer angry.

I remember thinking at first—wasn't Jesús being a bit hypocritical? He had joined a theater group, after all, where acting was in fact precisely what he did, and here he was telling me that after joining a group of actors, he finally felt he no longer had to act. How can acting not be acting? A hypocrite after all is really just an actor, so if all hypocrites are actors, are all actors therefore hypocrites, too? But I didn't think of Jesús as a hypocrite, because what separates the hypocrite from the actor is the spirit of the act itself. The hypocrite acts for narcissism, but the actor acts for altruism. Either way, one must act—it is all we can do. But not all acts are the same, and some acts are better than others. The trick is to know the difference.

That is how I came to know Jesús, one morning, outside the church, in the garden. I might have come to know more of his story, but at that moment, Maria walked toward us and pointed to me.

—Today it is your turn to act, she said with conviction.

I wasn't supposed to act. I was the journalist, the tag-along, the person who records and observes, not the person who acts. I was the outsider, the traveler on an unfamiliar road. But people had already gathered at the front of the church, and Maria wanted to perform the story of the Good Samaritan, and that story required four people. Given our numbers, Maria told me I needed to act, so that Joe could prepare for his little drama while we performed ours. Maria asked me to play the role of the injured traveler, something which, given my current situation, wasn't really much of a stretch and wouldn't require much acting skill.

There wasn't a large audience that day, but one thing I would soon learn with this troupe is that no matter the size of the audience, ten or ten thousand, every one of them gave the exact same performance. This was their passion.

I was given simple directions by Maria as to how to play my role. In hindsight, I could say that it was Maria who taught me really and truly to act. My role in this moment was simply to lie down, look weary and injured, and look like I needed help. Again, given my situation, that would not have been difficult to do. I was supposed to be at the side of the road, so she improvised and had me lie down at the edge of the concrete walkway that led out of the front of the church, and then covered me with one of the fake blankets we had slept under the night before.

I will confess that I had never lain on the ground like that, especially under a blanket and especially in front of a group of people, and the moment I took my position on that concrete walkway, the moment when I began to play my role, I began to think unexpected thoughts and to feel unexpected things. As I waited for the drama to begin, I began to think how strange it was to lie down on the sidewalk, how uncomfortable it felt, how strange it was to have people staring at me, and how strange it was to pretend that I did not notice them staring at me. I felt vulnerable. Then I thought of all the people in the world who lie down on concrete like this every night, not to act but to sleep, or to find a moment's refuge, and I wondered how they could sleep on concrete, and how they could pretend not to notice the people that stare at them as they walk by. I felt a tremendous rush of both compassion and guilt. Why had I never felt this way before?

As I lie there lost in my emotional tempest, Si approached me, knelt down beside me, gave a look of fear, then stood up and hurried off. It was strange to have Si look at me like that, to look at me as if I were someone to fear. We had just been on the bus together, slept in the same space. Next, Jesús walked by, and, just as Si had done, knelt down beside me, stared a moment, only this time with a look of disdain and disgust rather than fear. Then he also walked away. I thought to myself, why would Jesús look at me that way? What had I done? We had just spent time talking intimately in the garden, and now it is if he were trying to deny me, to deny we ever spoke. I was acting, and I knew I was acting, and yet, why and how did I feel this emotion? What had happened?

At last, Maria approached me. She was the Good Samaritan, the one who would help me, the one who would set things right and make things better. She knelt down beside me, as the others had done, only this time she looked at me with kindness and compassion. She reached out and laid her hand on my head, with a tenderness and genuineness that I found almost disorienting, and suddenly the sorrow and anxiety that

I did not know I carried with me came flowing out. I felt as if I would cry. Maria put her other hand on my shoulder and told me to rise, and I found myself in need of her help to get to my feet. She wrapped the blanket around me, put her arm around my shoulders, and asked me to walk with her.

—I will help you, she said.

And walk with her I did, off to the direction of the church. The small crowd offered small applause.

I did not act any more that day, though the others did so for a little while more. Someone in the audience tried to start a collection afterward, but Maria stopped the effort and said we would not accept money, though someone did insist on giving her a coupon for a local car wash, which seemed more of a statement about the appearance of our bus than it did an act of charitable kindness. We had a last meal at the church, and the head priest even gave us some money for gas, which Maria only accepted with reluctance and after a long round of insistence and reassurance from the priest that it was an act of gratitude, not one of payment for services rendered. We then packed up the few belongings that we had and headed off to wherever our next destination was. Night was falling, and as we drove off, Joe put the radio on. The voice of Bob Marley wafted through the bus, his words bringing solace to the night. *No Woman, No Cry.*

I stared out the window and reflected on everything that had happened in the day. Why had I reacted the way I did? How could something I knew not to be real, and a story whose drama I knew from beginning to end, evoke such emotional turmoil within me? How could Maria's act of dramatic compassion bring me genuine comfort and relief? I also thought of those who looked on, those in the audience who were genuinely moved by what for them could only have been a well-acted performance, the plot-line and ending of which they already well knew. Was their applause for the acting? For the story? Or for the way our acting invoked emotion for them as well? An actor always knows he is acting, but do others? I wasn't sure what the answers were, and more importantly, I wasn't sure if the answers mattered. There was a great mystery in much of this, and in that moment, I was content to let the mystery be.

When the sun goes down in the desert, it is like a complete change of scenery. Isolated lights in the distance appear as reflections of isolated stars in the sky. One becomes aware of distance. The night shift moves in to take its place. Even the air transforms—there is a precise moment when you feel that first wisp of charmed, cool air. You know the night has arrived, the day is over, and what had been the present is now slowly transforming into the past. The lingering scent of roasted chilies and spent piñon filled the air. People in New Mexico often light fires in the evenings, even when it isn't cold. It's a ritual, a habit they can't seem to break. Or maybe they can break it but just don't want to. Either way it is the same, and no one would ever know the difference. No one would want to know.

7

In Artesia, New Mexico, which can be found rather conveniently where US 82 and US 285 make a cross in the road, a simple alteration of perspective can change the way you see the entire world, provided of course you accept Artesia as the entire world, which you would if you were in Artesia. Stand in Artesia and look to the west, and you will see the old town with its old stone buildings and staid way of life. Look to the east, and you will see a behemoth oil refinery, with its modern metallic labyrinths and steam-venting towers and carefully calibrated patterns of work. Same Artesia, different horizons. The type of town you want Artesia to be depends on which direction you want to face.

Nearby Clovis is the home of Clovis Man, what is sometimes called the oldest known culture of the New World. Yes, that's right—the *oldest* civilization of the *new* world. White lab-coat scientists often laugh with derision at the white robe religious fools of the world who believe in scriptural time, but scientific time is really no different. Our sense of time is based on faith. Different belief systems create different beliefs in time. Time itself doesn't change. Only our beliefs do. Same time, different horizons. The type of time you want to experience depends on which chronological direction you want to face, on which set of vestments you prefer. A new civilization in the old world occupies the same moment as an old civilization in the new.

Is it an illusion? An act of self-deceptive folly? Imagine, for instance, a flat bed of concrete. Yes, of course, it could be dirt, or even grass—no need to get lost in technical details—but whatever the place and whatever the material, there will be a platform of sorts, the first sign that some sort of structure is soon to follow. Next there is a brick, only one to start with, and then another, and another. Perhaps there will also be some wood, or clay, or any one of a number of other primordial materials. At what point does our perception change? What is it? What will it be? At this point, it could be anything, really. But then something magical happens—and where and when that exact point is remains something of a mystery—the structure is transformed from an inchoate collection of materials into something intimately recognizable. This is never an accident. It is always intentional, always part of the design.

I stared at the façade of Nuestra Señora del Refugio, in a place called Puerto de Luna—just south of Santa Rosa and just west of Artesia—which turned out to be our next stop, our next performance, our next act of acts. There are a lot churches that sanctify the landscape in New Mexico, and Nuestra Señora del Refugio is only one such church. It is an old church, but you can only see that when you look at the church from the front, when you see its antique façade. Behind that, the church has been refurbished in a rather stern, unsanctimonious style, with bland tan siding, a metal roof, and a couple of nondescript windows. From the side it could be taken for a house, a barn, or even a restaurant. Like the city of Artesia, the type of church you want to see depends on which direction you want to face.

But why, I asked myself, why make a church that calls attention to itself as an illusory architectural performance? The front of the church, the make-up, so to speak, is designed to invoke some sort of emotive response from those who look on its visage: strength, or peace, or awe, or refuge, or inspiration, or humility. Yet look behind the visage of Nuestra Señora del Refugio, and you'll see only the standard construction materials that compose any standard structure. It's like having a performance in a theater, and then at some point the scaffolding falls and all the props and lights and technical wizardry that make the show possible are revealed.

Sometimes people don't like to see what is behind everything. There's no mystery in that, and mystery is the garden of faith.

But what exactly makes a church a church, and not something else? When does it start to be a church? When does it stop? In the early days of Christianity, churches were really just houses, Christian houses where other Christians would congregate. Was the house, once transformed into a church, always and ever a church thereafter? Or was it a church only in certain moments, and a house in all others? And what made it a church? Did God show up only for brief appearances? Or was it the liturgical drama, the mass, that made it a church? Or the audience? Can there by a mass if no one is present to see it? And if there is no mass, is there then no church? Why do churches have different names? Why do they have names at all? Why not just Church?

My mind wandered everywhere, brought on by the puzzle of this one solitary old wall of Nuestra Señora del Refugio, at which I stared for long enough that any passer-by would have thought me a lunatic. I don't know how long I stood there, enraptured by this wall of stone, knowing it was only a façade, but not knowing whether I cared, or whether it mattered. I was startled to hear the voice of Si right beside me.

—Dude, you look righteous, he said with a gentle snicker.

I hadn't even noticed that the performance had already finished, that the audience had dispersed and gone their separate ways, and that the others had loaded up the bus and were ready to head off to the next stop. Only after Si pulled me out of my trance did I notice that the shadows were getting longer and the day was moving on. On the bus, we drove down the highway in silence, watching the desiccated landscape flow by and imbibing the nascent coolness of the wind blowing through the windows. Outside, the red earth mesas stretched to the horizon, a disappearing act foiled only by the cactus and yucca and black mesquite jutting defiantly skyward. From time to time, I could see dust devils rise up from the desert floor, perform their arid pirouettes, then disappear like earthy spirits back into the dusty landscape from which they came.

Si switched on the radio. At first there was only the crackle and sputter and hum of a radio coming to life, then sounds began to form out of the airwaves, until the metallic bristle turned gently into melodious harmonies, with different voices in different tongues emerging ethereally from the void. There were hints of fiddly country music, snippets of the always misnamed alternative genre, tinges of timeless Tejano, corridos from Los Reyes, defiant grunge that had now become classic rock, and even mariachi death metal fusion, which was apparently a thing. But in the end, Si settled on the spoken word, perhaps because it came through so clearly, and in a moment we all turned our ears to hear a story from the electric radio voice.

A white llama had been discovered running loose in southern New Mexico, right near Las Palomas and just across the border from Mexico itself. My first thought on hearing this was how strange it was to assume that a llama would be running loose—isn't that really the natural condition of a llama? It's the tethered llamas of the world that are unnatural. Nevertheless, this particular llama had attracted considerable attention because, first of all, it was impeccably white, in spite of running around through all sorts of things that by right should have left it blemished or stained or sullied. When something is bright white like that, people tend to ascribe it a special meaning—no reason is given. It's assumed. If you see a dove in a tree, it's a dove in a tree. If you see a white dove in a tree, it's an omen, a symbol, a talisman—anything other than a white dove sitting in a tree. So a white llama? It's got to mean something, and according to the story on the radio, there was no shortage of people who claimed they knew what it meant, including one local resident from Las Palomas who thought it meant he should buy lottery tickets.

There was also a dispute as to where it had come from. Had it crossed over the border from Mexico? One angry farmer thought the border patrol had some

explaining to do, since if they couldn't spot a white llama coming across the border, they probably couldn't
spot anything. What was the point of having a border
patrol in the first place? Another official tried to speak
to the llama in Spanish, with the idea that if the llama
responded in some cognizant way then it most likely
came from Mexico. The possibility that it might be
from some other Spanish speaking country—Spain,
for instance, or Ecuador—was not entertained. One
public health official worried that it might have a disease that would threaten other animals in the area,
due to the llama's questionable origins, and so she suggested that the animal be destroyed. This led almost
immediately to a Save the Llama campaign that quickly spread from southern New Mexico to nearly all the
rest of the state.

No farmer on either side of the border claimed the
llama, and no other llama did for that matter as well.
People came great distances to see the white llama,
each of them staring at it, trying to discern its meaning. There was talk of putting the llama in a zoo, but
there was public fuss and outcry against that, since it
would no longer be able to run loose. Finally there was
a most unexpected end to the story when a Buddhist
monastery in the wilderness outside of Taos offered
to adopt the llama, to take care of it and to let it roam
free. The head monk claimed that the llama appeared
to be a wise soul, perhaps a reincarnation of some spiritual leader, a claim that he made with such conviction

that the residents of New Mexico, those with religious leanings and also those without, could agree that this was the most logical solution. Even the mayor of Las Palomas waxed politically eloquent about New Mexico once again being the land of enchantment. There was another press conference when the Buddhist monks came to claim their new spiritual friend, and after a brief ceremony that no one understood except the monks and perhaps the wise white llama (though many onlookers pretended to understand by nodding in affectively spiritual ways), the saffron-and-red-robed monks and their impeccably white furred llama went off to return to the monastery. The monks had even chosen an appropriate name for their new companion—Dolly.

—Funny, said Joe.

After a few contemplative moments, Si turned the radio off.

—Dude, do you think Jesus ever told jokes to his disciples? he asked of none of us in particular.

—Why would Jesus have to tell jokes? asked Joe.

—Dude, he wouldn't *have* to. He would *want* to.

—Okay, but why would he want to tell jokes? replied Joe.

—Dude, why wouldn't he want to? said Si.

I thought about Si's point. It made good sense. Why wouldn't Jesus want to tell a joke from time to time? I mean, it would make Him so much more believable and approachable. Imagine the disciples are in the boat, afraid of the storm, and Jesus walks across the water to help them.

Hey, Jesus, you're walking on water! they all exclaim.

That's nothing, you should see me walk on land! responds Jesus without skipping a beat.

—But that's a lot of pressure on Jesus, I said. His jokes would have to be perfect. If Jesus told a bad joke, what would it mean?

—That God has a sense of humor, said Jim.

—How about this one, said Joe. Knock knock.

A few moments of unanticipatory silence pass.

—Knock knock, repeated Joe, this time more suggestively.

—Who's there? I replied, with an ambient sigh.

—Jesus.

—Jesus who?

—Jesus Christ.

—Dude, said Si cautiously. Isn't that like sacrilege?

—Not if Jesus said it, explained Joe.

—But Dude, Jesus didn't say it, you said it.

—Yes, I said it, but I said as if I were Jesus.

—Dude, you're not Jesus.

—Yes, I *know*, said Joe. I said it as if I were pretending to be Jesus telling a joke that he actually never told.

—But then Jesus didn't say it, Dude. You did.

Si had been playing Joe all along, and Joe fell for it. Joe waved him off dismissively, and sulked momentarily in the defeated embarrassment of having been played.

—Seriously, continued Jim. Think about Jesus outside of the stories we know about Him. Do you think he ever stubbed His toe? Lost His balance? Tripped and fell? Skinned His knee? Fretted over a splinter?

—He was the son of a carpenter, Jesús added.

—What's your point? asked Joe, having moved past his temporary defeat.

—My point is that Jesus grew up. He traveled, He met people, He did things, He ate dinner with friends every night. Do you really think in His whole life He never laughed? Never told a joke?

Sometimes I feel like I have to believe that Jesus could laugh, that He did laugh.

I remember at that moment hearing something I had never really heard before, and that was the sound of Maria laughing. I hadn't heard her laugh before—not like that.. It wasn't a hysterical laugh, certainly not a guffaw or a chortle, but there was a good-natured, warm, and reassuring sound to her laughter. She was sitting behind all of us, and had been listening to our every word. Finally, she spoke.

—I think it would be good if we can make people laugh, she said.

The rest of us exchanged glances, not knowing exactly what she meant.

—How do you mean? asked Joe. You mean, in general?

—No, said Maria. I mean us, in what we do.

—But we're not comedians, said Si, whose seriousness was reflected in the way he momentarily addressed no one as Dude.

—We should do more than just act, said Maria. We should act *out*. Laughter is empowering.

There was an awkward sentiment in the air as we tried to grasp precisely what Maria meant.

—We need to change everything, she added.

And that was that. So many performances and so many creative ideas, yet neither Maria nor the troupe had ever thought to put on any sort of comic twist to any of the acts. Why should religious drama always be somber, serious, and morose? Sure, there was plenty of suffering to be found in the long record of religious plaint, but somewhere in all of it there had to be some humor, something to laugh at, some element of comedy to offer hope in the endless litany of tragedy that so glibly dominates the scriptural records of the world, past and present. No one was suggesting some new institution, of course—no Our Lady of the Sarcastic Quip or Church of the Holy Pun. But what Maria was suggesting was that a bit of humor might be a powerful thing for the troupe, something that would link actor and audience in a shared moment, acting *with* rather than acting *for*. It was time for a change, time to try something new, though at the moment I don't think any of us had any idea how radical this idea was. And all of us wondered why we hadn't thought of it before, all of us, of course, except Maria, who in fact had already thought it.

—Knock knock.

This time it was Jesús, who had emerged from his momentary quietude. We all looked at each other.

—Knock knock, he said again.

—Who's there? offered Joe, to see how it would play out.

—Jesus, said Jesús.

—Jesus who?

—It's just me, Jesús. Don't you even know my name? And I thought you guys were my friends.

I had to reflect for a moment on laughter, and what a strange and wonderful thing it is. What if laughter were inseparable from religion and faith and piety and spirituality? Was laughter always a profane element of humanity, the thing that took us away from our sacred center? Or was it an essential part of that sacred center? Maybe laughter was just a shared ritual that the unsaintly and impious kept among themselves—God had his mysterious secrets that we could never fathom, so we had our mysterious laughter that He tolerated even if He could never quite relate. Or maybe God has a sense of humor, or maybe our sense of humor is part of our divinity. If God had a sense of humor, after all, laughter would be sacred.

I asked Maria for a piece of paper and a pen and scribbled something down. I still have that piece of paper, and it is pinned to the wall in front of me as I write. Here is what it says. *I will never truly know if God has a sense of humor, but I do know that anyone without a sense of humor can never truly believe in God.*

8

It seems an oddly mathematical maneuver for being in the middle of the desert. One road, with a number of 40, turns into another road, with a number of 41, by way of a precise 90-degree left turn. The signs said we were turning toward Albuquerque, ABQ as the local folks call it, but along the way we made another turn, a left turn to be precise, and now faced south, with signs pointing to the unnecessarily named Mountainair. I could feel we were circling. We were slowly being drawn into the orbit of Albuquerque, ABQ, the center of the universe, if New Mexico were a universe. Which it is, especially if you're in ABQ.

Maria was sitting in the back of the bus. She had been scribbling in a notebook all along the way, generating a meditative and intense mood about her. The notebook was black with no markings on the outside, and no indication of what sort of information was contained on the inside. I could tell from the occasional crescendo of sound emanating from the affective friction of pen on paper that Maria was trying to articulate something from deep within her inner emotional circuitry. There was a frenetic grace to her movements, and Maria often seemed unaware that anyone or anything else existed as she worked. There was her, her notebook, her pen, and her written word—all else was simply a void.

The content of the nondescript, black notebook was not the only mystery that I could not fathom about Maria. The other was the mysterious way that she arranged everything—there was always a place to be, and when we arrived there, there was always someone expecting us, something ready for us to do. I talked with Joe, I talked with Si, I talked with Jim, and I talked with Jesús, and none of them ever saw Maria on the phone, on a computer, or on any other device. I never saw it either. No one knew how she did these things— we could only accept that she did, and each of us bore witness to it.

—I can't make any sense of it, Joe once said to me. But really, is there any point in trying? It is what it is, and that's cool.

We were southeast of ABQ and it was a new day. At a later point in time, when I would return to this place to retrace the very path I was now on, I would learn that here, in the land of the Manzano Mountains, there was a long history of human drama that would make everything that was about to happen resonate much more clearly that I could have imagined. There were ruins of old pueblos in this area, and there were missions, too, most built on top of those ruins. For the Spanish governors who thought they controlled this landscape and for the people that walked upon it, the hard and durable walls of the missions foretold a permanent presence of power that would eternally outlast the crumbled ruins of what came before. But what the governors did not know, and what they could never have imagined, was that the people over whom they tried to exert their eternal authority, and the very people they forced to build the missions themselves, rebuilt those ruins right underneath the missions so that the ruins were no longer ruins and the missions were not really missions.

The local residents, sometimes with the connivance of local priests who showed one mask to the authorities above and another to the faithful below, embedded their own ceremonial structures into the foundation of the missions and the houses that surrounded them. Only those engaged in their acts of worship knew the true objects of their devoted inspiration. When the Spanish governors came to town, they saw what appeared to be devout Christians worshipping in the mission church under the mission bell. When the Spanish governors left town, of course, nothing changed, but that was really the whole point—nothing had ever changed. The Spanish authorities believed that everyone had become believers, but what everyone believed was that the Spanish authorities were fools. As for the residents and the priests who served them, they were devout, no doubt, but what they were devout about was known only to them and to the spirits that believed them.

Tour buses became more frequent on the road numbered 41 as we came nearer to the sites that tourists believed were important to see. In a final act of dramatic irony, the ruins under the missions are now preserved and the missions themselves are now ruins. The state authorities set aside funds to make sure both are cared for, and the tourists flock to see both as part of the same pre-paid packaged pilgrimage. According to the writing on the tour buses, the experience was guaranteed to be authentic, and New Mexico was the land of enchantment, so all were guaranteed to be authentically enchanted.

Maria took notice of the tour buses. I could tell because she would look up from her notebook and the scribbles she was inscribing every time we saw a tour bus, and when she saw one, her eyebrows would furl and her furrow would brow. Maria was thinking something, that much I could tell, but what she was thinking was something I could only guess at.

—You okay back there? I asked, having no cause for concern but having concern nevertheless.

No reply.

—I see you looking at the buses, I said.

—They have their bus, we have ours, she said.

That was all.

We pulled into the Mountainair Church of The Nazarene, which I remember well because of the oddity of the name. Technically all churches are churches of the Nazarene by default, so why the clarification? Has anyone ever seen a Christian church and been confused as to which Jesus the church embraces? *Excuse me, is this a church of Jesus the Nazarene or Jesus the Vancouverite?* Then again, we were in a place called Mountainair, and I half expected the next town to be called Earthground or some such other uninspired name. We all climbed out of the bus, with Maria the last out. She looked pensive, but there was mischief in her eyes as well.

—Today everything changes, she said.

The rest of us exchanged furtive glances. Uncertainty was the mood of the moment.

—Should we go inside? asked Joe.

—We're not going inside, said Maria.

At that point someone came out of the church into the parking lot, which was empty, except for us and the bus. I remember there was a cool breeze blowing, only because I remember that Maria's hair was billowing and she was remarkably indifferent to the movement.

—Father Da Silva, she said.

—It's good to see you, Maria, said the man, whom I presumed to be Father Da Silva.

—You will be performing here today before the service, as usual? asked Father Da Silva.

—No, Father. Today, nothing will be as usual. We will perform, but not here, answered Maria.

—So, you are not performing for the Church today?

—I did not say that, said Maria.

Father Da Silva looked gently confused and bit his lower lip in anticipation, awaiting some sort of answer from Maria. Actually we were all awaiting some sort of answer from Maria.

—We will perform today, but not here, began Maria.

She then explained what would happen and why. We needed to reach more people, and we needed to reach them in different ways. The spirit of the performance would still be the same, but the audience had to change along with the role of the actors. We were going to make people laugh and we were going to make them see things they would not otherwise see, or would choose not to see. Maria had the insight that we were really only re-enacting religious stories that everyone already knew. They were good stories, and they needed to be told, but they were not enough. Nor was it enough to let a small audience come to us. It was time for us to go to the audience, to create a new audience, to let people know they were in the audience whether they were aware of it or not.

I will confess to being both inspired and bewildered in the moments when Maria was speaking. I felt stirred, even awakened, even if I did not always understand the meaning of her words.

—Father Da Silva, said Maria suddenly in a serious tone. We are going to do something that may have consequences, for us and for you. I would like to leave our bus here, and we will retrieve it shortly and leave quickly. If you do not want to be involved, please say so. No one will think any less of you.

Father Da Silva looked to the ground, then to the sky, then to Maria.

—There is no act that does not have consequences. Whatever it is you intend to do, you have my support and my blessings.

Maria looked at him and smiled easily. Then she looked at all of us, keeping that smile, and with a slight jump in her step, started walking. The five of us looked at one another, then looked at Father Da Silva, who gave an almost imperceptible nod, and in unison we walked after Maria, as if it were the most natural thing to do. Maria never looked back to see if we would follow. She did not have to.

We walked along Piñon Street, where the church emptied into the street, and from there continued along through a mishmash of houses and local businesses, which included two scruffy bars and a disheveled restaurant called El Burro Loco, until we arrived at a precisely perpendicular intersection where the road with the number 55 met the street with the name Cedar. Technically it was East Cedar Street, and I would learn shortly, on the way out of town, that there was also a West Cedar Street. This was the same street, it just changed its name and direction at a specific point, as did all the streets in Mountainair, except for the ones with numbers for names. At the intersection, Maria waved for us to stop, exaggerating her hand movement in a way that made it clear that we were to stay where we were.

Maria then walked directly and purposefully into the street, directly into the intersection, unconcerned and undistracted by any signs and signals. We stood aside and gazed with wonder and trepidation, for she was walking right into traffic, and we were frightened for her. She walked without fear. I don't think any of us could have done that, at least not then. The traffic seemed to part ways around her, following her lead and following her movement. Cars slowed down, then they stopped. And as they stopped, and as people got out of their cars to see this vision of a woman on the road in the traffic without fear, Maria began to do what she had come here to do.

She slowly worked herself into a much more extravagant version of herself, exaggerating her movements more than I had ever seen her do before, and projecting her voice in a way that seemed to overwhelm the sleepy suburban landscape. It wasn't just the volume that surprised and startled me, it was the ease with which she took on different voices as she began to tell a story. Much like a circus director in the main tent, Maria was introducing the main act, and yet, the main act was Maria herself. The story she told was one that at first was unfamiliar to me, only because I was expecting something from the usual scripturally scripted repertoire.

She told the story of a local mayor—the name of the mayor I now forget, and in any case, it's irrelevant. She acted out the story as she told it, taking on all roles and speaking in all different voices. The story, which turned out to be true, or mostly so, was a tale about a mayor had tried to reverse his own signature on a bill legalizing prostitution by claiming he was too drunk when he signed it for the act to be legally valid. After his opponents decried his approval of the bill, citing it as evidence that he was morally unfit to govern, he attempted to prove his capacity to govern by claiming he was incapacitated when he committed the act that allegedly displayed his lack of capacity.

I remember being amused by the story, I remember expressing a cynical chuckle, but Maria had turned the story into a fable of human folly, a parable on the arrogance of power, a sermon on the seduction of authority. She did so with the flourish of a public performance that created an audience where none had existed only moments before. She had made an audience appear out of thin mountain air. She portrayed every character, and played every voice—she was male and female, she was ruler and ruled, she was oppressor and oppressed, she was good and evil—and not only was it wonderful, it was wonderfully funny. Maria had found a way to make people laugh, and yet as they laughed, she also made them think. This had become Maria's new passion.

Some people came out of their houses to watch, staring in amazement or disbelief. Who was this woman in the street? Was she crazy? Traffic had stopped, people were out of their cars, standing and listening, as if mesmerized. Some wanted to listen, while others listened in the hopes of finding a reason not to listen. Yet as with all moments like this, for every person that grows curious, there is another that grows suspicious. Any time a person attracts an audience, they attract other things as well.

Here a driver honked the horn, there a neighbor got on the phone. Some people got angry, others got angry that others were angry. Yet Maria was an expert in her element, and in the middle of the scene, facing the people, she was able to watch them in their actions, even as they watched her in hers. She wound down her performance with the same seamless ease with which she had ramped it up minutes before, then walked back to the side of the road where we had been standing and watching all along.

—*Vámanos*, she said.

We walked back to the church, where we found Father Da Silva still standing outside. Maria approached him.

—Thank you, Father Da Silva, she said.

—Nothing to thank, he replied.

We all climbed into the bus, with a sense that something had just happened, something had changed, but we weren't sure what it was. There wasn't a large audience at the intersection, barely twenty people, as I recall it. Yet Maria's conviction in what she had done, in knowing that what she had done was exactly what she wanted to do, had left an impression. There was more to this than any of us knew. Things had been set in motion, that much we knew. What those things were, only Maria knew.

We drove out of town, heading west on East Cedar. A police car passed us, heading east from West Cedar, with sirens wailing and lights flashing. I wondered where it was going, but did not ask. Perhaps the others wondered as well. I had the feeling that I had just witnessed the start of something important, though now that I reflect on it, I'm not sure if part of that feeling is something I have only now, knowing as I do everything that was soon to come. Perhaps it doesn't matter. You never see the start of a revolution until the revolution is at its end.

Maria turned to me.

—You should write this down, she said. All that has happened.

I fumbled for something to write with and something to write on, knowing I didn't have either, in the same way that people look at their wrist when asked the time, though they know they are not wearing a watch.

—Dude, you should start a blog, said Si.

—I don't like blogs, I said. I don't trust them.

Maria reached over the seat from behind me. In her hand was a pen. I took it from her, and stared at the pen. I now knew my task was to witness, to observe, to record. I was back in the role I started with, before I ever left on this journey. What had been my end was now my beginning—a reincarnation, or rebirth, of sorts. Maria had created this role for me, and I wanted to play it right this time. I thought for a moment of what I would write, if I had to describe everything that I had just seen, everything that had happened.

—Take this, she said.

Maria had handed me something else, something wrapped in plastic. I rubbed it, as one might rub a magic lantern, and removed the plastic. Now I had a black notebook of my own.

9

Who are the true believers, and what do they believe? To call someone a true believer is rarely a compliment, and yet, at the end of the day, it seems rather ridiculous to think that there could be believers who are anything other than true. If you are a believer, then by definition you believe something to be true. It is possible to be a true disbeliever, I suppose, in that a person could be quite resolved not to believe something at all and remain true to that disbelief, but anything in between seems either not to be true or not to be belief. Belief can only be true—otherwise it's not belief.

I struggled with this idea at the time. I had only been with the theater troupe for a few days, though it felt like much longer. It felt like I was among friends, or at least among companions, but then again, calling someone a friend is really just another act of faith. Did

I have friends, or did I only believe I had friends? How would I know the difference? I struggled with doubt as much as I struggled with belief. I wanted certainty and clarity—to know or not to know, to believe or not to believe—but found myself continuously foundering in rhythmic swells of opacity and diffidence.

I distracted myself as often as I could by writing. Now that I had a notebook and a mission, I had a sense of purpose, even if I sometimes mistook the distraction of writing for the purpose itself. I had much to write about in those days. We made a series of performances with a series of stops, all of them repeating the same guerilla theater tactics—that's how the media would later describe it—that Maria had first unveiled in Mountainair, where audience and actor appeared and disappeared only moments apart. We made our way, performance by performance, through towns like Bernardo, Abeytas, Sabinal, Bosque, Jarales, Belen, and further north into Los Lunas. With each show, the others got better and better at this new way of doing things, and they became more comfortable with transforming the old repertoire into the new. I had difficulty at first understanding what Maria was trying to do, but as we made our way to Albuquerque, it started to become clear.

—Dude, we made the news, said Si.

And indeed we had. One isolated performance of a woman disrupting traffic at an intersection is just an incident, a good story to tell others, and perhaps an interesting police report. A series of performances, especially when the same set of characters are present every time, quickly becomes a social phenomenon. There is structure and intent, and it's only a matter of time before people sit up and take notice. I understand now, only much later, why Maria wasn't concerned if the number of people who saw these new types of performances was small. Once the media picked up on the story, and once people started to talk in the way they are prone to talk, it didn't matter who had actually seen the performance. What mattered is that people were talking, and when that happened, it was as if those who had truly witnessed a performance acted as if they were among the chosen. Those who had only heard the stories wanted to see things for themselves, to bear witness, to be among the chosen. The tales became taller with every telling. Social media lit up like an electronic bonfire, with many a person praying to the digital deities that they procure viral status—an affective affliction sometimes bestowed upon the especially needy and narcissistic. Some told the story so many times they actually came to believe it, to believe they had seen what they had never seen.

The audience, whether real or imaginary, grew rapidly. It was there on the radio, it was there on the television, it was of course there all over the internet. Bloggers picked it up, trolls followed suit, and many people tried desperately to be in the right place at the right time in the hope of being a part of something that was not theirs to be a part of.

—There's a woman here who's upset about our performance in Veguita, said Joe. She called it a publicity stunt.

—We didn't do a performance in Veguita, said Jim.

—That doesn't seem to have stopped her from saying we did, replied Joe, with a whispered chuckle and a visage of disbelief that people often have when they glimpse humans falling to temptation.

People were taking notice, and people were taking notice of the fact that people were taking notice. As short as they were when they lasted—maybe five minutes or so—the new-fashioned street performances had taken on a life of their own. This is how legends and traditions get started—legends being the things we tell *to* each other, and traditions being the things we perform *for* each other. Not that I thought we were starting a legend or a tradition in that moment, but you could at least catch a glimpse of how it might occur, had it happened. Which it didn't. At least not then.

By far the oddest thing that occurred was the competition among a specific group of bloggers for the right to tell the story of what had happened and what it meant. In just one day, four bloggers had taken to the blogosphere to write their own version of the performances, and while all of them got the gist of the story right, they differed in significant details and they differed in what they wished to emphasize about what happened. It was like reading four different versions of the same story, and somehow you had to read between the lines to piece together some version of what must have happened, even though the pieced together version is really just another version. Jim began to read them aloud.

One blogger chose to focus on the role of Maria. In that version, Maria took on a primeval role whose actions represented the fundamental human aspiration for freedom, created, as the blogger gleefully pointed out, by a woman. The people who were complaining and the authorities who were concerned were in truth just upset by the fact that a woman had taken the lead, that a woman had come first. This turned the whole order of society upside down, and threatened existing structures of power, all of which, according to the author of this account, were patriarchal. If society could be transformed into something matriarchal, then the human urge to freedom, long ago blocked by the evil tribe of men, would be liberated and restored to humanity. The world cannot handle strong women, said the blogger, because they represent a threat to the powers that be, and thus, people could not handle the actions of Maria. Those actions, which were described by the blogger as taking place high on a hill, showed that if women led the world, the world would be free and the world would be at peace. Maria was the embodiment, the corporeal confirmation, that women were the solution to all that ailed the world.

—If you want to consider women equal, said Maria, then you shouldn't consider them different.

The second version saw the theatrical spectacles of the troupe in terms of political commentary. There was a long history of satire in America—this blogger called it an American tradition—and satire was the lifeblood of democracy. The random street performances—in this version they took place on a wide, grassy plain, an interesting accomplishment for something titled *street* theater—were a revival of American democracy, and through them American democracy had been born again. The fact that people were upset about the rebirth of American democracy, the fact that people were complaining about these *flash* performances (his words, not mine) and that the police were *concerned* for public safety showed how far America had fallen as a beacon of democracy. America had lost its way, we had forgotten our democratic tradition, and these performances were evidence both of the fall of American democracy and of the hope of the revival to come. Democracy was eternal, said the blogger, and so these performances must be celebrated by all. They were the spark that lit the fire of democracy.

—That's a bit dramatic, said Joe.

—Dude, so are we, said Si.

—Not me, said Jesús.

—Especially you, said Jim.

Then there was the third blogger, who wrote about the community of actors, that is, about us, the troupe. All of them seemed to get along, noted the blogger, and so why couldn't the rest of us be like those actors? This was by far the shortest blog we read, and described the performances in terse and sparse prose—well-chosen words, just fewer of them. The actors, said the blogger, were a village, a commune, a utopia, a small group of people who got along as all people would get along, if only the state didn't intervene. Government was the antithesis of the people, but the people didn't know that. This was the wake up call. If we all lived as the actors lived, if we all acted as the actors did, we wouldn't need the state, and we wouldn't need government. We would only need ourselves. We could make our own rules to live by. The agents of the state knew it, and that was why the police—and this blogger compared them to the soldiers of the Roman Empire—were worried about the performances as a threat to public safety. But no, said the blogger, the people always had their safety, and it was the government who took it away from us, over and over again, as history was a witness.

—Sounds like we've got ourselves an anarchist, said Joe.

—Dude, I bet he wears a trench coat.

—The irony, I added.

—Irony? asked Joe.

—The trench coat was developed for troops to fight in trenches in the First World War, I explained. It's a symbol of the state.

—Maybe he's an ironist, said Jim.

—That's not a thing, clarified Maria definitively.

The fourth account saw everything as an act of subversion. *Guerilla theater*, as she called it. I will admit I thought it was a catchy title—I even made a note to myself to use it later when I wrote everything out. The author of this blog pointed out that the spontaneous acts of theater—which weren't actually spontaneous, but she didn't know that—conformed to the rules of guerilla warfare, of lightning attacks against an adversary in situations of power asymmetry.

—Power asymmetry? asked Jesús. Who talks like that?

Jim scrolled.

—The author is a graduate student of liberation theology at Incarnate Word College, said Jim, reading directly from the screen.

—*Dios mio*, sighed Jesús, looking slightly skyward.

What made these acts of guerilla theater so powerful, said the aspiring student theologian, is that the guerilla strategy had been grafted onto a form of struggle that was inherently nonviolent. Words had replaced weapons, words had become nonviolent weapons, and in doing so, the rebel actors of guerilla theater had displayed exactly the sort of struggle that Jesus would have wanted. WWJD, the blogger pondered.

—WWJD? asked Jesús.

—What Would Jesus Do, said Jim.

Jesús pressed his forehead to the palm of his hand, a perfectly executed facepalm, which is what Jesús would do when he was at a loss for words.

—So, Jesus would be an actor? asked Joe.

—Maybe He was, answered Jim.

—Dude, He was a carpenter, said Si.

—Or maybe He just acted like one, countered Jim.

—If he did, then he nailed it, said Joe.

Jesús intensified his face-palm in pained silence, while Maria, who had been quiet throughout this exchange, shed some somber light.

—I don't think nail jokes are something we should say about Jesus, she said, feigning crossness.

Maria started to scribble in her notebook. A few minutes later so did I. All this writing, all these words, so much faith in so many words. Ancient Egypt had its hieroglyphs, sacred scribbles on stone slabs. Ancient India had its learned class of Brahmins, whose literacy gave them access to the sacred scribbles of sages. Ancient China had its scapulimancy, sacred marks on tortoise shells and oracle bones, with meanings known only to those who knew how to read them, to see things no one else could see. Leonardo Da Vinci had his own secret code, to occlude his knowledge so that only his own eyes could see the signs. All this writing, all these words, so much faith in so many words.

I thought about the blogs that we had read. Four people saw the same thing and yet wrote four different accounts of what they had seen. Which one to believe? Should we believe them all? Should we believe only what we see with our own eyes? Should we believe only what we ourselves write, so that we all have our own secret code, our own hidden signs? Word had gotten out about us, and now words were being written about us. I suppressed the urge to write my own account, to set things straight, to tell the truth, because really, what truth would I tell? I knew very well that even if those of us in the bus wrote out our own version of events, the stories we each told would be as different as those of the four bloggers we read earlier. Humanity seems compelled to write story after story, hoping one day perhaps someone will understand, yet knowing that no one ever will. Not completely, at least. The rest we have to take on faith.

We passed the sign for Petroglyph National Monument, an ancient landscape of sacred scribbles and scratchings out in the West Mesa of Albuquerque. Lots of people go there to see the signs, to see the carvings, and local tribes claim the land is a sacred landscape. Yet no one knows what these carved signs and etched emblems really mean, no one except perhaps those who carved and etched them in the first place. Some years ago, a couple built and consecrated a Tibetan stupa on the same landscape. When the government took over the land to preserve the petroglyphs, using legal documents written in words that only those of the lawyer clan can understand, they left the Tibetan stupa on the landscape, but they had no qualms demolishing the home of the couple and every other non-sacred structure on the site. Perhaps the couple should have consecrated their home, but then again, had they done so, their home would have become a temple, and the only people who live in temples are either priests or gods.

We skirted the sacred landscape and drove north toward Albuquerque. We stopped at one point to get some food, and while we were stopped, Maria told us why we were going to Albuquerque and what we were going to do there on the next day. There was to be a festival in honor of Saint Genesius, and we were to perform there. This would be the largest crowd by far that the troupe had ever performed for, and with the rumor and babble of our recent charades skipping across the electric landscape, there was every reason to believe that crowd would be even larger than expected. For the first time since I had been with them, the troupe seemed genuinely aware of an ominous weight descending upon their shoulders. We returned to the bus and drove north. We passed the sign for

Albuquerque city limits, and entered the city with a grave silence, cradling our burritos from Las Palmas, a taqueria with real palm trees, fake adobe, multilingual graffiti, and a house-made hot sauce that they call El Diablo.

10

The city of Albuquerque straddles both sides of the big river, the flowing monument known as the Rio Grande. The arid outskirts of town generously and unselfishly offer up the red dusty residue that coats the boots and tires of every urban cowboy and every iron horse. Every child of ABQ knows the sting and watery eyes borne from the silty dust that lies in wait where the city lights begin to thin, waiting for the smallest wisp of breeze to carry it into town. The sound and scent and sight of the river serve to remind the good citizens of ABQ of the fragility of their lives. Without the river, the dust would never be washed away. It would invade the town and triumph in its undeclared battle against the ever-resistant river. An endless thirst would prevail, life would come to an end, and ABQ would be a ghost town. From up on high, say, from the spired pinnacles of the Sandia mountains that lie due east of town, one can look down on this eternal battle, looking at an endless sea of brown parchment tundra cut through by an azure river that refuses to back down, and refuses to stop giving life to everything around it. From up on high, ABQ looks like an earthen stage in a giant ethereal amphitheater.

We pulled into that great amphitheater and headed for an event that Maria had promised would be quite a show.

—Trust me, she said.

We were scheduled to appear at a festival at the San Felipe de Neri Church, located in what ABQ folks like to call Old Town, apparently because it's the part of town that is old. It was quite a famous church, however, as I was soon to discover.

—It's historic, said a woman to me later that day.

Considering that history is nothing other than the record of things that transpire in time, there isn't anything on earth that isn't historic in some way or other. I thought of pointing this out to the woman, but a disputation on the meaning of history was not my purpose that day, so I merely nodded to acknowledge her observation, and we went our separate ways into our separate days.

Not long before I had this historic conversation with the woman, we had pulled into ABQ, all of us emotionally jostled by the strange combination of weariness from the road and excitement for the event, all of us woefully unprepared, except perhaps Maria, for the drama that the day would eventually offer up. The city seemed peaceful enough, with the good people of ABQ running about in the subtle rhythms of everyday life, but as we got closer to the church, everything seemed to slow down, literally so. Apparently this was to be quite the festival, judging by the way the traffic began to congeal like blood on an open wound with every block closer we crawled toward the church grounds. Eventually we decided it would be best to break our journey at a distance and walk, rather than suffer through the interminable blood sludge of traffic, more flood than flow, and so after a circuitous search through the streets that skirted Old Town, we found a place to park. We departed the yellow bus, taking all our earthly belongings with us, and leaving her parked at the corner of Hollywood and Rio Grande. What we didn't know in that moment was that it would be the last time any of us ever saw that yellow bus again.

We walked towards the church. I could glimpse hints of the spires through the trees as we approached, and gradually the whole grand edifice revealed itself. At the time I thought it was a big, impressive church, which it was, and still is. The pinkish hue of the mud clay walls gives the church an air of defiance, rising as it does with pretensions of permanence out of the landscape of red silty earth, the very earth from which it was made, and the very earth to which it will one day inevitably return. The thick walls of the church were a testament to the presumptuousness of human architecture. Sacred or not, one day, they, too, would be ruins. Only later did I learn that the original church that had been built here had been dissolved by rain in 1792. The church was eventually rebuilt—same church, but also somehow not—with a rather grandiose vision, its ambition reminiscent more of human folly than divine power. It's the oldest building in town—making it historic, as the woman told me—and therefore forms the foundation of Old Town. Incidentally, there is a plaza located right across the street from the church, and in keeping with New Mexico's curiously revered tradition of peculiar place-naming, the plaza in the Old Town is called Old Town Plaza.

The plaza was being used on that day as part of the festival venue. Crowds of people mingled and meandered inside and outside the church, and from the church grounds into the streets and into the plaza. I remember thinking as I approached the church that it seemed more carnival than caritas, but for far more of humanity than humanity would like to think, caritas is not possible without at least some element of carnival, so either everything or nothing was exactly as it should have been on that day. There were signs everywhere advertising all sorts of things, from local retreats to far away pilgrimages, with many odds and ends in between, most of which I found odd and some of which predicted the end, which for as long as anyone can remember has always been nigh and near.

The five of us did what we usually ended up doing, following Maria, as she seemed to be the only one of us who knew exactly where we were supposed to go. We ended up at a registration kiosk where we were supposed to check-in. To get there, we first we had to walk underneath an arch of flying bowling pins, which were being juggled across the pathway into the church compound by two young men who to my mind seemed way too happy to be engaged in such a needlessly and mindlessly repetitive task. I suppose the same thing could be said about writing, although no one has ever accused a writer of being way too happy about anything. Indeed, no one has ever accused a writer of being happy at all. I wandered off into a momentary daydream that consisted mostly of me juggling typewriters, but my daydream was cut short by the overly enthusiastic voice of the woman behind the kiosk counter.

—May I help you? she asked.

She glanced at all of us in a way that clearly showed a rush to some sort of judgment, followed by a smile that showed she had made her judgment but was going to keep it to herself, because she considered herself too good a person to rush to judgment.

—We are here to perform, said Maria.

—All of you? asked the woman behind the kiosk.

—Yes, said Maria. We are all actors.

The woman seemed skeptical, although I could not think of a single reason why anyone would or could be skeptical of the claim. She began to shuffle some papers, as if she were trying to get them into some sort of proper order, even as that order mercilessly eluded her. She seemed inexplicably protective of these papers, as if they were full of powerful charms and secret incantations. In reality, as I would learn later, and only when it became an issue, they were legal waivers for all festival performers to sign. Next to her was a woman counting money in a peculiarly repetitive way, silently voicing numbers that made it appear like she was evoking spirits or casting spells on each individual bill or coin, and next to her was another woman selling tickets to the festival, who kept saying thank you to everyone in a ritualized voice that carried all the emotional depth of a juggled bowling pin. I watched all of this, but slowly found myself watching Maria watching all of this. Something was happening, I just didn't know what.

—Is Father Markovic here? asked Maria, rather directly.

The woman behind the kiosk tightened her grip on the papers she held in her hands.

—Father Markovic is busy, she said, with an emphasis on the word busy that carried a sense of menace and malice, followed by a smile that indicated she considered herself too good a person to express menace or malice.

—How do you know he is busy? asked Maria, with a clear tone that showed she was going to lead this conversation.

—I know he is busy because I know Father Markowicz, said the woman. He trusts me to take care of his things.

—How do you know he doesn't trust everyone with his things? inquired Maria.

—It's like people say, behind every strong man stands an even stronger woman, she replied.

She looked at Maria again with a smile that showed she clearly perceived herself to be the stronger woman, though she was too good a person to consider herself the stronger woman. She was evidently pleased with her observation, which carried all the profundity of a greeting card, without the greeting.

—God is behind everyone, said Maria.

—Are you saying God is a woman?

—God only knows.

—Are you being sarcastic?

—Mostly sardonic.

—I don't know what that means.

—God does.

Maria made a motion with her hand that indicated we were to follow her, which we did, past the ticket booth—Thank you, said the ticket-seller ritualistically, though we had bought no tickets—and into the church compound. Maria told us to wait while she ascended a set of stairs, where moments later we heard the sounds of muffled talking echoing in the reflective way that things always seem to echo in a church. I recognized only one of the voices, which was Maria's. The other voice was clearly a man's voice, but beyond that, nothing was clear.

Maria descended the stairs and had a look about her that I could not fathom. If I had to give it a word, I would have called it gravity, though gravity isn't really a look so much as a mood, and an unfathomable one at that. She explained to us the details of what we were to do, when we were to perform, and what we were to perform. Apparently, we were going to perform a play on the corruption of authority, and apparently there was quite a bit of expectation in the air since Father Markovic may or may not have spread a few stories here and there about us, if nothing else to generate a sense of anticipation. I forgot that we had been in the news as of late, and apparently this Father Markovic, whom I had not yet seen but had almost certainly heard, had a flair for the dramatic or a good sense of showmanship, or perhaps a bit of both. Maria was mysteriously scant on any hint of dialog for our play, which was, as I had learned, almost always intentional, even if the intent remained known only to her, which it almost always did.

We whiled away a few hours in a mostly empty room in the building next to the church. It was full of construction equipment for some reason, though whether the room was being built up or torn down was unclear. We weren't really rehearsing anything, but rather going through the motions of what a rehearsal would look like, if we had to rehearse. Jim and I were to play persons of authority, and so spent a fair amount of time trying to figure out how to act as if we had authority. Maria suggested we needed some sort of costume, something that represented the authority that Jim and I were supposed to have, or supposed to act like we have, and so she improvised two Roman helmets out of two red construction hats and some red bristle brushes.

—So our play is set in Roman times? I asked.

—No, said Maria.

Apparently when Christians see a Roman soldier they know it means authority, and not the good kind.

Si was to play a merchant, so he kept jangling change in his hand, which isn't really a skill that takes practice, but he practiced it nevertheless, until he felt confident that his change jangling was done in a sufficiently determined and calculated manner. Joe was to play the part of a beggar, so he was supposed to look like he needed help, which we all helped him practice. Jesús was to play an undocumented worker, which seemed a little too close to reality, except that, as Maria pointed out, no one ever suspects an actor of being the thing they are. Maria was to play—and these were her exact words—a voice of conscience. None of us had any idea what that meant, but Maria did, and that was enough. She reached into her bag and pulled out a fake beard—for any other person in the world I would have found that strange—and when she put it on she had the appearance of a wise man, or a wise woman, albeit one with a beard. I remember wondering if anyone would have mistaken her costume, thinking for instance that she was a hipster, but it wasn't really that kind of beard and besides, no one has ever mistaken a bearded hipster for a wise man.

After what seemed a long while a young man stepped into the room.

—It's time, he said.

What happened next is what some might call the stuff of legend, or maybe only I call it that, since I was there then to bear witness to the events, and now that I write about it, I certainly think it could be, or should be, a legend. The young man led us to a small raised stage in a large open courtyard, and no sooner did we hit the stage than Maria began the hitherto unrehearsed performance.

—Why do we need festivals to give money to the church? she shouted plaintively.

That wasn't really the opening any of us were expecting. Judging from the reactions of many in the crowd, they clearly weren't expecting it either.

Maria continued.

—Why do we not want to see the poor until we think that God sees us seeing the poor?

Si jangled his coins, while Joe appeared to beg for them. Jim and I looked on with authoritative awkwardness, while Jesús stood still-life-like with a sense of apprehension and fear, but whether it was his character or the events that were responsible, I could not say.

Maria continued her sermonesque soliloquy, mimicking the talking heads and babbling bloggers who couldn't wait to talk about us over the past few days but never once talked to us. She ridiculed everything from holy days to holidays, and asked repeatedly the simplest of questions.

—Why is it so hard for us to be better than the people we have become?

When a few people in the audience responded with choked chortles and gruntled guffaws, Maria became intensely aware of the distance between her and the people around her and became equally determined to close that distance. She slapped the hand of Si the merchant, sending his coins flying over the head of Joe the beggar, whose begging career ended in that very moment. As members of the audience went to their knees to filch the flung coinage—*This is what brings you to your knees at a church?* Maria exclaimed with exasperation—Maria left the stage and walked into and through the crowd. The rest of us followed.

Maria continued her words of conscience and her measured movements, leading out to the main gate. The crowd on the inside flowed outward into the crowd on the outside, like a river of confused humanity. Maria walked by the booths of the ticket seller and the festival manager, stopped pensively, and then in a moment overturned their tables with great panache, flinging money and tickets and trinkets to the ground, which sent some people to their knees and some people to their feet. People on the streets and in the plaza turned toward the commotion. Few were indifferent, some were inscrutable.

—She looks like Jesus, said a passerby.

—She looks crazy, said another.

—She is crazy, said another still.

I can't repeat every detail of what Maria said and did in those dramatic moments and to be truthful, I don't have to. Anyone there would tell you the same story, or at least some variation of it, I am quite sure. For the life of me I can't recall how long everything went on. I do remember at some point Jim and I removed our improvised Roman helmets and gave them to two young children, who immediately put them on and began fighting authoritatively with one another. I remember crowds of people moving about furtively and anxiously. At some point I heard the sound of breaking glass. Car alarms went off, and it was clear that people wanted to panic, but failed to do so, at least initially, due to religious restraint and pious propriety. It was a strange crowd in a strange town. The noise level rose, and the restraint receded accordingly. I wouldn't call it a riot, but others might. Riots tend to break out at the transition point where outward action becomes preferable to inward reflection. Maria had asked them for inward reflection. The crowd responded with outward action.

I remember watching people struggle to overturn a car. I remember watching a woman holding her young daughter while a man beside her struggled to punch another man. I remember a shirtless man with both arms raised in the air jumping with unrestrained joy, his face bearing a rather unsettling smile that suggested this is how he had hoped the evening would end all along. I remember the sound of sirens in the distance. I remember a white van pulling up, and a familiar voice—the same voice I had heard up the stairs earlier conversing with Maria—shouting for us to get in. I remember getting into the van, and I remember looking out the window at all the lost souls wandering around us. I remember driving out of town. I remember how we were all so tired, and how everything became silent and still as the town receded into the distance. I remember Maria sitting next to me, and how she slowly drifted off to sleep. I remember that as she fell asleep, her head came to rest on my shoulder. I remember thinking it was a very beautiful thing.

PRIESTS

1

Father Andelko Markovic was born in Croatia, though I don't know when. I never asked. He doesn't know a word of Croatian, and speaks with an accent that seems not to be who he is, though it is. That's because he grew up in Papua New Guinea, the child of two missionaries who decided that Papua New Guinea was the place to which their God had called them, and so the young Andelko grew up in a village in the Papuan highlands, whose name I can neither precisely remember nor accurately pronounce. He was raised in what he described as an Edenic land-scape that revealed a deep and ineffable sense of beauty, one that existed simultaneously with a gritty reality that persistently shattered the innocent moments of idealism and inspiration that every child craves. The one thing I remember him saying quite ecstatically was that to this day he holds a profound reverence for butterflies.

—The people of the village would look at butterflies and imagine them to be the protective spirits of their ancestors, he told me. I always looked at them as little angels.

—Did you eventually learn to see them as ancestral spirits? I asked.

—What I learned was there was no difference.

As Fate would have it, or perhaps it was Grace— the Angels can fight over that one—Father Andelko left Papua New Guinea many years later, when he was old enough to pursue his own calling, and after years of study in a seminary, received his first posting to a church in Asunción, Paraguay. The first official act he performed as a priest on the very first day of his very first mission was to baptize a newborn girl named Maria. And yes, the very same.

That's the distilled essence of what I have in my notebook about my first conversation with Father Andelko, in the days after we fled from ABQ and the church festival. On the same page there's also a sketch I made of a cactus, displaying the skills I have that answer the question of why I never became an artist. There's also a note to myself to read Willa Cather, amusing insofar as I never looked at that note again until now, which means I still haven't read Willa Cather, even though according to my rediscovered note I certainly should. At the bottom of the page there is a phone number that I underlined three times, reminding me of the habit I have of writing down phone numbers without writing down the names they belong to. I have no idea who this one belongs to either. It will always be there, as I can't bring myself to scratch it out since it could still have meaning. I also know I will never call it. I'm not sure what that says about me, and one day I will think about that, but today isn't that day.

When we fled from the festival, we drove west. I knew we were headed west from the angle of the bright North Star in the clear desert sky, which I could see through the window. There were other, more obvious signs as well, such as those by the side of the highway that stated we were on I-40 West. There were six of us in a white van that was meant for twelve. Jim asked Father Andelko where we were going.

—Tohajilee, he said.

Tohajilee is an Indian reservation just west of Albuquerque, part of the Navajo nation. It was the first native land we would come to after we left Albuquerque. The first of many, as it turned out.

—Dude, are we going on a spirit quest? asked Si.

—You should never be *off* a spirit quest, said Father Andelko. And my name's not Dude.

—Sorry, Dude, said Si.

—Father Andelko? queried Jim.

—Call me Andrew.

—But that's not really your name, said Jim.

—And I'm not really your father. Is that going to be a problem, too?

—Can we call you Andy? asked Joe.

—No.

—Why not?

—Because that's not really my name.

Father Andelko, now christened Andrew, explained to us that we were going on a jurisdiction quest, which was sort of like a spirit quest, except that instead of searching for spiritual giudance we were searching for legal shelter.

—We need to find places where the law can't reach us, said Andrew. You left behind quite a mess in Albuquerque. Word will travel fast, and as it travels, it will change shape. The high priests of ABQ will want someone to pay.

—But we didn't do anything, said Joe.

—What you did is less important than what people believe you did, replied Andrew.

So that was it. Maria had made a scene, and too many people had seen the scene. The problem with things like that is when people see things they do not understand, they start to tell themselves a story about what they had seen, in order to understand it. Those stories take on a life of their own, and pass from one person to the next, taking on a new life and a new meaning in every retelling. Eventually they become a story of their own. It is how the actions of ordinary people become extraordinary epics. Things grow to be larger than life, legends and tales are born. And yet, for every story that grows in this way, that grows on the aspirations of both those who want to tell stories and those who want to hear them, there will always be those who want to take what is larger than life and make it small again. For every person who wants to believe that something extraordinary could be true, there will always be another person who goes to extraordinary lengths to prove it is not.

When we arrived at Tohajilee it was dark and dusky. The highway had given way to a smaller road, and the smaller road had given way to an even smaller one, until at last that road turned to dust and we arrived at what appeared to be a small house. Maria stirred at the changed sound thrown from the tires when they traded smooth asphalt for rough dust, accompanied as the transformation was by a few rocks that rudely varied the way. Jesús had climbed into the very back seat and had fallen into a deep sleep. Andrew alone got out of the van, and was greeted at the door by someone dressed exactly as you would expect someone to dress in these parts. A conversation ensued between the two men, of which I heard not a word. Andrew shook the man's hand affectively, and returned to the van.

He sighed.

—We have to move on, he said. We can't stay here.

Apparently there had been some people who had been making drugs on reservation land, in an RV, as later reports would explain, to keep mobile and avoid detection. This had already attracted unwanted attention from law enforcement about illegal activity on native lands, and then with a recent shootout that left two DEA agents dead, there were federal officials everywhere. On top of that there were film crews everywhere asking for permission to film, hoping to turn these real-life events into some sort of made-for-television drama. With cameras and officials in every here and every there, it wouldn't take long to find the white van, and so we, the tribe of the white van, had to move on. Which we did.

We retraced our steps back to the interstate and followed the asphalt trail a few miles further down the road, passing through Mesita before arriving at the heart of Laguna territory, which was Laguna Pueblo itself. We pulled in front of the church, which with its bright white plaster walls looked rather spirit-like in the incomplete darkness of the starlit night that had now fallen definitively. The front of the building had only a doorway, one central window above it, and two smaller openings in the parapet in which were set two brass bells. In the light of the night the white of the church seemed to glow, making the recesses of the door and the window and the two parapet bells all appear black. I began to see a face in that façade, eyes where the bells were, for instance. It was oddly reassuring, though even now I can't explain why.

Andrew had entered the church as soon as we arrived and after a few minutes, the very same minutes in which I was night-dreaming the visage of the spirited church, he returned with the news that we had been offered shelter for the night, which was a great relief to us all as we were at that point quite weary and decidedly worn. The priest of the church at Laguna, which I would soon learn was the San José Mission Church, wanted us to gather in the church so that he could give us his blessing, so we all tumbled out of the van and wandered purposefully into the mouth of the church. The luminescent white of the outside of the church was Quaker plain, but the inside of the church was a festival for both sense and soul. Long and narrow, and lit only with candle-light, ornate wood work and carvings of unctuous stone ensconced the interior, and even as the tactile senses were drawn to texture, the visual senses were dazzled by the inspired splashes of red, yellow, orange, and green, flowing listlessly along the interior surfaces. The ceiling had the sun and the moon and the stars and every color of the rainbow, mostly because on it was painted a rainbow, with every color that a rainbow should properly have.

We approached the altar, which was covered with a large animal skin—something I found that unsettling. It was one thing to imagine that wine could be changed into blood, or that bread could be turned into flesh, but to see the remnants of death so close to what is supposed to be the fount of life was something that confused me. It still does. I stood between the thick, massive walls and the thin, lithe skin, uncertain of where to be. I looked up and noticed the many symbols of the Laguna spirit-world interwoven with the many symbols of the church's spirit-world. I wanted them to resolve to one side or the other, but looking back on that moment now, I can think only of Andrew and his butterflies. Not everything has to resolve.

The priest, a pensive man whose weathered and textured face appeared at one with the chiseled and carved ornaments that surrounded him wall by wall, gave his blessing to each of us one at a time with the same careful and caring attention. His devotion undermined the inertia of ritual. He blessed us not in English, nor in Spanish or even Latin, but rather in his own language, which was Keresan. I was blessed with words whose exact meaning I would never know, though I do still have a note to myself in my notebook, accompanied for some reason with two stars, to learn some Keresan words. But I suppose when it comes to a blessing, what matters is not that I understand it, but that I have it.

After the blessing, we were led outside and shown the way to a small dormitory off to the side of the church. The priest had asked some of the church staff to prepare a simple meal for us, and I remember feeling immensely grateful that evening for the food, for the bed, and for the kindness. I had always mistrusted kindness as something that people did because they wanted something in return, like it was a feigned act or an incomplete transaction. But that evening I felt a kind of ease of heart that was unfamiliar to my usual way of seeing things. Or maybe I was just tired from the events of the day, though weariness can be a good teacher if you are open to the seduction of learning.

While we ate our meal together—corn and potato porridge with chilies—the priest told us of his own eventful day. Apparently a shepherd with a flock of sheep had crossed the border from Mexico into the United States, and had simply kept going north, making it all the way to the outskirts of Albuquerque before someone finally called the police. I'm not sure why someone would think to call the police—a person walking with a flock of sheep might be unusual but it certainly isn't suspicious. The man apparently had no identification on him whatsoever, leading one local news station to refer to him as the Man with No Name. No one could figure out what to do with someone who had no name and no identity, except for being a shepherd. And when the young shepherd told his story, no one believed he could just walk across the border with a flock of sheep and make it as far as ABQ without being noticed. The reputation of many a public official was at stake. How could this happen? To complicate matters even further, the man and his sheep had unknowingly wandered into Isleta territory, tribal land on the outskirts of ABQ, so authorities had to work with Native American tribal leaders to come up with a solution.

—Are there still shepherds in this day and age? asked Jim.

—Wherever you find sheep, you will always find shepherds, answered the priest.

—And wherever you find shepherds, you will always find sheep, said Maria, breaking her long evening silence.

The Isleta leaders reached out to some of the other tribal groups to find a solution. Since the shepherd had no opposition to the idea of returning to Mexico, he simply volunteered to go back, though authorities claimed they officially had to deport him, to make a statement about the law and its power. The problem was the sheep. No one knew what to do with the sheep. Officials in Mexico also decided to add their own difficulties to the matter by stating that they had no way of knowing if the shepherd was actually from Mexico, since he had no identification, and suggested that perhaps he was just an undesirable character that the United States wanted to foist off on Mexico. Mexico also referred to the shepherd's sheep as dangerous beasts that might be harboring American pests—that's what they actually said—and stated emphatically that even if they were to take back the shepherd, there was no way they could take back the sheep. The shepherd was distraught, for a shepherd without sheep is truly a lost soul.

—A shepherd goes for a walk with his sheep, and somehow it becomes an international incident, said the priest. What a world.

After dinner, we all helped to clean the dishes and the kitchen, and then wandered off to our rooms. The rooms were small and clean and comfortable and I think we all appreciated having a room to ourselves and a place for some solitary sanctuary. There are times to be with others and there are times to be alone. I was tired but restless and so I went outside. I walked back to the church, which was now dark except for what little light flowed in through the upper window. I was drawn to that light, and so I walked up the narrow set of stairs that led to the choir balcony, at the back of which was the window. I walked to the window and opened it, letting in the cool night air. I leaned on the sill and could see the world below. The lights of the pueblo looked like stars on the land, and the stars in the sky looked like pueblos in the heavens.

I heard the door of the church open—it had a particular creak to it—and the sound of footsteps coming up the stairs. It was Andrew, who seemed not at all surprised to find me there. He joined me at the sill, and we had a long talk about all sorts of things, most of which I can no longer remember, but some of which I do.

There was at one moment a bright shooting star that fired up the night sky horizon. I looked over at Andrew to see if he had seen it, too, and I remember he had a serene smile on his face.

—Did you make a wish? I asked.

—I said a prayer.

—Is there a difference?

—Only in the address to which it is sent.

In another moment a moth flew by the window, a large one, as I remember. It seemed to hover momentarily in front of us, as if she were as inquisitive of who we were and why we were there as we were of her (assuming she was a her for no particular reason). Then she flew off into the night.

—Why are there no butterflies at night? I asked ponderously.

—Maybe there are.

—But I've never seen one.

—That doesn't mean they aren't there.

Later that night, as I tried to fall asleep in my room, I remembered the story of Zhuangzi, the Chinese philosopher—if philosopher is an occupation—who fell asleep one day and dreamed he was a butterfly. When he awoke, he realized he had no way to tell if he was Zhuangzi dreaming of a butterfly or a butterfly dreaming of Zhuangzi. The great insight of Zhuangzi was that it didn't matter which vision was true, and any effort to prove one over the other was pointless. I fell asleep that night hoping to dream I was butterfly in the desert night. I don't remember having that dream, but that doesn't mean it didn't happen.

2

Somewhere in New Mexico, not far from where we were, there stood a man in uniform, looking out over the landscape and knowing that somewhere, someone was doing something wrong. For this man, the world was a dangerous place, a place where the forces of disorder always threatened the inherent fragility of order, a place in need of constant care and careful vigilance, a place where every wrong and every injustice, no matter how small or insignificant, needed to be set right. For this man, the world had no use for nuance, no need for shades of grey. There was either black or there was white. There was either day or there was night. There was either either or there was or. There was either right or there was wrong. There was simply no other way for the world to exist. This man believed every word that was contained in the great book, by which I mean of course the Criminal Code of the Great State of New Mexico. For this man, the law may as well have been carved on stone tablets, for the law was eternal, and should therefore by eternally enforced. This man never uttered the word law without the word order, for they were inseparable. The world was a wrongful place, and only the law could save the world from its state of eternal dissipation and dereliction. This man knew the law and he knew how to enforce the law. He was the sheriff of the county, and his name was Lex Lieberman.

Sheriff Lex, as he was known, was a rugged man, born and raised in ABQ. New Mexico was his world, and he loved the land of enchantment, just so long as it remained legally enchanted. He didn't like to waste words, and he spoke neither more nor less than was absolutely necessary. Never a woman or man was there that called him loquacious, and in his whole life no one ever told him to be quiet, for he most often was. Sheriff Lex was a disciplined man. His uniform was always impeccably pressed, fresh and crisp with just enough starch to hold its look from the start of the day to the end. The six-point star, the sign of the sheriff, was always shiny and polished, and always perfectly aligned, never tilting to one side or the other. He wore sunglasses with dark, impenetrable lenses and he wore them always, even when the weather or the waning light of day made their darkness redundant. He was the lawman's lawman, and he knew it. He was exactly the kind of lawman you would want if you were writing a novel and needed a larger-than-life lawman to lay down the law of the land.

At the time of these events, of course, I didn't know any of this about Sheriff Lex. I didn't even know who Sheriff Lex was. It was only much later, after all of these events transpired, that I came to know more about who he was, mostly from those who knew him, with a bit from Sheriff Lex himself. All I knew at the time, and the first I learned of it was the morning after our first night in Laguna, was that there was chatter on the airwaves, chatter that confirmed everything that Andrew had foretold. The law was after us, and not just any law—the law of Sheriff Lex. Tribal police monitored the police frequencies and picked up on this chatter, and early that morning a police courtesy request had come through to the tribal authorities asking if anyone had seen us or knew our whereabouts.

—We can't stay here, said Andrew to all of us.

—You are among friends, said the priest.

We all knew what the priest meant. We were safe, at least for now, and the tribal leaders would protect us. But Andrew also knew we were putting them in a difficult position. So we agreed that we needed to keep moving, staying within native lands as much as we could to hide behind the blurred and confused lines of legal jurisdiction that crisscrossed this part of the country.

—So we are on the run, I said blankly.

—Story of my life, said Maria, with an equal blankness.

We had a simple breakfast and then we were on our way. From Laguna we continued west on I-40. Technically we were still on tribal lands, but the interstate itself was one long road of open vulnerability, since it fell under the legal spell of state and federal authorities. Andrew seemed nervous as he drove, looking furtively in the rear view mirror.

—Maybe we should travel at night by the cover of darkness, said Jim.

—We're in a white van, said Maria. We may as well drive a glow stick.

—Maria is right, said Andrew. Our best bet is to keep off the main roads and keep to the side roads as much as possible. Plus I can't drive a stick.

Not long after we passed the Sky City Casino, one of those monolithic monstrosities that many, many years from now, archaeologists will unearth and study as some sort of temple complex for an incomprehensible cult where people gave up all their money for no discernible reason and believed against all odds that one day they would get it back. At San Fidel we turned off the highway and drove south past Acomita Lake, and when we reached a sign with a straight-ahead arrow that said Alaska—yes, that's right, Alaska—we veered right onto Fatima Hill Road. Then we made a left onto a black tarmac that went almost perfectly straight into the distance and had no dividing line, though drivers still followed the appropriate ritual and kept to one side, even when no other car could be seen from one horizon to the other.

—This seems like a lot of effort just to avoid the law, said Joe.

—We're not avoiding the law, said Maria. We are following a different one.

—A man puts on a uniform and suddenly he thinks he has the power to rule the world, said Joe, imbuing the air with ambient cynicism.

—I wear a uniform, said Andrew.

Awkward pause.

—That's different, said Joe with adept futility.

—How is it different? continued Andrew. A sheriff wears a uniform that no one except a sheriff may wear. It's a cloth of the profession, decked with accessories that embody the power of the law. Each element has a meaning and function. That's little different from me in my vestments, except that the power and the law they embody are different.

—But Dude, a policeman and a priest aren't the same thing, countered Si. They can't be. I mean, you don't put on your uniform and suddenly feel like you can lord over everyone.

—There's a lot of lording in what I do, clarified Andrew. Different kind of lording, of course, but a Lord is involved nevertheless.

—But you don't always wear your uniform, countered Jim.

—And a policeman doesn't always wear his, said Andrew. And yet, he is always a policeman, just as I am always a priest.

—But without your uniform, you're just one of us, said Jim, his voice finding the sweet spot between desperation and exasperation.

—People can always spot a priest, even without the vestments, said Andrew. There are always signs. No one has ever mistaken me for a barista.

—I could use some coffee, said Maria.

At the end of the long, unmarked, and undivided road we came to the foot of a mesa that rose up out of the valley like an earthen altar. This was Acoma Sky City, which I knew because of the sign that read Acoma Sky City, with additional information promising guided tours, a gift shop, and a snack bar.

—Maybe they have coffee, I said to Maria.

—If only one of us were a barista, said Maria, with desert dryness.

—Maybe one of us is, said Andrew aridly.

Getting to the Sky City pueblo is a bit like ascending into heaven, except that there are no pearly gates, God isn't directly involved, and you can drive a car there, or in our case, a white van which may or may not have resembled a glow stick. I guess in that sense it isn't like ascending to heaven at all. But still, since you can't see the pueblo from the narrow, lineless road that leads across the plain, you really have no idea that a whole pueblo sits there atop the mesa. It's a small pueblo, but a pueblo nevertheless. And it's quite beautiful, especially upon first sight.

—Jesus, said Jesús.

We pulled up to the Church of San Esteban del Rey. In some ways, it's the center of gravity for the pueblo, and though it isn't necessarily the most dramatic structure in New Mexico, it's the kind of building that art books would call iconic, usually when they can't think of a better word. When I saw the church, I remembered once seeing an Ansel Adams photograph of the very same, though I couldn't remember where I had seen it or when. It frustrates me sometimes that I can't remember how or where things happened, which happens more frequently than I wish were the case. But I figure if I get the gist of things, that's probably enough. Not sure. In any case, I remembered the Ansel Adams picture of the church, and I remember it made the church look very iconic.

An elderly man with a distinguished walk and a distinctive face came out of the church, and walked up to Andrew and greeted him with a handshake and a one-armed hug that spoke of friendship and trust. They knew one another, that was clear. As I would find out shortly, this man was the priest of the Church of San Esteban del Rey, and he welcomed us to the pueblo and then invited us to share a meal. We walked together to one of the houses, Andrew and the priest talking in front and the rest of us gaggling behind. We walked up an external ladder—such was the way of the pueblo—to a second-story shaded patio with chairs, where a kind woman who smiled a lot began to serve us food. We had a simple meal of thick stew made with beans, squash, corn, and chilies, served with thin corn bread, all of which had been cooked in a clay, wood-fueled, outdoor oven, blackened just so by everyday use.

There are those who would want to see more to this pueblo than there actually is. Sometimes we want to believe there is more to something than what is there, when in fact the truly brave thing to do is to believe in what is only and actually there and be content with it. We are all prone to exaggerate things—I certainly am—and want to find comfort in thinking that everyone else is like that, too. The pueblo of Sky City is considered a Shangri-La by some, by many in fact, a place where life is simple and life is old and life is traditional, running every day along well-worn lines of tradition and ritual, each of which is good and true and right. The reality, however, is that Shangri-La is really just a different way of saying someplace else. It *must* always be someplace else. No one actually lives in Shangri-La, because if you live in Shangri-La, it isn't Shangri-La. It's just the place where you live. The only people who think Sky City is Shangri-La are the people who don't live in Sky City. For the people who live in Sky City, it's just their pueblo.

—The sheriff is definitely on your trail, said a man to all of us, having just walked up the laddered stairs.

—We already know that, said Maria.

—Did you know he is seeking special dispensation? the man asked.

—No, said Maria. Probably because I don't know what that means.

—It means he's made his claim to us, interrupted Andrew. It means his authority is now valid all through the state, for the sole purpose of finding us and bringing us to justice.

—Bringing us to his justice, you mean, added Maria.

—Maybe we should bring him to ours, said Joe.

—You're safe here in the pueblo, said the man whose name I did not know and never would.

—Besides, said Andrew, if anyone says they saw us in Sky City, everyone will think they mean the casino.

—That's a bit of a gamble, don't you think? asked Jim.

—Not when God rolls the dice, answered Andrew.

—Does God really gamble? queried Joe.

—Yes, but He always wins.

—Then He doesn't really gamble, does he?

—That's why He's God.

—Because He doesn't gamble?

—Because He doesn't have to.

It was easy to feel safe and protected, high on a mountain, up on a roof, in a house, down an alley, in a pueblo. The danger of the world below, the temptations of the plains, the risks of life among others, among outsiders, meant a life of permanent uncertainty, a life of endless gamble, the odds of which were unknown, and the rules of which were uncertain. I found myself lulled once again by the idea of having a community, a place where I felt I belonged and a place where I felt safe, and then found myself annoyed yet again that I had allowed myself to feel that way. The desire for Shangri-La is deception, and yet the loss of Shangri-La is despair. I wondered if faith were really just the ongoing struggle to suppress deception. I was angry that Sheriff Lex was on our trail, but I slowly understood that Sheriff Lex had his own Shangri-La. His was a Shangri-La of law and order. Disorder revealed the deception of his Shangri-La, and so the only way to suppress that deception was to suppress disorder and live by the word of the law. Why question the law when it was easier to believe that the law was good and true and right? To blindly follow is always easier than to truly believe.

I walked over to sit next to Andrew, my mind laden with deception and despair.

—Can I confess something? I asked.

—In the religious sense? replied Andrew.

—In a personal sense.

—Go on.

—I don't understand things.

—No one does.

—I find it hard to believe things.

—Everyone does.

—But you're a priest. It comes easily to you, this belief thing.

—No, it doesn't. If it did I wouldn't be a priest.

—I don't understand.

—You already said that.

—I mean how can a priest not believe?

—I didn't say I don't believe.

—But you don't believe completely.

—No one can.

—But you're a priest. You have to believe.

—I don't have to do anything. I choose to believe. That is my faith.

—Then how do you make others believe? How do you lead the mass? Is it all an act?

—I can't make anyone believe anything. And I don't lead the mass.

—Then who leads the mass?

—God does. All I do is translate.

—So you impersonate God during the mass?

—No. I prefer to see Him as my Altar Ego.

—I don't understand.

—You won't let yourself understand. You won't let yourself believe.

—But I want to.

—You're not there. Not yet.

Later, when evening started to fall into night, I went up to the very top of the house. There was no one there but me, and I lay down on the rooftop, arms crossed behind my head, to stare up at the sky and await the arrival of what some call God's sweet lanterns. Others simply call them stars. A short while later Maria came up to the roof, and lay down alongside me, arms crossed behind her head just like mine. She said nothing to me, and I said nothing to her. A shooting star graced the sky, only for a moment. Such is their nature. I glanced over and saw that Maria was smiling. I couldn't help feeling that she and I saw different things. She saw the heavens. I so wanted to see her heavens, too. But for me there was only sky.

3

U p in the heavens, looking down on earth, one could be forgiven for thinking that earth was a strange text, composed from an alphabet of infinite letters with characters and hieroglyphs thrown in by a beneficently literate God, and written on a spherical scroll such that no matter where an aspiring reader might start, the beginning and the end are exactly the same. The first sentence is the last, the last sentence is the first, in a script that is read over and over again, every single day. Whether that makes the story an eternal one or one of circular reincarnation, well, there's no point in quibbling over that, though sadly, many have and many still do.

The roads and pathways and alleys and byways and trails and highways that cover the surface of the earth—these are the scrawlings and scribblings that, at least from high in the heavens, or on any decent map, begin to reveal the hidden text, the etched earthen braille tale, the concrete calligraphy, that tells the story of humankind doing whatever it is that humankind thinks it's doing. Keep in mind that humankind tells just one part of the story. There are animal trails and paths and tracks, each of which has its own contribution, just as there are rivers and creeks and valleys and deserts and oases and so many other things that have their own story to tell as well. Humans write only a small part of this story, and understand even less of it, though in their defense, they do keep trying. And though the story has remained the same after all these years, some parts have been added anew while old parts have been partially erased or entirely destroyed. Earth the Cosmic Palimpsest. No wonder that for many, all they can do is put their faith in the Great Editor.

We were following part of that tale on the trail known as I-40, though what part of the tale we were following we didn't know. We couldn't know. We all had a feeling of vulnerability when we left Acoma land and ventured out into the great wide open. We knew that Sheriff Lex was out there, somewhere, maybe near or maybe far, but definitely there. We left Acoma land and headed toward Grants, the self-appointed uranium capital of the world, where the half-life always threatens to usurp whatever plans for the whole life any person may aspire to. A different kind of ash and a different kind of dust in a mineral reign of endless decay.

There were other realms with other laws out there in the great wide open, and what had once been familiar suddenly seemed quite foreign. We had entered the realm of Sheriff Lex, and we were in his country and we were with his law, and the taxpayers had to pay for it, whether they agreed with it or not. We had our law, too, though our law had a different realm and a different enforcer and was also tax-exempt, though not exempt from taxpayer law. To the south of us was El Malpaís, the Badlands, and to the north of us was the Cibola Forest. To the south, a valley of death, and to the north, a forest of Eden. Neither was our destination. At that moment, we had nowhere to go, and were certainly on our way there.

—Why do they call it El Malpaís? asked Jesús.

—Because it's a place where bad things happen, said Jim.

—That's not the earth's fault, countered Jesús. It doesn't make the *país mal*.

—They say nothing grows there, said Joe.

—Dude, it's full of volcanoes, said Si. They burn the earth.

—They are the earth, said Maria, firmly.

—So, is the whole earth El Malpaís? pondered Jesús.

—There is no El Malpaís, said Maria. There are no bad lands. There are only bad people on those lands.

—So why not call it El Pueblo Malo? asked Jesús.

—Because not all people are bad, stated Maria, flatly.

—Volcanoes have always been associated with divinity, I added, thinking I added something.

Maria looked at me quizzically.

—I mean, you can't have a vulcanologist without first having Vulcan, I added with supreme diffidence.

—What do you know about being a vulcanologist? asked Jim.

—I know where they work, I said.

A moment passes.

—In a lavatory.

We had veered south onto a small rural route right round Grants. Andrew had been listening to us but had said nothing, and was driving with mindful caution. I noticed that he had been glancing in the rearview mirror more often than seemed necessary. We still had the woodlands on the right and the badlands on the left, but straight ahead there were other signs. One told us we were on the Trail of the Ancients Byway.

—Every trail is a trail of the ancients, noted Maria.

There were lines and trails and paths everywhere, some seen and some unseen. There was the chain of craters, the continental divide, even the tree line, above which the pine and fir and cedar and aspen would no longer grow. There was the trail that led through The

Land of Fire and Ice, or so a sign dramatically promised. Below the ground there was ice, above the ground there was fire. A land of stark opposites, as if the west air rose in the east. A landscape that at any moment threatened to destroy life as much as it promised to begin it. A landscape of fear and awe and uncertainty and wonder. So many beliefs have been created by this landscape, not to make sense of the landscape itself, but to calm the emotional storms it generates within those who walk across it, each one leaving their own trail, each one following another, even as another follows them. Whether the people believed the beliefs of their systems, no one knows save for them. And even if they said they believed them, we would still have to decide whether to believe them, those who said they believed.

—We're on Navajo land now, said Andrew.

All of us felt a sense of relief at that moment. The landscape now somehow seemed less menacing, or maybe I only wanted to believe that. I didn't know for sure, but the refuge of belief was better than the anxiety of uncertainty. There are stories of people who commit atrocious crimes and seemingly get away with it, and yet years later they turn themselves in to face the law and accept their punishment. Many people believe this only shows the eventual triumph of good over evil, that eventually even bad people understand that what is wrong is wrong. People who do bad things need to set things right and liberate themselves from the weight of guilt. But guilt may not be the ultimate catalyst at work here. It could also be the unbearable anxiety of wondering when and if they'll be found out. Once they turn themselves in and confess, the anxiety of uncertainty, of wondering each day if that's the day when they'll get caught, disappears. They aren't liberated from guilt, they are absolved from uncertainty.

Joe announced that he had to answer the call of nature, and since nature is nothing if not one giant lavatory, Andrew decided to stop. Joe walked off in that strange gait that humans use to disguise the fact that they are heading to answer the call of nature, and yet in doing so, unmistakably reveal that they are going off to do precisely that. It's a strange saunter that uses feigned nonchalance to mask the guilt and shame we have when everyone knows we are about to perform a natural function, even though we all know that at some point, our time will come, most likely soon, and fairly regularly, if all goes according to plan. As Joe began to search for the perfect spot behind the perfect bush in a way that shows we are never as different from animals as we like to think, the rest of us walked toward a huge promontory of rock. Like wanderers making their way through the desert in search of something more than a toilet, we were drawn to this structure that seemed to rise up out of the earth in ways that both defied and confirmed the laws of nature. As we approached, we saw what appeared to be strange lines and shapes. Nature of course is full of lines and shapes, which only seem strange to those who no longer live close enough to nature to remember their meaning. But these lines and shapes seemed strange in unnatural ways, as if someone or something had decided to add commentary onto earth's enticingly incomplete manuscript.

There were rows and rows of inscriptions, some of them names, some of them messages, some of them names with messages. Nearly all of them recorded a specific year—itself a message, but an incomplete one. Why is the year always assumed to be the most important marker of time? John Smith, winter. Kim Heesu, Tuesday. No one ever writes that. Romesh Bhandari, bored. Jean Valjean, miserable. No one ever writes that either. Names and years, that's all. As if that's the sum of humanity. There was at least a handprint, with no name or date, which only made me wonder who that person was and what year they were here. No one ever puts footprints on a wall, or handprints on a path, something that would puzzle evolutionists and religionists alike. There were hieroglyphs and petroglyphs, too, and first I pondered their meaning, and then I pondered why we always assume that whatever an ancient person wrote long ago must somehow have meaning, one that is both true and profound. Later I learned that like the Acoma pueblo, people had tried to build a settlement on top of the promontory, though this one failed and all we have left are the ruins, which are nevertheless their own sort of inscription. Whether they built their community on high to be closer to God or further from people, we will never know. The only lesson to be drawn from this is that nothing is written in stone.

We all wandered back to the van like a band unambitious pilgrims, and drove on to a small Navajo village, really little more than a cluster of houses and a church that looked like all of the other houses except for a handmade sign that said it was a church. We all got out of the van and followed Andrew toward a weathered wooden door, above which was inscribed in capital letters that all ran together THELORDSWORD.

—What's The Lord Sword? I asked.

—You mean, The Lord's Word? replied Andrew.

—Oh, right, I said.

—I thought you were a writer, said Andrew.

—So did I.

A man as weathered as the door greeted us.

—So you're the outlaws, he said, with a gentle grin, nearly a smirk.

This was Father Zeus—yes, that's right, Father Zeus. Even in my notebook I had this circled with a note to myself—in parentheses and for some reason also circled—that said *real name*, under which I had written the date of our meeting. I suppose when his parents named him they never thought he would become a priest. Still, becoming a priest was probably preferable to becoming a doctor, for title reasons alone, as Doctor Zeus sounds positively cartoonish.

—You're safe here, said Father Zeus, his fingertips pressed together in the way that people often do when they wish to add gravity to their words.

—But, he added, also with gravity, there's no place for you to stay here.

Andrew had his mouth open in the way that people often do when they wish to measure their words, but Maria, whose words had no measure, broke in first.

—So what do you suggest we do? she asked.

—I'm thinking, Father Zeus said, fingertips still together and eyes looking at the ground in the way that people often do to show that they are thinking in meaningful ways. I'm thinking you should go to Candy Kitchen.

—Candy Kitchen? said Andrew.

—Dude, what's Candy Kitchen? asked Si.

Candy Kitchen—and I would never have believed a place could be named such had I not seen it with my own eyes—was a community of misfits, outcasts, radicals, activists, artists, individualists, nonconformists, survivalists and other aspirational and inspirational rebels, all so united in their disdain for belonging in society that they came together to form a society where they could all belong. Half of the people didn't have phones, for instance—didn't want them—and the other half had phones but didn't want to answer them. The one thing they had going for them, and the one thing that Father Zeus knew he could rely on, was a strong sense of privacy. Nobody asked questions, and if anyone did, no one answered them, except to ask why someone was asking questions. Whoever you were, that was who you are, and that was no one's business but your own.

—No one's gonna look for you there, said Father Zeus. And if they do, they'll never find you.

So off we went, Father Zeus with us as our guide, down a small road, to an even smaller road, then to a dirt road, then to no road, then to a camper with a gas lamp. A woman came out of the camper and walked up to the van.

—Father Zeus, Father Andrew, she said.

—Father Susan, they both said, almost simultaneously.

Father Susan was born a man, except that later in life, she was born again as a woman. As I would soon discover during our short stay in Candy Kitchen, spirituality and not religion was the ambient flair of the community. Nobody asked what you religion you practiced, but everyone assumed you at least believed. Father Susan was a community leader, as well as a spirit guide, though if she followed any specific religious pathway, no one would have known. But I was at least thrown by the title, Father Susan, not by the gender part, which by the unwritten rules of Candy Kitchen was also no one's business, but by the title, and by the way that Andrew and Father Zeus addressed her with the title.

—Does a priest really need a religion? she asked, answering my question with a question of her own.

I had no true answer. So I turned to Andrew, to Father Zeus.

—She believes, she guides, and others seek her guidance, said Andrew. Isn't that enough?

—But why do you call her Father, if she isn't a part of the church? I asked.

—What church do you mean, exactly? queried Andrew.

—Any church? I clarified with uncertainty.

—We call her Father because everyone else does in this community, said Father Zeus. It was you who assumed that in calling her Father she could only be one thing.

—There was a man who came to the shelter in Albuquerque nearly every day, said Andrew. He wore a threadbare tweed jacket and he loved to talk of all sorts of things, and so we all called him Professor. Whether he had a PhD or not, well, no one really cared. He used his mind to good ends, and that was enough.

—And I once knew a man who had a PhD, in History as I recall, who insisted that we all call him Professor, said Zeus. He was a tremendous idiot.

Perhaps it was the altitude's thin air, or perhaps it was being in the midst of a community that was cooked from an odd cauldron that drew laws from lawlessness, rules from unruliness, friends from strangers, and comfort from fear. But I had no reason to doubt any of the words I had heard. I thought of Andrew in his church, of Father Zeus and his Lord's Word, of Father Susan in her Candy Kitchen, of Vulcan in his Fire Kitchen, of Sheriff Lex in his Police Station. Temples and Laws, all. I thought of myself, and the blank paper world in front of me. Next to me was my notebook, with its own strange inscriptions and drawings and graffiti and scribblings, only some of which I understand, even now. Perhaps all of us are simply priests of one sort or other, each with our different rules and laws, each with our different communities and different temples, and each with our different stories to believe in. And of course, each of us equally determined to convince others that our stories are true and worthy of belief. Is it any wonder that so many believe in what they consider to be the greatest story ever told?

That evening we all dispersed to separate places in Candy Kitchen. Maria and I ended up in the same place, a small house with a kindly couple who had no electricity and who loved to read and tell stories by the light of a gas flame.

—The light of the universe is a gas flame, they said.

Maria slept in the spare bedroom while I slept in a bedroll on a couch in the front room, the only other room in the house besides the kitchen, which also had only a gas flame. Before we slept, Maria and I had a moment outside, sitting on two folding chairs with a gas lantern burning between us and the stars burning above us.

—Do you think you'll dream tonight? Maria asked me.

—I hadn't thought about it, I said.

—That's your biggest problem, you know, she said.

I wanted to ask what she meant by that, but she was already gone, and the night was already there. I climbed into my bedroll, closed my eyes, and waited.

4

Why is it so hard to speak, when we speak of love? This one word, this one, little, beguiling word, twists our emotions into the most exquisite of knots. With love, we can't say what we want, even when we know in our hearts what it is we want. No other emotion can be conveyed so completely with complete silence—imagine two lovers on a bench, watching a river go by, hand in hand, saying nothing to one another. In that nothing, there is more love than words could convey. To speak in such a moment would be pure folly. Better to squeeze the hand ever so gently of the person whose heart you treasure more than any other treasure on earth. Cynics may dismiss love with a roll of their cynical eyes and a shake their disbelieving heads, philosophers may expose love as a dubious delusion of the mind, anthropologists may disavow love as nothing more than a cultural construct—so many people in the world, past and present, have offered us an endless list of reasons not to love. What these great detractors fail to understand is that the more they tell us not to love, the more we know we must. I can't explain why that is, and I don't want to. One does not need a reason to love. One just loves.

How else can I explain why the people of Candy Kitchen kept us hidden from the outside world and safe in their inside world? In the morning we were served breakfast, vegan of course, which we ate sitting at a picnic table in front of Father Susan's trailer. I still have the recipe for the mountain berry scones that Father Susan made, which I asked her for because they were so delicious, and which she gave me because she was the kind of person who gave things to others—not because she didn't want them, but because others did. The last line of the handwritten recipe, which she wrote on a scrap piece of a paper cut from a brown paper bag—*paper is paper, fancy or not*, she said—says to Bake with love, Share with others. I've never once made the recipe, though I hold on to that piece of paper religiously, stuck as it is between the pages of my notebook.

In any other place, if someone handed me a scone and told me it was baked with love, I'd probably consider the gesture at best half-baked and most likely overdone. And though there were many people in Candy Kitchen who were undoubtedly fully baked—it wasn't just the smoky scent of spent piñon that waft-ed through the herbaceous mountain air—I had no reason to think that the love the people had for their community, and the love that Father Susan wanted me to carry along with me on my journey, wherever that journey went, with or without a scone, was anything other than a real and beautiful thing. And yet at the time, I still remember struggling hard to find a reason not to believe it was true. I was different then. Doubt was a refuge. I wanted to find a reason to believe that Candy Kitchen was something other than what it was. I know better now.

After breakfast, someone known as a runner ar-rived. A runner is someone who knows where the scat-tered residents of Candy Kitchen live, someone who is trusted by those residents, and someone who brings news of the outside world to those who have chosen to cut themselves off from it. The arrival of a runner serves to reestablish that connection, momentarily at least, so the reconnection is bittersweet, usually with a sense of resignation, reluctance, and reservation. This time the runner had a message for us.

—Sherriff Lex is waiting for you, he said.

Andrew looked taciturn, Father Susan looked amused, Father Zeus looked concerned, Joe and Jim looked indifferent, Jesús looked for another scone, Maria looked coyly annoyed.

—He's waiting for us, is he? she asked with subtle defiance. And where might he be?

—In Gallup, said the runner. He knows what you are trying to do.

—Sheriff Lex only thinks he knows, said Andrew.

Gallup, by the way, is a strange little town, but one not without its charms, shambolic though they may be. It sits at the intersection of the quintessential American highway, Route 66, the Mother Road that leads to California, and Route 666. Though the federal government isn't supposed to do anything that smacks of religious persuasion, the number and sign of Route 666 were changed a few years back to Route 491, apparently to keep Satan hence. People around here still call it the Devil's Highway, in spite of the efforts to the contrary of the federal government, which may or may not be run by Satan, depending on which conspiracy theory you believe. Gallup likes to call itself the Indian Capital of the World, which seems a little pretentious and self-indulgent. With its natural cloak of red sandstone cliffs and the rocky daggers of the Hogback Mountains, the town and its surroundings effortlessly evoke the spirit of the Wild West, both as stereotype and artifact. The town itself looks like it was built as a film set for a film made about a town like Gallup.

—Why is Sheriff Lex so keen on getting us? asked Joe. What is this, the Wild West?

—Not if Sheriff Lex is there, answered Andrew. Sheriff Lex would never tolerate Wild. It would just be West.

—He says you disturbed the peace, said the runner.

—He is disturbing my peace, replied Maria.

—He says you threatened the public order, said the runner.

—His order publicly threatens mine, said Maria.

Awkward pause to acknowledge that the conversation is going nowhere.

—Please, I'm only a messenger, said the runner.

—So am I, said Maria.

Nowhere indeed.

Andrew and Father Zeus stepped aside to have a huddled conversation, in essence, a random performance of murmur and gesture that intimates meaning and purpose without any indication of content. Something was afoot, a moment was at hand—at least that much I could surmise—but knowing what was afoot or at hand would have to wait until the huddled conversation became unhuddled, which it did momentarily.

—Father Zeus thinks it would be unwise if we tried to drive through Gallup, said Andrew. Sheriff Lex has ways of knowing things, and Father Zeus thinks there is a good chance we would be caught.

—Dude, what are we going to do? said Si.

Brief pause for a crescendo of awareness by Father Zeus.

—He calls you Dude? asked Father Zeus of Andrew.

—He calls everyone Dude, replied Andrew.

—Even God? asked Father Zeus quizzically.

—Dude, He's the Greatest Dude, explained Si.

Father Zeus nodded, clearly searching for a counterargument, but unable to do so, muttered a hum of resigned theological acceptance.

—I can abide by that, he said, looking at Si like a coincidental brother.

—Father Zeus says we should head to Zuni Pueblo and wait things out another night, said Andrew.

—They'll be expecting you, said Father Zeus.

—They're good people, said Joe.

—So are all of you, said Father Zeus.

We headed out to another path, another road, another destination, another stage in another journey on another day in another town. We followed an unmarked road that led west from Candy Kitchen, a road not found on any map except for the hand-drawn one that Father Zeus gave us when we left, which was really little more than just a squiggly pencil scribble on a page of my notebook. If I showed that page to you today, you would think it to be a child's first effort at writing cursive. In any case, the map was unnecessary because there was really no way to get lost. There was only one road to follow. The unmarked road eventually emptied into Route 36, where just as Father Zeus had said, a wiggly tree stood as if it were a gatekeeper, and right next to it, inexplicably, was a small flower stand with two girls selling flowers and watering cans, apparently to no one.

Father Zeus told us to turn right onto Route 36 at the wiggly tree with the two girls selling flowers, and so we did, as if on some sort of magical quest. We drove north and soon saw another sign, one that read, just as Father Zeus said it would, *You Are Entering Zuni Land: Welcome.* When we hit Route 53, we turned left and west, on the road to Zuni Pueblo. There we found a second sign welcoming us to Zuni Pueblo, with the added admonition: *Absolutely No Photography of Cultural Activities.* It was apparently fine to describe those cultural activities with words, but unacceptable to capture them with pictures. The gift of words is that words can embellish, and therefore liberate. The crime of photographs is that photographs capture, and therefore imprison. I could evoke an image, I just couldn't take one. And yet that was the very thing that started me on this evocative journey in the first place.

We drove directly to the Old Zuni Mission, oddly named simply because there wasn't a New one from which to distinguish the Old. The Old Zuni Mission rises up like an adobe mesa, mimicking the mesas that mark the landscape around the pueblo, but humble enough a structure in both build and tincture to understand it can only mimic and never imitate. A woman came out and gave us some food, pieces of cornbread and hot bean soup, which we ate with gratitude and without question. I remember thinking to myself that I would never do this in New York. In New York, you don't eat things given to you by strangers. Yet here it was like a cultural activity, which is why I can tell you about it but not share any photographs, of which there are none. Odd how culture can make us do things we would never otherwise do, and act in ways we would never otherwise act.

A short while later a priest came out to greet us, dressed as he was in flowing ochre robes that seemed sewn from the very earth upon which he walked. He hugged Andrew like an old soul and kindred spirit, kissing him gently on the forehead, and then greeted the rest of us with a gentle handshake, taking our hands in his, one by one by one, and then covering our joined hands with his other hand. I remember that his hands looked very youthful, though the lines on his face showed a life spent in many desert summers. He looked each of us in the eye, and I felt for some reason that when he looked at me, he looked at me differently. I didn't feel paranoid, but I felt as if he sensed something about me, perhaps something about me that I could not sense about myself. I wondered where and when I would cease to be a stranger. What things would I have to do, things I did not yet know and perhaps never would, to make that happen? I didn't want to be a stranger, but I was. I always was. At least then.

The priest beckoned us into the church, in order to give thanks for our safe arrival and offer his blessings for the journey to come. We entered through the doorway of Our Lady of Guadalupe, and the first thing we saw was the Virgin Mary. Her portrait, her image, welcomes all who enter this church. I flashed back to the moment this journey had begun for me—in a bar, in the rain, on a street, with these people. If you shift your focus from the front of the church to the back, you will see just behind the altar another portrait of the Virgin Mary. She is there at the front and there at the back, there at the beginning and there at the end. Above the altar is an image of Jesus, dressed in a Zuni blanket, and adorned with the turquoise for which the Zuni are famous. The Zuni had welcomed Him as one of their own, and He had welcomed them as one of His. Still other marvels of Our Lady of Guadalupe reveal themselves if you look up to the ceiling, for there, above the images of the Stations of the Cross, are murals of so many kachinas, the protective spirits of the Zuni people.

—They are our messengers, said the priest.

The priest paused for a moment to look upward with the rest of us.

—God's love is vast, he continued. It is more than any of us could ever understand. The kachinas bring the message to us in ways that help us understand that Love. When we want to return that Love, the kachinas take our words back to God, so that he may understand that we are capable of a Great Love, too.

—So they are like angels? asked Jesús.

—Of a kind, said the priest. Or perhaps angels are a kind of kachina.

The priest in the ochre robes led us to the front of the church and there offered his thanks for our safe journey and his blessings for the journey to come, just as he said he would do. I remember feeling very safe there, in that sanctuary of so many guardian spirits, and I remember thinking that, for a moment at least, I did not want to leave. This is always the great heart-break of finding sanctuary—you want it to last forever, but you know it never will. After we received our bless-ings, we returned to the less ethereal world of our cur-rent situation. We had to arrange for a place to stay for the night, which the priest of the ochre robe did for us, and we had to take care of all those practicalities of life that always bring us back down to the earth, no matter how deeply we wish we could remain in the heavens.

Our next stop, for instance, was the Zuni Coin Laundry, just down the street. The very same earthen landscape that inspires so many spirit-seekers, artists, and other searchers in these parts, when it gets on your clothing, well, then it's just dirt. Through the in-tercession of the priest of the ochre robe, the manager of the laundromat did not charge us, which was a bless-ing, since we pretty much had no money among us. I'm not sure laundry would be considered a cultural prac-tice, let alone a spiritual one, but when you are watch-ing laundry go round and round, first in the washer, then in the dryer, it does give you time to contemplate things. Did Jesus wash his own clothes? If not, who did? When He ate with His disciples, did any of them ever spill food on themselves, maybe a little hummus here or olive oil there? These are the things that Holy Books never tell us. Yet we are constantly reminded to be cleansed of our sins, or to lead a clean life, which really means that the spiritual life itself is an endless struggle between clean and unclean. Just like laundry.

We also picked up some additional clothes, after the manager showed us a backroom that contained baskets of unclaimed clothing, some dating back many years. Seriously, who does laundry and then forgets their clothes? In any case, it helped us solve the great laundry dilemma that all laundry-seekers face: you want everything to be clean on laundry day, but whatever you wear while doing your laundry is already taking you back into the realm of the unclean. We each chose an outfit from the baskets of unclaimed laundry, and then we dressed in someone else's clothing while we each laundered our own.

I walked outside to get some fresh air, and found Andrew sitting on a bench in the shade, amusingly dressed in a white Zig-Zag t-shirt. On the wall behind him was an amateurish bit of graffiti that read God is Love.

—God is Love, I read aloud.

—Yes He is, replied Andrew.

—I was just reading the writing on the wall, I said.

—Does that make it less true? he asked.

—I don't know if it is true or not.

—It's not about knowing. It's about believing.

—How can you believe what you don't know?

—If I knew it I wouldn't need to believe it.

—Why is that?

—Faith is faith. It cannot be collapsed into reason. It is certainty in the face of uncertainty. If I knew everything there is to know about God, then I would be a philosopher and not a priest.

—But I can understand Love. If God is Love, why can't I understand God?

—Your premise is flawed. You cannot understand Love. You can only believe in it.

In my notebook, at the bottom of the page that contains a few rudimentary sketches of the kachinas in the church, there is scribbled my own bit of personal graffiti. It reads simply—*I believe in Love.*

5

On the grounds of the Old Zuni Mission, surrounding the church of Our Lady of Guadalupe, there is a cemetery. Surrounding the cemetery, around the grounds of the Old Zuni Mission, there are fields and gardens growing all sorts of vegetables and flowers. It is the same soil and the same earth that sprawls from the steps of the church into the fields, yet if you walk a straight line in any direction, you first must cross over the soil that covers the dead and only then will you reach the soil that nurtures the living. We like to think of the living and the dead as two eternal opposites, and yet the two never seem to be so far apart. Where you find one, you will always find the other. In the cemetery, there is the community of the dead, those who have passed on to wherever it is that they go when they leave us. Those beyond the cemetery, in the fields and the houses, are the community of the living, those who are still among us, those who have not yet passed on.

We of the living say that we are haunted when an exception has been made, when those who have passed on have returned to be among us, we who are still living. We of the living believe that such spirits should know their proper place—they should rest in peace, meaning they should stay where they are, wherever that is. Yet we also believe there are other spirited beings—the angels, the kachinas, the guardian spirits, the reincarnated souls—who can move freely between the worlds of the present and the passed, and these spirits we want always to be here among us. Indeed, we pray to them for consolation and guidance, and ask them to watch over us and keep us from harm. They rarely respond to our prayers or speak with us, much to our dismay, or perhaps they always speak with us, only in a language that we have long ago forgotten, that we can no longer readily understand.

I thought of this on the morning of the next day, walking across the grounds of the church, and coming upon not one but two white vans, similar to one another up close, and from a distance, indistinguishable. They were parked side by side, one of them empty and being tended to by Andrew, the other with what looked to be five passengers and being tended to by the priest in the ochre robe, whom I now knew to be Father Ramón and who in any case was no longer enrobed in ochre. All of the others slowly assembled together, and we beheld the sight of the two white vans in the bright light of a cloudless New Mexico morning.

—Dude, said Si.

We walked closer and soon saw that the five passengers in the van were neither among the living, nor had they passed on—nor could they pass on. Five mannequins sat in the van, four male and one female, dressed in ways that made them appear unsettlingly like us, and donning wigs that looked like they had seen too much of this world. Andrew and Father Ramón were likewise dressed in similar ways. I was amused and disturbed by the whole situation, roughly in equal measure.

—Where did you get the mannequins? asked Maria.

—From the tribal shop, said Father Ramón. Until a short while ago, they were adorned in blankets and turquoise.

—And the clothes? she continued.

—From Zuni Coin Laundry, said Andrew.

—Who dressed me? asked Maria.

—I did, said Andrew. Do you like it?

—No.

Over breakfast we discussed the plan of the two white vans. Father Ramón and his five inorganic companions would leave first, twenty minutes before us, and would drive straight through Gallup. We, on the other hand—that is, Andrew and his five more organic associates—would sidestep Gallup and follow an alternative route northward to Navajo land. The hope was that if Sheriff Lex were lying in wait for us in Gallup, as we had been told, he would go after the decoy van, with Father Ramón at the wheel, leaving us free to seek shelter and refuge elsewhere. It seemed a simple but effective plan.

After breakfast, we all climbed into our white van, with Andrew at the wheel. We all looked over at the other van, each of us peering into the window to look at our spiritless counterparts, our duplicitous doubles, wondering how anyone could mistake them for us. But the whole ruse rested on someone doing exactly that. We had to believe they would. We had to believe they could.

—Yep, that's pretty creepy, said Jim.

Father Ramón started his van, and turned to us with a meaningful wave of his hand.

—Godspeed, my friends, he said.

Father Ramón drove off in a trail of dust, some of which fell onto our van, some on his, the rest cast to the wind to find something else to sully. The eternal conflict continues—clean and unclean, just as with good and evil, sacred and profane, spiritual and material, and so on and so on, for all of eternity. As for us, we had twenty minutes to sit and wait, and as it turns out, six people in a white van with twenty minutes to wait isn't the sort of thing that constitutes epic drama. It's one of those moments that directors never film, and writers never write, unless perhaps they are German, and even then, only if they are absurdly so.

I mean, Chaucer never wrote a tale in which his merry pilgrims ran out of stories to tell and so rode on in awkward silence, bored to tears with nothing left to say to each other and staring off into the distance for any distraction that might make the time pass even a hint more quickly. There's nothing in the Gospels that tells us what Jesus and his often less-than-merry disciples did in between all the teaching and the preaching and the healing and the spiriting, but there had to be at least one moment where Peter yawned flagrantly and then fought off a nap or Thomas complained resentfully that his feet hurt from a journey that went on just a bit longer than any of them expected. Certainly there had to be at least one awkward pause in the conversation at the Last Supper, or a moment when one disciple made odd facial gestures trying to use his tongue to remove some bit of food that was obstinately stuck in his teeth. Does the thought of such mundane moments diminish their sacred essence? Sacredness doesn't just occur in dramatic moments. Indeed, mundane sacredness is perhaps more beautiful than dramatic sacredness, if for no other reason that it is gloriously unexpected.

Meanwhile, back in the van of the living, all of us were now going through all of those seemingly unintentional movements and gestures—many of which turn out in fact to be quite intentional—to make subtle noises and movements to break the silence that is called awkward because of the way it calls attention to itself. Silence is golden, as many a cliché-peddler would tell us, but more often than not, it's just awkward. Jim scratched an itch that probably didn't itch at that moment. Joe adjusted his position on the seat, though the previous position was probably just fine. Si inspected a smudge on the window which had been there all along and which required no momentary inspection as there was nothing in the least bit extraordinary or suspicious about the smudge. Andrew pulled the sun visor down and then just as quickly put it back up, then looked down at the floor mat, apparently to make sure it was still there and hadn't been removed by unseen forces or malevolent spirits. Jesús tapped out a drum beat to a song that was playing only in his head, and mouthing words that may or may not have been the lyrics to his imaginary soundtrack. I flipped through the pages of my notebook, as if searching for something, though in reality I was searching for nothing at all, which I am sure the others knew but appreciated nevertheless.

Only Maria sat still and was at peace with her silence. When Maria decided to break the silence, she did so in a way that was definitive and resolute.

—Maybe we should cut Sheriff Lex some slack, she said.

The rest of us stopped our unnecessary pantomime with a sense of relief and residual embarrassment, which we quickly covered over with our eager acceptance of Maria's invitation to dialog.

—You mean, we should just turn ourselves in? replied Andrew.

—No, said Maria. He's wrong, but he's not so different.

—Are you worried that we are vilifying him? asked Jim.

—No, said Maria. I am worried that we are glorifying ourselves.

—But we are doing the right thing, said Jim.

—No, we are doing what we believe to be the right thing, said Maria. There is a difference.

—Are you beginning to have doubts? asked Joe.

—No, said Maria. I never have doubts.

—Dudes, I'm confused, said Si, confused.

—He has his law and we have ours, continued Maria. He believes in his as much as we believe in ours.

—So, are you saying we should render unto Caesar, or are you saying that any belief is as good as another? asked Andrew.

—No, said Maria. Not that. It's just that, he's coming toward us from his belief, just as we are moving away from him due to ours.

—Jesus was a rebel, said Jesús, rebelliously.

—Yes he was, replied Maria firmly. But he was a policeman as well.

—Dude, Jesus was a cop? asked Si, with perplexity.

—In some ways, yes, continued Maria. Different laws and different crimes, it is true, but all he wanted was for people to follow the law, even if that law was to love those who had different laws. Right to the end, He never condemned the soldiers or the police or their laws. He merely tried to show that there was a better way, a better law. A different law.

—In other words, said Andrew, if Sheriff Lex is wrong, let him be wrong on his own terms?

—I don't know, said Joe. Sheriff Lex is like us, but not like us. He appears the same, but he isn't.

—The world isn't always just police and thieves, affirmed Maria. Sometimes the clash is something other than what we believe.

It was at that point that Andrew said our time was at hand, and he started the van and we drove off. The plan was to follow the same route as Father Ramón and his mannequin companions, but just before Gallup we would veer off onto a loop road, bypass Gallup and circle back circuitously into Navajo country further north. If Sheriff Lex, with his love of law, were really lying in wait for us, we with our law of love, then he should be distracted just long enough by Father Ramón's decoy van to let us make our way to safer country.

As it turns out, the plan worked flawlessly. At just about the exact moment we reached Church Rock, a few miles east of Gallup, Sheriff Lex decided to make his move and stop Father Ramón's white van, which he did in Yah-ta-hey, north of Gallup, after trailing him for several miles. As we would find out later, Sheriff Lex was none too happy at being deceived, and went to great lengths to find something in his law books with which to charge Father Ramón. But it turns out that filling a white van full of mannequins and taking them for a scenic drive isn't against the law, though I am sure there are those who might see it as peculiar. After a long bit of questioning and some well-tempered venting of simmering rage by Sheriff Lex, Father Ramón was allowed to continue on his way, although there was some doubt about whether he would be allowed to take the mannequins with him.

When he told us the story of the encounter later that day, Father Ramón related with a bit of giddiness what he said to Sheriff Lex when Sheriff Lex said he was taking the mannequins.

—Do you need them for further questioning?

Apparently at that moment Sheriff Lex realized the absurdity of the request, that and the awkwardness of putting six poorly-dressed mannequins into a police car and driving them back to the police station, to serve as evidence for a crime that never happened in the first place.

In Church Rock, we stopped for a while to have a look around and hiked out to see the eponymous Church Rock, which is a rock that looks something like a church, if you see it from the right angle. It's less of a Shangri-La sight and more of a rock-sculpted church mannequin, or churchequin, if that is a thing, which it probably isn't, or shouldn't be. Church Rock itself is composed of red rock, which is visibly red, of course, but for those who have trouble naming basic and obvious colors, you are given a gentle reminder by the brilliantly named Red Rock Park, in which Church Rock sits, which is a park full of trails that wind through—and I know this will come as a surprise—red rock. Further up the frontage road is what for many people really is a genuine imitation of Shangri-La, in the form of Fire Rock Casino. The rock here isn't particularly bright or incendiary so why they had to create a geologic stunt-double and call it fire rock rather than red rock is beyond me. I don't name the landscape, I simply wander through it. Perhaps fire rock sounds more exciting and dramatic, or perhaps fire rock is reminiscent of the money that people burn through when they visit. Church Rock also has yellow rock, by which I mean uranium, and there are grim reminders—mostly in the form of warning signs that tell people to stay out of the river and not to drink its water—that not all of the dust of the earth is made from the same rock. This yellow rock might create yellow dust that looks like any other rocky dust, except that this yellow rock causes people to build casino-sized buildings and machines to tear it from the ground, ultimately to build weapons that they gamble they will never have to use, but if they do, will sadly turn rock of all colors into fire.

We followed a long and winding route, with long expanses of the landscape accompanied by long expanses of silence inside the van, until we met up with Father Ramón in Twin Lakes. There we had a picnic of simple food, and there Father Ramón told us the story of his encounter with Sheriff Lex. It was an odd picnic, to say the least. Andrew and Father Ramón were dressed alike and sitting side by side, while we ate in full view of the watchful eyes of the mannequins created in our image.

Father Ramón warned us that Sheriff Lex would not be deceived for long, and seemed more determined now than ever to find us. Father Ramón apparently found the whole encounter with Sheriff Lex quite amusing, which only fueled Sheriff Lex's indignity, for Sheriff Lex did not share in the humor, only in the situation. Two men, with two different visions of the same events.

—Sheriff Lex was not happy to be deceived, said Father Ramón. It was a clever ruse and it worked, but it will only buy you limited time before the day of reckoning with Sheriff Lex and his book of laws.

—Maybe he can charge us with impersonating a mannequin, said Maria. Even a badly-dressed one, she added with a glance to Andrew.

We parted ways after the picnic—Father Ramón gave each of us a life-affirming hug before we left—and decided we should put some distance between ourselves and wherever we imagined Sheriff Lex to be, namely in or around Gallup. We headed north on 491, while Father Ramón headed south back to Zuni Pueblo. It was a long and silent drive into the north. We passed signs that spoke of the Bisti Wilderness and the desolate badlands of De-Na-Zin—haunting for some, enchanting for others. We were tempted to wander in the desert, but we resisted temptation and stayed on the Devil's Highway instead. We passed Two Grey Hills, spectacularly named because there are two grey hills there. We drove further and further north, until we finally came to our destination, which was Shiprock. Shiprock is named for a rock formation that apparently looks like a ship. To my mind, however, it looks more like a church than Church Rock, and Church Rock, with its three tall mast-like formations, looks more like a ship than a church. Both are illusions in any case, formed as they were long before ships and churches were things to imagine in the landscape. The landscape itself is indifferent to those who confer upon it names. Does it really matter that Shiprock looks like a ship? Not in the least—about that I harbor no illusions.

6

It juts out of the flat earthy basin, rudely so, impossibly so, heretically so. It's a flagrant middle finger to those in the world who want to believe that the world is flat, or should be flat. It's an unsettling monument, this thing they call Shiprock, and it is no wonder that all who have cast eyes upon it have tried to explain why it is there—to give it a name, to tell its story, no matter how improbable that story may be. It provokes, it irritates, it agitates, it overwhelms, it inspires, it daunts, it haunts, it troubles, it irks—it offends with its geologic arrogance to rise so dramatically into the horizon. Yes, it's a heretic, alright. Does it look like a ship? Only if you know what a ship should look like, if a ship were made of rock, and even then, to say it looks like a ship already identifies the identifier as an outsider, for who would ever think of a ship in the middle of an arid, rocky desert?

The shipless Navajo have other stories that explain this red rock imposter, one being that it was the great bird that brought them here from somewhere else, which only calls attention to the fact that even the Navajo saw this monolith as something foreign, something that had to have come from somewhere else, something that didn't quite fit, something that had to be explained—something that had to have a story. The Navajo say they used to live on that rock, until one day the sky sent down a lightning bolt so fierce and violent it obliterated all pathways in or out, leaving the people there to die a slow and agonizing death, bereft of food and water, and no doubt spending their last moments cursing the earth and sky for something that seemed to make no sense and have no reason. To this day, the Navajo forbid humans to go on the rock, lest they inadvertently stir up the angry ghosts of those who perished long ago on its rugged heights.

—Yep, that's a big rock, said Jim, staring at Shiprock alongside the rest of us.

—It looks even less like a bird than a ship, commented Joe.

—Dude, it definitely looks like something holy, said Si.

—Peter means rock, said Andrew. That's why Jesus told Peter to build the church, because he wanted it to be on a rock, to be unshakeable.

—So the writings of the church are all petroglyphs, added Maria.

—That's one way of putting it, said Andrew.

—It's my way of putting it, said Maria definitively.

—Maybe we should call it San Pedro, commented Jesús. It's a holy rock, no?

—The rock doesn't need a name, said Maria. It is we who need to name it.

Back in the town of Shiprock, named rather witlessly after the eponymous rock, we stopped in at the Bureau for Indian Affairs as a courtesy. We also wanted to consult with someone recommended to us by Father Ramón. As we walked in, Andrew tried to introduce himself but was cut off.

—We know who you are, said a young man in a dark suit with a black bolo tie standing behind the counter.

—Is it that obvious? asked Andrew.

—There's no mistaking you for anyone else, said the man. You are who you are.

The young man led us back to a small office, where we were introduced to Peter. Peter greeted Andrew as if he already knew him, though he didn't, and Andrew acted as if he wasn't surprised, though he was. Peter was a big man, with a personable spirit that made him seem even bigger. He was a Beatles fan, judging from the poster-sized print of the Abbey Road cover that adorned the wall of his office.

Peter turned to the young man with the bolo tie.

—Thanks, Jude, he said to him.

We all shuffled into Peter's office and told him what had happened and what our vision was of what should happen next. We didn't want to stay on the run forever, but we didn't want to give up or give in either.

—What you need is to find a way to disappear, said Peter.

—Can you help us with that? asked Andrew.

—I'm a Navajo, said Peter. Not a magician.

Maria was lost in the Abbey Road poster, and I was scribbling in my notebook as Andrew and Peter spoke. There was a point where a momentary silence brought the ambient noise of pen sketching on paper into the foreground. Peter noticed and looked at me, then looked back at Andrew.

—Does he always do this? asked Peter.

—No, not always, answered Andrew. Often though.

Peter turned to me.

—What are you scribbling so furiously? asked Peter of me.

—I'm trying to sketch Shiprock, I said.

—The rock or the town? asked Peter.

—The rock, I said.

—Can you show me what you've got so far? asked Peter.

I turned my notebook around to show him my sketch. Peter looked at it intently for a moment.

—I would never have thought that was Shiprock, he said. It looks nothing like it.

—I'm a writer, I said.

—I hope you write better than you draw, said Peter.

—I can't say if I do, I replied.

Peter told us we were safe in Shiprock, but probably not for long. Shiprock was no big city, but it was the biggest town in the area, a place where being seen was easier than not. We had thrown Sheriff Lex off our trail, and driven the long solitary road northward to Shiprock. But how long would the ruse last? Where would we go next? How long would this go on? How could we disappear?

Peter told us he would make a few calls and arrange a place for us to stay. He told us to head out for a bit and to come back in an hour or two.

—You should take my truck, he said. Park your white van in the back, behind the building.

—Why is that? asked Andrew.

—All of you driving around in a white van? said Peter. You may as well be sailing around on a shiprock.

We climbed into Peter's truck, one of those trucks that shouldn't still run but somehow does. Andrew, Jim, and Joe sat in the cab, while Maria, Jesús and I sat in the back in the open-air bed. As we drove through the streets of town, we talked among ourselves about who the people of Shiprock were and why they lived there. Shiprock isn't a big town. One hesitates to call it a town at all. You wonder why anyone would live here, as it seems the kind of place where everyone dreams of being somewhere else. You live in Shiprock only until you can think of where else you want to live. Travelers that come through use Shiprock as a junction, a means to an end, a place to pass through on your way to somewhere else. Perhaps the Great Ship, or the Great Bird, stopped here by accident. Perhaps Shiprock was supposed to be somewhere other than where it is. Maybe it should be Shipwreck rather than Shiprock.

We went to a flea market to pass some time. Flea markets are marvelously powerful reminders of just how much useless junk exists in the world. Flea markets are places where large numbers of people come together to exchange things they don't want for things they don't need. It's like a pilgrimage site for the endless reincarnation of things that should have died a final death long ago. Trinkets that would otherwise be trash find new life as a trove among those who think them treasure. At one booth, a self-styled artist was selling what was apparently his specialty craft, namely small three-masted ships made of plastic that he glued rather amateurishly onto small rocks. No Two are Alike, said the sign, which seemed unnecessary, since as far as I could tell, No One had ever been purchased. Still, I had to admire his faith and optimism, this one-hit-wonder of an artist, who sat behind the counter in between a box of rocks and a box of plastic ships, glue gun in hand and entirely unnecessary safety goggles on his face, making ever more of these persistently unwanted works. I think he truly believed that one day that first customer would finally walk up to the counter, money in hand. One day, he believed, his plastic ship would come in.

We eventually made our way back to Peter's office, driving the truck that every day defied the ways of the mechanical gods. Peter had brought food for us, some tamales filled with squash and chilies, and said he was waiting for a phone call from a priest at a local church who was making the necessary arrangements for us to stay the night. We ate in Peter's office, and Peter ate with us, sitting as he was behind the desk.

—Is Peter your real name? asked Joe.

—What kind of question is that? asked Peter, equally amused and perplexed.

—It's just that Peter doesn't sound like a Navajo name, explained Joe.

—What does a Navajo name sound like? said Peter.

—Not like that, said Joe, ineffectively.

Peter thought for a few moments while he pondered Joe's inquiry.

—My Navajo name is Tse, said Peter.

—Dude, like Guevara? asked Si, suddenly animated.

—Not Che, said Peter. Tse.

The phone rang, and Peter did one of those momentary mental inventories to survey what options you have when you need to pick up the phone but your fingers are covered with tamales and hot sauce.

—You mind if I put it on speaker? he asked.

None of us had an issue with that, especially considering how our hands and fingers were similarly indisposed, and so Peter surveyed his hand to see which finger was least covered with food, which turned out to be his left pinky, and deftly pushed the button on the phone.

—This is Peter, he said.

A voice crackled through from the other side.

—Hello, Peter? the voice asked, as if unsure that it was really Peter.

—Padre, said Peter, with genuine warmth. I was expecting your call. Is everything on schedule with the arrangements for our guests?

—Yes, about that, continued the voice. It's just that, well, something's come up.

—What's the problem? asked Peter, with some concern in his voice.

There was a pause on the other end of the phone.

—It's the sheriff, said the voice. He was just here.

The room quickly fell silent and still. Peter slowly reached for a napkin and began to wipe the food from his hands as he pondered and wondered.

—This is Sheriff Lex we're talking about? asked Peter.

—Yes, said the voice. It's him.

A moment passed.

—Peter? asked the voice.

—Yes?

—There's just one more thing.

—What's that?

—He's coming to see you.

—Now?

—Yes, now. You've got about five minutes, maybe less.

Peter stared blankly at his desk while he continued to wipe his hands. He slowly reached his hand over to the phone.

—Thank you, Padre, he said.

Peter pushed the button to end the call, his eyes moving slowly and furtively as if he were looking for some sort of answer as to how this could have happened, how Sheriff Lex could have found us, could have known we were there. Suddenly he looked up, as if in a moment of revelation, and uttered one simple word as he exhaled slowly.

—Jude.

Suddenly Peter stood up, as if he had resolved to take action and yet had no idea of what action to take. The rest of us followed his cue and began quickly to move about—pushing our food aside and doing things that made little sense but at least made us feel like we were doing something.

—We can leave out the back way and get in the van and go, said Andrew.

—No, said Peter. It's too late for that, and besides, you have to drive out the front, and he'll surely see you.

We all looked at each other, feeling helpless and hopeless.

—I've got an idea, said Peter. All of you stay right here. Don't move and don't make a sound.

Peter got up to leave the office, and stood at the doorway with one hand on the doorknob and the other on the light switch.

—I hope you're not afraid of the dark, he said.

And with that, he threw the light switch and closed the door behind him, leaving us all in an impenetrable and palpable darkness. We could not see each other. We couldn't see anything. In what seemed like only a few seconds, we heard a bell ring. It was the bell on the front door of the building, and for the first time, we all heard the voice of the man who was trying to track us down. It was unmistakably the voice of Sheriff Lex.

The conversation between Peter and Sheriff Lex was muddled. We could hear timbre but not meaning. Occasionally a word or a phrase would come through clearly. Sheriff Lex's voice was deep and sonorous, with a slight southern accent and an unnerving sense of calm. None of us had seen him before, except Andrew, and in the darkness and in my mind I was trying to sketch the face of the man whom I only knew at this point as a disembodied voice. We could hear a few muffled pleasantries and what sounded like an uneasy politeness that could give way at any moment to something decidedly unpleasant. I heard a hand knock on the counter every few moments, and I assumed that Peter was trying to head Sheriff Lex off, to keep him on the front side of the counter. Sheriff Lex must have sensed something was up. It sounded like he said he wanted to have a look around, and Peter rebuffed him.

The one thing I heard very clearly at one point was Peter's resolute voice.

—This is sovereign Navajo land, he said firmly and definitively.

Moments later we all heard the unmistakable clip-clop of boot-heels moving away from us, and the bell on the door told us that someone, presumably Sheriff Lex, had left the building. A few moments went by, probably just Peter waiting to make sure Sheriff Lex was truly gone, and when we all heard the sound of a car starting up and driving away, then and only then did Peter open the office door and turn on the lights.

—He's gone, but probably not far or for too long, said Peter gravely. You shouldn't stay here tonight.

—We know, said Andrew. We'll go now.

—Head east to Jicarilla, said Peter. I'll call them to let you know you are on the way. It's the least I can do for you.

We walked out of the office and did a quick check to make sure we hadn't forgotten anything. The young man with the black bolo tie was still seated behind the counter, doing his best not to look at any of us.

—Hey Jude, said Maria, almost tenderly, to let him know that we knew.

We climbed back into the van and headed east on what turned out to be a long and winding road into the desert mountains, in between Angel Peak and Cedar Hill and on through Navajo City and beyond.

Night was falling and it was falling quickly, and the move back into darkness made us all a little uneasy.

—I don't like this, said Jim. He makes us feel like we're criminals, or worse, heretics.

—We're his heretics, said Joe.

—And he is ours, said Maria.

I looked out the window at the dark desert landscape and imagined a world full of heretics, ghosts, spirits, and demons. Inside, we all fell into silence. For a moment, Maria put her hand on my shoulder.

The white van drove on into the dark night.

7

We drove that night through the darkness, trailing an asphalt thread through a needle eye of rock, water, and wood, saddling a point somewhere between Cedar Hill and Angel Peak. We passed many things that I did not then know were there. Only later, when I retraced this very journey and drove this route in the light of day, did I know the sights I had not seen. Only later did I learn that I could trust my senses. But that night, that night as we drove on through the darkness, I did not know where we were and did not know what was passing by outside the window. I could not see through the darkness. I sensed water at times, though I'm not sure why. Perhaps there is some innate sentiment in all of us that draws us back to our watery origins, something that takes us back to the moment when some cosmic spark fired and the thing which we are and which no one else can ever be came into existence. Later, even deeper into that dark night, I felt we were heading through a forest. I could not see the trees, yet I could feel the forest. Maria once told me that enlightenment comes only to those who first learn to close their eyes, and though I did not understand her words then, I certainly understand them now. I more than understand them. I believe them.

It was a very long drive that night. Andrew was at the wheel, and one by one the others dozed off slowly. Maria was the last to fall asleep. I alone remained awake for the entire journey for the simple reason that, at the time at least, I was nervous to fall asleep in a car in motion. I feared that if I fell asleep, there was nothing that would prevent the driver from doing the same. Every time I was in a situation like this, I would make a plan in my head, a plan to plot out what I would do if the driver fell asleep. Would I have enough time to grab the wheel? Stop the car? No, there was no way I could sleep. I also felt guilty for thinking that way, as I could not shake the feeling that somehow it meant I did not fully trust Andrew to stay awake, to drive us all safely to where we were going, wherever that was. It was an unsettling emotional cocktail of fear, mistrust, and guilt, and it kept me awake, in spite of the fatigue.

—Are you tired? I would ask Andrew.

—No.

A short while would pass.

—Are you tired?

—No.

And finally later.

—Are you tired?

—Only of you asking.

—Do you want me to stop?

—I never wanted you to start.

When we arrived at wherever it was we were, it was late. Or I should say, It felt late. It was that palpable moment when it felt too late to be night, but too early to be morning. There is a stillness in that moment that is like no other time. You don't know exactly what time it is and you don't need to. We had pulled up to what looked like a house with a dim light on the small porch of the entrance. We all tumbled out of the van, sleepy zombies in our gait, and followed Andrew inside. We were shown to a room with a carpeted floor, and on that floor were six blankets and six pillows arranged with surprising geometric order. We were all too tired to care where we would sleep. I found a blanket and a pillow, and went horizontal without effort. I closed my eyes.

I opened my eyes. Thick cloth curtains were drawn over the windows, but I could sense that it was daylight, that morning had arrived. Someone was preparing food. A sweet smell hung in the air, like yeasty caramel, if that's a thing, along with the bitter hint of coffee. A few of us were already up and about, judging from the empty spaces where blankets had been the night before. Only Si, I, and Jesús were still under our blankets, and even we were on the verge of stirring.

I walked over to the window and drew back one side of the curtain. I was assaulted by a massive flash of light and immediately recoiled, the way a vampire might do in a bad vampire movie. I closed my eyes. There was a momentary, subtle pain from the light flash, and I spent a few moments watching the afterglow images slowly decay into the visions we see when our eyes are closed but we nevertheless keep trying to see. I opened my eyes. Now, with eyes adjusted and accustomed, I could make out a large water tank not too far away and just up a gentle sloping hill. Dulce. That's what the tank said. Dulce.

Dulce. So that's where we were. I had never been to Dulce before, not many people ever get there. Not many people ever want to get there. Though few people have seen it, everybody knows or claims to know at least one thing about Dulce. That one thing that everybody claims to know is the story of the great alien shoot-out, the day when, a few decades back, secretive military types building a hidden underground base came face-to-face with secretive alien types, who were also building a hidden underground base, and a gunfight broke out at the less-than-okay corral. Sixty humans allegedly lost their lives that day. By some accounts the aliens and nonaliens were actually sharing the premises at the time, in some sort of dual-use arrangement, and then something—perhaps a dispute over rent, anger over alien gentrification, the inability to phone home, or just the general stress of living underground—led to a moment of extraordinary intergalactic violence.

How Dulce came to be some sort of alien Shangri-La is a mystery. How it is that a group of super-intelligent space aliens, with the technology to go anywhere in the universe, would pull out a map of the universe and collectively decide—*Dulce. Yeah, Dulce. Definitely. That's the place*—is a bit of a mystery. There were also reports in the area of farmers finding cows in the fields that had been turned inside out, evidence, some said, of alien activity. But how is this evidence of alien activity? Why would aliens come all the way here, to the great paradise of Dulce, build a secret base underground—and by the way apparently aliens are bad at keeping secrets because the so-called secret base was known by pretty much everyone in and around Dulce—and then engage in some bizarre form of cow origami? The only thing more amazing than the story itself is just how many people believe it. Whether they want to believe or need to believe is impossible to discern. That they believe is impossible to doubt.

I followed the scent trail and made my way to the kitchen, where I found the others already eating breakfast, which consisted of freshly-made beignets with caramel sauce and fresh strawberries served with Italian coffee.

—Beignets? I asked.

—What were you expecting, Belgian waffles? replied Maria.

Nothing made any sense here, at least not yet. I woke up on the floor of a house that might best be described as a museum of 1960s architecture—the bad kind, not the good—walked into a kitchen with old-style wood paneling—the kind that no one would ever mistake for actual wood—and find freshly-baked beignets and some of the best coffee I had had since I left New York.

—Who made all of this? I asked, incredulously.

—Stone did, said Andrew.

Then you have one of those moments when you know you really need to ask the obvious question, and you know that the person who just said something to you knows the question you are going to ask but makes you ask it anyway.

—Um…and who is Stone? I asked.

—Stone Parker, answered Andrew. He's the head of the local Apache Tribal Council.

—He's also a chef, said Maria, reading a newspaper that was yellowed with age.

—Hence the beignets, I said, following the line of reasoning to its unexpected, pastry-based end.

—Hence the beignets, affirmed Maria, without looking up from the old newspaper she was reading.

—And where is Stone? I asked.

—He went off south to the park, said Andrew.

After breakfast Jim and I wandered outside. One can't really wander far in Dulce. You're more likely to wander out of Dulce. We came across a place called The Hawk's Den, which I remember well because my first thought was the oddity of the name. Hawks don't live in dens. They live in nests. So why not call this The Hawk's Nest? Is a nest less welcoming than a den? Outside there was a sign advertising *Gifts and Jewelry*, as if jewelry could not be a gift. Also on the sign: *Native Crafts*. I came to develop a genuine dislike for the word crafts, as it was a word that implied something was more or other than what it was, which was simply something someone had made. In New York, lots of things had always been made by lots of people, but those who called themselves craft-makers did so because they thought what they had made was a bit better than what someone else had made. The coup de grace on The Hawk's Den sign was the little tidbit at the very bottom of the sign, highlighted as it was in red: *UFO Information*. Jim and I wandered in.

It was an odd place, but then again, so was all of Dulce. I suppose an odd place in an already odd place isn't really odd. There was a man behind the counter, and the entire place seemed to have no order to it whatsoever, yet without in fact being in disarray.

—Can I help you? asked the man.

Jim and I exchanged a quick glance, and from the look on Jim's face, I suspected mischief was afoot.

—We'd like some UFO information, said Jim.

And the game was joined.

—Okay, what do you want to know? asked the man.

—For starters, where are they? asked Jim.

—They live in the mountain, said the man.

—Seems like a lot of effort, said Jim.

—They don't want anyone to see them, said the man.

—Are they shy? asked Jim.

—Not sure, said the man.

—Have you seen them? asked Jim.

—No, said the man.

—How do you know they're there? asked Jim.

—I believe, said the man quick as a fox.

—So you can't see them but you believe they are there? queried Jim.

—Yes.

—So, they're like angels?

—Angels are sent by God.

—So who sent the aliens?

—The aliens sent themselves.

—So the aliens are their own gods?

—I don't know about that.

—So perhaps they are ghosts?

—I don't believe in ghosts, especially from other planets.

—If you didn't believe in them then they wouldn't come from anywhere because they just wouldn't be?

—No need to get technical.

—Do you believe in unicorns? I asked, to join in.

—I don't disbelieve.

—Are the aliens like unicorns then?

—We don't know if unicorns exist, the man said. But we know aliens do.

—Because you believe? asked Jim.

—Yes.

—Do you think aliens believe in people? I asked.

In front of me on the counter there was a box that said Video Rentals, and in the Video Rentals box was a DVD jewel case for *Terminator 2*, which as a DVD was not technically a video and in any case could not be for rent because when I opened the jewel case it was empty.

—Are you two brothers? asked the man of me and Jim.

—You might say he's my brother from another planet, I said.

The man looked flummoxed or amused, I couldn't tell which.

—Are you gentlemen going to buy anything? he asked after a moment.

—What do you think, Jim, should we buy some crafts?

—That depends, said Jim.

—On what? asked the man.

—Do you have any space crafts?

Jim and I made a quick walk through The Hawk's Den while the man behind the counter became utterly indifferent of whether we were there or not. We made the short walk back to the house, which still was filled with the scent of beignets, caramel, strawberries, and coffee. Andrew was loading some things into the van.

—We need to keep moving, said Andrew.

—Aliens? I asked, thinking I was being clever, but wasn't.

Andrew did not acknowledge what I said, though I saw him raise one eyebrow so I know he heard it. The others had come out of the house and we were all gathered around. Andrew shut the rear door of the van and turned to Jim and me, looking straight past us.

—Father Timothy, he said. So nice to see you.

Jim and I turned round to see the man from behind the counter of The Hawk's Den.

—Father? Jim asked.

—That's me, said the man who was Father Timothy.

—You're a priest? Jim asked incredulously. I thought that was a twenty-four seven sort of thing.

—Tell me, said Father Timothy, do you have to be in a church to pray?

—No, said Jim, with uncertain intonation.

—Then why do I have to be in a church to preach? said Father Timothy, with a subtly triumphant air.

—So you knew who we were? asked Jim. You knew we were just having a bit of fun?

—Yep.

—But why then? asked Jim.

—No worries, my friend, said Father Timothy. In the desert, you see, Satan had to tempt Jesus, but Jesus had to let him try.

—Wait, so which of us is Satan? asked Jim, with temerity.

Andrew started the van and we all climbed in. Jim's brow was furrowed with worried thought.

—Father Timothy, said Andrew, when you see Stone please give him our deepest thanks.

Father Timothy nodded his head, then leaned in the window, looking at Jim, and me. He chuckled slightly.

—Players got played, he said.

We drove off, and Dulce gently receded.

8

All acts of creation are shrouded in mystery. Even those who engage in creation sometimes fail to understand the origins and consequences of their own acts. Their own creation remains a mystery even to them. Worlds are made and unmade, created and destroyed, destroyed and remade. A writer writes a word, a painter paints a line, a sculptor sculpts a shape, a singer sings a note—acts of creation brought to life in a single moment, before which they did not exist, before which there was nothing. How does the creator, the artist, know when to start? When to finish? When to say the work is done, and that it is good? A writer, for instance, writes a word, then another, then continues to write and to create a whole separate world, lording over the creation like a priest or a deity. Characters come to life, do things and say things, all at the whim of the writer-creator. They experience

acts of cruelty or kindness that they can never understand. Why were they put into this world in the first
place? And all that separates the madman from the
artist is the ability to convince others to believe in the
created world. Singular madness is insanity, collective
madness is art.

—Did you ever wonder what it means to say that
God created man in His own image? asked Jim, seemingly out of nowhere.

—Seriously? said Andrew. This is what you've been
pondering since breakfast?

—No, said Jim. Not like that. It's just one of those
things that popped into my head. I think everyone
wonders.

—Dude, it's like the aliens, said Si.

—Wait, what? said Joe, turning to Si with puzzled
expectation.

—Think about it, dude, continued Si, imbued with
inspired reason. Every time you see a drawing of an
alien, they look suspiciously like us, don't they?

—So, we created aliens in our own image? replied
Joe, with incomplete conviction.

—I would love to see the day, said Maria staring
out the window, when a spaceship lands on earth and
when the door opens, out runs a bunch of ocelots.

—Lots and lots of ocelots, said Jesús, as if the sce-
nario made sense and only the number of ocelots were
in question.

—Superintelligent ocelots? asked Jim.

—I'm not sure how intelligent they would be, said Jesús, truly in doubt on this point.

—Intelligent enough to build a spaceship, said Joe.

—Maybe all ocelots are superintelligent, said Maria. They just haven't revealed themselves as such to us yet.

—Dude, awesome, said Si.

—Are we seriously having this conversation? asked Andrew.

We had been driving for about an hour. Apparently, according to Andrew, there had been some more Sheriff Lex sightings and it seemed prudent to move on early and often. Sheriff Lex sightings were becoming like alien sightings—suddenly he was here, suddenly he was there, yet no solid evidence had really turned up that he was anywhere in particular. Come to think of it, I didn't really know where we were either, ever since we had left Dulce. So I asked.

—We've just passed through Chama, now we're heading south, said Andrew. Toward Santa Fe.

—You mean Fanta Se? said Joe.

—Dude, is Santa Fe full of aliens, too? asked Si.

—Even worse, said Andrew. It's full of artists.

Santa Fe had a reputation for being for being a community that was too artistic for it's own good, for having its own form of madness that no one believed outside of Santa Fe. Hence the name, Fanta Se. People talked about Santa Fe as some sort of retreat, though what people were retreating from was never made clear.

Perhaps people in the rest of New Mexico were retreating from Santa Fe. Hard to say, and no one would say anyway if they knew, which they didn't. Everyone in Santa Fe seemed to fancy themselves some sort of artist, some sort of sacred vessel of creativity, and though all of these self-styled artists swore up and down that they suffered through the artistic process for the love of art itself, the number of art galleries in Santa Fe and the number on the price tags in those galleries revealed at least one alternative source of motivation. There were ongoing bouts of banter and bickering in Santa Fe about which artists had sold out and which artists had stayed true to their calling. The prevailing opinion was that the poorer the artist, the truer the art. It was also equally true that the poorer the artist, the more likely they were to believe the prevailing opinion. Santa Fe itself was like a work of art, with each building required to imitate truthfully the local style and to be created carefully in Santa Fe's own image.

—It's not real adobe, clarified Andrew. It's plaster and stucco designed to look like adobe. It's an act of deception.

—All art is an act of deception, said Maria.

—So all art is a lie? asked Joe.

—That's not what I said, said Maria.

—But you said all art is an act of deception, repeated Joe. Isn't that the same as lying?

—Would you say then that all of our performances have been lies? asked Maria.

—Well…no, said Joe, discomfited.

—You see a movie, you know it's not real, continued Maria. And yet in one scene it makes you cry. Are the tears not real?

—Wait, so if you believe a lie, does it make the lie true? asked Joe.

—No, said Maria. The lie is still a lie, but the belief is true.

—So if we can't prove that God exists, but we believe He does, then is religion just a collection of lies we believe?

—Belief is a response, never a source, said Andrew theologically.

—So what is the role of scripture? asked Joe.

—Scripture is a form of sacred art, replied Maria with conviction.

—So scripture is an act of deception? continued Joe, with diffident logic.

—Not to those who believe it, replied Maria, with logical confidence.

—I'm confused, said Joe.

—Faith resolves confusion, replied Maria.

The landscape was changing, gradually but perceptibly. We passed a place called Echo Amphitheater, which I remember well because there were several signs about it one after another leading up to the turn off, which I thought might be someone's idea of a joke so clever that no one got it. After that we approached Ghost Ranch, which in Spanish is referred to as *El Rancho de los Brujos*. I never figured that one out, not then and not now. A *brujo* is a sorcerer, so whoever thought a ghost was a sorcerer either didn't know Spanish or didn't know ghosts. And in any case, why would a sorcerer or a ghost need a ranch? To rustle up ghost cattle? Unlikely. To make things even more odd, the whole place is now run by Presbyterians, who as far as I can tell are neither sorcerers nor ghosts, though I could see how it might look that way to someone who came from afar—aliens, for instance. A person dressed in white and surrounded by candles with the amazing power to turn bread into flesh and wine into blood, through the incantation of precise words and gestures—that all makes sense to those who are familiar with such everyday miracles. But to the uninitiated, it might seem a rather frightening power for someone to possess, and a rather difficult concept to grasp. And don't get me started on the doctrine of the Trinity.

We had been driving for a while and the sun was at that angle in the sky where it seems to stand still. It becomes difficult to gauge the day by its shadows.

—What time is it? I asked.

—3:10, replied Andrew, quite specifically.

We drove past Ghost Ranch, and there were two old men by the side of the road, dressed as one might expect a cowboy to dress. They looked a bit red from the heat.

—What are they doing out here by the roadside? asked Joe.

—They shouldn't be out here in the country, said Jim. This is no place for them.

—Cowboys? asked Andrew.

—Nah, said Jim. Probably just city slickers.

—How can you tell? I asked.

—By the way they're dressed, said Jim.

—Like cowboys? I continued.

—Real cowboys don't dress like that, said Jim, who would know.

We hadn't driven much further when Jesús said he was tired of being in the van. It was an exceptionally long day of driving, and while the landscape seemed seductively enchanting, the interior of the van, much less so.

—We'll stop in Abiquiu, said Andrew.

A short while later, as the signs told us we were near Abiquiu, Andrew turned the van off the main road and onto a dusty side road with no markings. We continued down that dusty road for several miles, and just when I was convinced that we had made a wrong turn, that there was nothing down this road that spoke of rest or refuge, we came upon a cluster of buildings. We came to a stop right in front of a sign that said Christ in the Desert Monastery.

—A monastery? asked Jesús.

—I have friends here, said Andrew. They can help us.

Andrew went inside what looked to be the main part of the monastery. There were a few people walking around, all of them looking pensive, or perhaps bored. It's hard to tell the difference sometimes, when one has only an appearance to go on. We all climbed out of the van to stretch and walk around a bit. A man came out of the building that Andrew had entered into, and walked over to offer us bottles of cool water and freshly-baked bread. It was exactly what we needed at that moment. We thanked the man, and he bowed smilingly but made it clear through his gestures that he could not say anything. He had taken a vow of silence. He wouldn't speak, on account of that vow, but he could communicate, as he did with us through gestures. So language wasn't the issue, but rather speech itself. Or the noise of speech. It was, after all, a vow of silence, and not a vow of unintelligibility. The *logos* was there, as it had always been, but the sound was not. Perhaps the sound got in the way of the *logos*.

Andrew returned shortly thereafter carrying a piece of paper and thankfully more of that freshly-baked bread.

—We need to keep moving, he said.

—What's the rush? asked Joe.

—Sheriff Lex has been busy, said Andrew.

—Busy with what? followed Joe.

—Finding us, said Andrew with perturbation and resignation.

Andrew looked at the piece of paper and I noticed that there was writing all over one side of the page.

—The man who served us bread and water wouldn't talk to us, noted Jim.

—No one here is talking to anyone, said Andrew.

—Everyone has taken a vow of silence? asked Joe.

—For forty days, said Andrew. Starting today.

—Forty days of silence in the desert, noted Joe out loud.

—Christ in the Desert, said Maria.

—What's on the paper? asked Jim.

—An ingenious plan, said Andrew, without another word.

We left by the same way we came in. As far as I could tell, that was the only way in and the only way out, the dusty road through the desert. We were vulnerable again, and we all knew it. We were on holy land, though technically I suppose all land is holy, it's just a matter of recognition. We were on private land, too, though the holiness was accessible to the general public. But once we left the monastery, we weren't on native land any more, though technically I suppose all land is native, it's just a matter of recognition. But Sheriff Lex didn't care about technicalities or speculation. What he cared about was what the law said, and what the the law said was that when we turned back onto the main road, we were on land that Sheriff Lex considered wholly native to the great book of the Criminal Code of the great state of New Mexico.

We drove through the village of Abiquiu, passing by Bode's general store, at which point I thought we'd take a break, especially since across the street was the Church of Santo Tomas, but in fact we continued onward. South of Abiquiu we turned off onto another, smaller road. I remember crossing over a river in a shallow valley, only because I remember it being deep green with life, stark blue with water, and blood red with rock on both sides. After the river we turned left again, onto an even smaller road, yet another dusty road, and drove further and further into the desert wilderness. We eventually pulled up to an unexpectedly white adobe structure that appeared as something of an architectural oasis in the otherwise flat arid landscape.

—Dar al Islam? asked Joe, reading the sign.

—Perfect, said Maria, with an omniscient smile.

—But we're not Muslims, said Jim.

—I don't think they care, said Andrew.

—I don't think God does either, said Maria.

We parked the van in what appeared to be a parking area—really just desert that looked slightly more arranged than the surrounding landscape—and no sooner had we done so than a man came out to greet us.

—You must be Father Andrew, said the man, with a warm smile.

—You must be Khalil, said Andrew.

Khalil looked inside the van and smiled again.

—Welcome to Dar al Islam, he said.

Khalil told us to pull the van around to the back. Though at this point it was covered with dust, it was still the great white van.

—What are we doing here? asked Joe.

—We're staying here, said Andrew.

—This is the ingenious plan? followed Jim, obtusely perplexed.

—Think about it, said Andrew. If you had to search for a Catholic priest, no one, not even Sheriff Lex, would think to look in a mosque.

We parked, got out, and walked back round to the entrance, where Khalil was standing. Here, too, we were given fresh bread and cool water, except that the bread was flatter and the water cooler. Though the sun was quite intense outside, inside the white adobe structure it was comfortable and soothing, almost meditative. Khalil introduced himself to us one at a time, each time placing his hand over his heart and offering a slight bow.

Khalil left us there, as he explained, to go to make the arrangements for our stay. When he left, the room fell to silence. We became aware of our surroundings, all of us, standing as we were in the same cool room. Beneath our feet was flat, hard marble, and all around were walls of the same, carved with exquisite and ornate geometric patterns, all of them similar yet no two alike. I remember following the lines around, each one leading to the next, like a maze with no solution or a script with no cipher. Periodically the maze was interrupted by black marble plaques upon which were written golden lines of calligraphy. I didn't know Arabic then, and I still don't know it now, but I could tell from the calligraphic elegance, neither opulent nor ostentatious in its eternal moment, that these were sacred words. Their meaning would remain a mystery to me, but their expression was absolutely clear. Only those with cold hearts and closed minds could not find cause to marvel.

We stood there for quite some time in silence. In one moment, I found myself side by side with Maria.

—I'm at a loss for words, I said.

—You talk too much, she replied.

Her smile was calligraphy to me.

9

I once read a story—or maybe I heard it, I can't really remember at this point—in which a determined young man resolved to become the greatest artist of his time. He cleared one of his rooms to create a studio, bought all of the necessary supplies and tools that an aspiring artist might need, and proceeded to alter his behavior and clothing accordingly as he thought an artist of his temperament should require. He let his hair grow a bit too long, and worked hard to find the exact balance between unkempt and unclean. His clothes, too, were chosen with equal care and flair, always searching for the sweet spot between disheveled and bedraggled. He kept late hours, cavorted rhapsodically with bohemians, ate poorly and drank well, and had impassioned love affairs with the sort of women who were relentlessly vulnerable to the unstable alchemy of art and artistry. He would talk at volume in quiet halls, and would sit quietly with a taciturn expression in loud gatherings. *He's an artist*, people would say in such settings, while others would nod as if to excuse the young man of the magnificently misunderstood temperament.

Yet there was one thing he was never able to do, and that was to create great art. He lived the great life of the artist he would never be. The only thing that makes the story more odd than it already is, is the fact that so many of those who knew him believed him to be a great artist, even though they could never recall seeing any of his art. The youthful artist died young, as this is after all what great, impassioned artists do, and after his death, his many companions and acquaintances were shocked to discover that his studio contained only a handful of unfinished canvasses, none of which showed any discernible talent and all of which had been defaced in one way or other by the artist. Could one be a great artist without creating great art? Could the young man's passion have come not from his deep wellspring of creative talent but from the hateful realization that the talent he so desired was so egregiously absent from his being? Why did so many people believe him to be a great artist, without any proof or evidence, without any hint or testament or testimony? Maybe the real work of art was the artist himself. Perhaps his entire life was simply a piece of dramatic performance art.

I told that story as dusk gave up its ghost to the night at Dar al Islam in front of a wood fire in a pit on a chair with a tear in the company of my companions. I know this because in my notebook there is a page that has a sketch of the gold Arabic scriptural calligraphy, odd in so far as I could not write Arabic so it is unclear how I could think to draw it, and beneath it there is a text box that says, The Young Artist Story. Beneath it, an appended note says *Is This Me?*—a note that I apparently tried to erase at some point, smudged as it was, though I don't remember when or why. On the facing page there is a drawing of an ocelot, which looks more like a deranged cat with skin lesions, mostly because I cannot draw well and because at the time I could not remember precisely what an ocelot looked like. I suppose if one draws something without knowing what it looks like, then the drawing is necessarily accurate, in that it is faithful to one's mistaken imagination, though not to reality, or one's imagination of reality, as mistaken as that may be. I remember years ago singing along rather fluently to a song by Cesária Évora, even though I didn't know a word of Portuguese or a whisper of what it meant. Not sure how I thought I could do that, but I suppose I could also say I never got the words wrong because I didn't know how to get them right.

—Everyone is a great artist, said Maria. The problem is that most people never find their right art.

—I wonder if he ever knew he wasn't a great artist, pondered Jim. Maybe he truly believed in himself, and so others did, too.

—Dude, maybe the artist didn't deface his art, said Si. Maybe the defacement was the art.

I thought of Khalil. Here was a man whose kindness and faith seems to walk hand in hand. But how did I know that the kindness or the faith were not merely art, decorous displays of decorum? I didn't know Khalil, at least not then, and I wondered to myself about the disturbingly thin line between artist and trickster. I realized if I were to think of Khalil in those terms, I had to think of everyone in those terms. I had to think of myself in those terms. After all, a really good artist, including a really good scam artist, doesn't just fool from a distance. They fool with great intimacy. How well do we know anyone else? How well do we know ourselves? Perhaps our sense of self is the greatest act of tomfoolery in human history. Perhaps everything we say and do is really just an endless performance in a language that in the end is endlessly indecipherable. We never understand one another, we never understand ourselves. Art is the pretense of understanding, an irreverent gesticulation that is simultaneously a dramatic work and a satire of that dramatic work. The deception of art and the art of deception become indistinguishable. We can only enjoy the first if we can accept the possibility of the second.

—Why do we make gestures when we pray? I asked aloud, startled that I asked it aloud as I had thought I was only thinking in my own internal thought world. I wondered what else I had said aloud, thinking I had only thought what I had in fact said.

Did everyone know my thoughts now?

—We make gestures when we talk to each other, so why wouldn't we do it when we talk to God? said Joe.

—If we talk to God as we talk to each other, then is God really just one of us? pondered Jim.

—By definition He isn't one of us, said Andrew.

—Jesus isn't one of us either, added Jesús.

—Then He would just be Jesús, said Jim. If He were, which He isn't.

—Dude, said Si.

—I once knew a journalist from Japan, I said. He would bow politely to people even when talking on the phone, even when no one could see that he was bowing. It was an empty gesture.

—How do you know it was empty? asked Maria, who as always was listening intently even when it appeared she was not listening at all.

—I suppose I don't, I said, now unsure. But still, the kneeling and the supplication and the plaintive gesture and the pleading speech—doesn't God already know we are praying? Doesn't He already know our sincerity? Only a fool believes he can fool God, so empty gestures won't solicit divine sympathy.

I wasn't sure if I said any of that or just thought it. But I know I thought it.

—I talk to God every day, said Andrew. But I don't talk to other people about it. They might get the wrong idea.

—What is the wrong idea to get?

—That I am trying to be holy, said Andrew. Or that I am crazy without trying.

—Why would they think you are crazy? asked Joe.

—A man who talks to God is devout, said Andrew. A man who believes he talks to God is crazy.

—But doesn't all faith require some form of insanity? continued Joe.

—Who are you, Kierkegaard? replied Andrew.

—Do you think God gets the wrong idea? pondered Jim.

—God never gets the wrong idea, said Andrew with linear emphasis. Otherwise he wouldn't be God.

—What sorts of things do you say to God? asked Jim.

—Only God knows, said Andrew.

—How do you talk to God if you never get a reply? queried Joe existentially.

—How do you know God doesn't reply? countered Andrew. Words aren't the only form of communication.

—The question isn't whether God responds, said Maria with her inveterate laconic precision. It's whether we understand His reply.

A woman came to us as we talked around the fire and told us that our accommodations were ready.

—You'll be sleeping in the yurts, she said. All of you will be staying in the same yurt except for the lady.

There were three yurts on the property of Dar al Islam, structures that had clearly been added recently and were not attached to the main buildings.

—Why do you have yurts here? I asked. They don't have yurts in the Middle East.

—We're not in the Middle East now, are we? said the woman, with a sincerity that belied her wit.

—Do Muslims sleep in yurts? asked Jim.

—Muslims can sleep anywhere, replied the woman. They're quite astonishing that way.

Jim's face bore that peculiar expression a person gets when they've said something they wish they hadn't, hoped no one noticed, then realized everyone did.

—Dinner will be served in an hour, said the woman. Tonight we are serving pizza.

—Pizza? asked Jim.

—What were you expecting, hummus?

The woman gracefully walked away, taking her enigmatic smile with her.

—I like her, said Maria with a subtle smile.

A yurt is a wonderful structure insofar as it has no corners. If you've built a yurt and it does have corners, then you're probably more mad than nomad, or perhaps just an absolute nomad beginner. But really, an amateur nomad is just someone who is lost, and someone who is lost probably has no business building a yurt. Thus the yurt is the preferred choice of structure for the professional or habitual nomad, but not for the amateur.

I suppose we were less nomads than outlaws, though an outlaw is also by default a nomad, and an outlaw by definition cannot be someone who is lost because their wandering has a purpose, even if it is without a destination. The yurts were comfortable enough, even cozy, and unlike true yurts that offer shelter from the great steppe winds, these were anchored to the ground and had indoor plumbing. One nice touch was the wood-burning stove that provided a bit of rustic, yurtish heat. But as anyone who has ever slept with fire knows, there is an intricate time-based two-step between wood-burning heat and fire-warmed sleep. The fire grows cold as the sleep grows deep, and the descent into cold pushes the ascent into wakefulness, wherein one rebuilds the fire and the dance begins anew, throughout the long, cold night.

Khalil assured us that such a dance would not be necessary here.

—Don't worry, he said. If the wood-fired stove goes out, the electric heat system will kick in and keep the yurt warm through the night.

The yurt had a back-up system, a fail-safe option that offered the charm of the wood-fired sleep without the concomitant dangers, annoyances, and inconveniences. So much energy and time spent on back-up systems. So much effort to cast out the doubt and uncertainty built directly into the design of things. Everything seems to have some sort of back up, some sort of safety catch or security blanket, except of course for faith. Some might argue that faith *is* the security back up. But to my mind, faith by definition is the absence of a security back up, for if it required a back up, it would really just be doubt. Faith is the only thing we have that asks us to take a leap into the unknown, all in or not at all, with no safety net and no guarantee of anything. It goes against everything we are told about security and self-preservation. Faith is therefore always an act of defiance.

Once we had settled into our yurts and figured out where things were and where things went, the woman with the enigmatic smile came to tell us that dinner was ready. We chose to eat our dinner outside by the open-pit fire, rather than inside the dining hall or inside the yurts. Andrew and Khalil walked off together into the building, leaving the rest of us to eat our pizzas—which were stylistically more like flatbreads—amongst ourselves. The open-pit fire roared anew with visceral energy as it consumed another wooden sacrifice now offered to it. In return, it bellowed and spewed its ash and ember into the sky, as if reaching for the fiery heavens.

—Did anyone notice the arrow on the inside of the yurt? asked Joe.

—It points in the direction of Mecca, said Maria, staring dreamily into the fire.

—It's for how they pray, right? asked Jesús to no one in particular.

—It's for how they live, said Maria, still staring into the fire. It's a spiritual compass point. They can wander their whole lives through, but if they know at least that one direction, then they can never be lost.

—So, like a sailor and the stars over the sea? asked Jim, again to no one.

—I once met a man from Mo'orea who said that even in the dead of night on a raging sea, if he could see the Southern Cross even for a moment, he knew where he was and how to get home, said Joe.

—Dude, in California I had to see the ocean to know which way was west, said Si confessionally.

—What do you do now in New Mexico? asked Joe.

—Dude, I have an app on my phone that tells me where I am, said Si, realizing the sadness of his statement as he said it.

Andrew and Khalil returned some time later, and as we finished our dinner, they told us of some new developments and the options we now had before us. Whatever hopes we may have had that Sheriff Lex was going to give up the search and let things pass were dashed by the latest chatter from Andrew's surprisingly extensive network of friends. Not only was Sheriff Lex determined not to be bested by a bunch of what he called ragtags and misfits—a phrase I found to be without accurate meaning or apposite relevance—but he was now more determined than ever to make an example out of us, the people who dared to bring disorder into the his otherwise well-ordered world. Sheriff Lex was a man of singular purpose, a missionary of the law with a mission to convert the world to a life of singular order. Order was peace, and peace was order. The enemy was disorder, and the agents who brought disorder into the world had to face the order of the law. Any act of mayhem, no matter how great or small, could not be allowed to stand.

We had two options, according to Andrew and Khalil. One was to head directly into Santa Fe, and then head south, back toward Las Cruces and toward the Texas border. The logic there was a risky one, which was that Sheriff Lex would not expect us to take so brazenly obvious a route and so would not be looking for us there. The second was to head east into the mountains, gaining some altitude and hoping that the more rugged wilderness would allow for a discreet passage to the dusty plains of eastern New Mexico. The small towns in the remote east, out toward Oklahoma, were a forgotten landscape, and thus, a good place to forget things, like us.

—We do have a third option, said Andrew.

A silence followed as we all stared listlessly into the fire.

—We could just turn ourselves in, said Andrew with a sigh.

—We've done nothing wrong, said Maria, resolutely.

—But according to Sheriff Lex, followed Jim, we've done something illegal.

—Just because something is illegal does not make it wrong, said Maria.

Another silence followed in which it became clear that none of us wanted to pursue the third option. We had come too far to end things that way. For a moment, the fire crackled and sputtered, sending embers into the air as if to engage a last moment of defiance before starting the inevitable decay into black cold ash.

—Khalil, said Jesús. Why are you helping us?

Khalil turned pensively toward Jesús.

—I don't understand, he said.

—Why are you helping us? repeated Jesús.

—I understand your question, said Khalil. What I don't understand is why you are asking it.

Jesús struggled, searching for words.

—You ask the wrong question, my friend, said Khalil.

—What is the right question? asked Jesús.

—How could I not help you? replied Khalil.

Weariness descended upon us and we began to retire to our yurts for the night. Khalil's words resounded in my ears. For so much of my life, I had been angry at the universe for never giving me the answers I needed. Now I was confronted with another possibility. Maybe all this time I had been asking all the wrong questions.

The fire crackled, as if it too were prepared to enter the inevitable night.

10

The greatest hubris of humanity is to confuse knowledge with understanding. There is an element of folly in this, in that humankind seems uniquely desirous to know all there is to know, and yet also knows that it can never know that. There will always be a vestige of the unknowable beyond the knowable, a residue of the immeasurable beyond the measurable, a remnant of the incomprehensible beyond the comprehensible, a hint of the invisible beyond the visible. The realm that lies beyond us is the realm of faith, awe, and wonder. Yet the pox on us is that the more we know the less we learn, for it is at the hands of those who have claimed not only to know but to understand that so much suffering and devastation has perennially plagued our fragile existence.

Consider the man on a spiritual quest to be the holiest man he can become, the quintessential practitioner of his faith. As he climbs his spiritual ladder from neophyte to acolyte, from acolyte to student, from student to priest, from priest to saint—at each stage he believes his knowledge has become understanding. In believing he has understood the words of his god, he believes he has found the favor of his god, that he is the chosen one of that god, the one for whom others bear witness. Yet it is precisely at this point that his faith imperceptibly transforms into sacrilege, the point where the saint commits his biggest sin—to claim that he can know what is by definition unknowable, to claim that he can comprehend what is infinitely incomprehensible. In believing he has truly understood the words of his god, and the exact meaning of his scriptures, he overlooks the simplest truth of all. Those who are most secure in their belief that they are going to heaven are always first in line on the path that leads to hell.

Such were my thoughts as I wandered around in the middle of the night outside my yurt. I could not sleep, as my mind was on fire with ideas and questions and doubts and uncertainties. I thought perhaps a walk in the cold desert air would set my mind and heart at ease. I stared into the night sky, which in New Mexico rarely disappoints those who seek its treasures. From one horizon to the other, there was an endless stream of beautiful stars, some shining red, some white, others blue, like perfectly sculpted gems reflecting light from an invisible sun. I once read a book, and not a good one, that claimed that religion was only necessary until humans evolved sufficient intelligence to understand the world. The wonder of the universe was conquered by the certainty of science. The flickering stars were no long heaven's embers or angels and gods in the sky. They were superheated spheres of gas produced by a universe whose age and manner of origin were now known. Science and religion had battled, and science had won, said the author. Only stubborn fools still held onto their faith, said the author. But I don't think science dispelled the wonder. I think the science is part of the wonder. I think the scientist, the philosopher, the priest, and the poet can all stare at the same night sky, and all of them can experience their own sense of wonder. For wonder is created in the realm beyond what we can fathom, and only the arrogant fool or the dead of heart cannot see the endless beauty of the starscape across the desert night sky.

I heard footsteps, and turned to find Maria walking toward me.

—Can't sleep either? I asked.

—Your footsteps awakened me, she said.

I remember thinking that night, right in that moment, that Maria was the most beautiful woman I had ever seen in my life, a statement that was as true then as it is now. I can't tell you why I think that, and I won't bother to describe the many things about her that made me think this way. No matter the quantity or the quality, words would only fail to convey what I want to convey. So instead I can only convey the thought that I felt something that I cannot convey, something that has no equivalent in the world of words.

A shooting star elegantly traced a light trail across the sky, before disappearing into the darkness from which it came.

—Make a wish, said Maria.

—Isn't that just a superstition? I offered.

—No, it's an elegant hope, she said.

A few moments pass, both of us staring into the sky.

—I always make a wish, she said.

—Do they ever come true? I asked.

—That isn't the point of a wish, she said.

I'll admit I had never considered until that moment that the wish itself was the precious substance, that the outcome of the wish was an entirely separate affair.

—Besides, she added. Would you really want to live in a world without wishes?

A firefly appeared and flashed its own brief incandescent exuberance. Why it did that, I'll never know. Perhaps it was inspired by the shooting star, or perhaps it was jealous of it. I had not seen a single firefly in New Mexico, and assumed that they didn't exist in these parts. Yet here was this firefly, rather extravagantly lighting up his own little world. I did not see any other fireflies. Just the one.

—Maybe he's lost, I said, staring ahead in anticipation of the firefly's next show.

—Maybe it's a she, said Maria. Maybe she knows exactly what she's doing. Maybe she is trying to tell you something.

—Should I make a wish? I asked.

—Do you want to make a wish?

—I don't know.

—Maybe it's an omen, she said.

—Good or bad? I asked.

Maria smiled slightly, and sighed.

—You with your expectations, she said.

We wandered back to our respective yurts, leaving the stars and the night and the firefly to carry on as they wished. I remembered chasing fireflies as a child, running through the tall grass of late summer, filled with awe and wonder in a world where everything seemed magically new and every moment seemed eternally endless. Had I lost my sense of wonder with the world? Had I simply buried my childish wonder under the rubble of my adult expectations? I wanted to know the answers and outcomes. I wanted the world to give me certainty and predictability. I wanted to understand things. But Maria was right. It is only in the acceptance of our imperfect grasp of the world that we can ever hope to find peace. I made a wish, and eventually found my way back to sleep.

In the morning we had breakfast in the main building and afterward helped to clean up. It was the least we could do. I'll admit that for most of my life I had always been suspicious of this kind of thing, this communal sort of help. I had always been suspicious of people who seemed genuinely good. I didn't trust them. Someone had washed our van, for no other reason than to be helpful and nice, and now it gleaned with an angelic white light as it reflected and dispersed the mid-morning sun. Never mind that within two minutes of leaving the place it would be just as dusty and dirty as it was before it had been washed. For now, it looked white-horse gallant.

As we were loading up the van and getting ready to leave, the woman from the previous day, the woman with the feisty wit and the inscrutable smile, brought us a neatly-packed box.

—You may have a long day's journey, she said. We've packed a lunch for all of you.

—Leftover pizza? asked Jim.

—No, it's hummus, she said rather wryly.

Khalil bid us farewell and wished us peace, a gentle *salam alaikum* with his hand over his heart, and off we went on the long dirt road, our white van surrounded by a dust-cloud aura. Andrew told us that he and Khalil thought it best for us to head east into the high desert and get past Taos. Heading to Santa Fe would have been a too risky, too much of a gamble, according to Andrew.

—Santa Fe is full of people who want to be noticed, he said. If you go to Santa Fe and try not to be noticed, everyone will notice.

Andrew was even reluctant to drive toward Santa Fe, so the more obvious route through civic-minded Española and spirit-guided Chimayo—the greatest pilgrimage site on American soil—was bypassed for the smaller byways that took us through El Rito and Ojo Caliente. El Rito has the oldest church in New Mexico, which comes as a surprise when arriving in El Rito as there is precious little to suggest its cultural and historical pedigree to anyone who wanders through. People were strangely friendly there. I remember them waving to us like they knew us when they didn't. Ojo Caliente is the kind of place where people come to cleanse their souls and their intestines, not necessarily in that order and often at the same time. There are signs promoting the healing waters of the mineral springs everywhere you look. There's also a perceptible Buddhist ambience to the place, and a spiritual pining for the religious essence of Tibet, not necessarily as it actually exists but as people imagine it to be, while sitting in sacred resort waters and eating goji berries in the herbal mountain air. Buddhist prayer flags can sometimes be seen fluttering in the wind. In other places this kind of spiritual blending might seem strange and confused. In New Mexico, it could never be any other way.

In Carson we stopped to take a break and to eat lunch. We unpacked the box of food and found that it did indeed contain hummus, along with several other things, such as flatbread, olives, cheese, and a cooked dish of lentils and rice. There was even some cold gingered lemonade, and of course a small tin of Hatch chilies, which for most people in New Mexico comes third only after air and water on the list of things essential to sustain human life. Carson is one of those places where the desert looks as if it wanted to change its mind and become something other than what it is. The rich green color of less arid foliage keeps breaking through here and there along the vast sandy plain, and the bare-earth red of so many a desert mountain elsewhere in New Mexico here becomes modestly clothed with generous greenery as the altitude becomes more insistent.

—When I look at this food, it makes me think of what they must have had at The Last Supper, said Jim.

—I doubt Jesus had a can of Hatch chilies, replied Joe.

Andrew found this terribly amusing.

—I've never understood the difference between supper and dinner, said Jesús.

What followed was a brief debate on the difference between supper and dinner, which produced the conclusion that supper and dinner are different things, that the words are used interchangeably even with the knowledge that they are not the same thing, and that the reason they are used interchangeably is that people know they are different but do not know what the difference is and so use them as if they are the same.

—In Spanish we call it *La Ultima Cena*, continued Jesús. The word *cena* is very precise. It means the evening meal.

—Evening is always the most ominous time of day, said Maria.

—Yes, said Jim after a moment. And besides, The Last Dinner doesn't have quite the same resonance.

As we finished eating, a windstorm suddenly stirred up its fury, sending us scrambling to secure things, to cover our eyes, and to take shelter in the van. The sky was clear, and there were no storm clouds on the horizon, so the sudden change was both unexpected and unsettling. I could feel the power of the wind while sitting in the van, which was being rocked back and forth. The pale, sandy dust stirred up by the winds engulfed the van, which had been so bright and shiny only a few hours before. Looking out the windows, I could see the trees swaying in the wind, while the smaller bushes were pushed frantically in this direction then that, struggling to hold fast to the earth that held them back. Every living thing sought shelter, except for the birds, for whom the air is water.

After about fifteen minutes, the windstorm that had so suddenly released its fury just as suddenly stopped and everything became calm and silent. The first thing I remember hearing was a crow caw from a nearby tree. I thought of my conversation with Maria the night before, under the stars. Did this frenetic windstorm mean something? Or was it just wind, doing what wind inevitably does? I wished I had known.

No one had said a word during the windstorm, and no one said a word for some time afterward.

—Perhaps we should wait a while before we set out, said Andrew, breaking the silence.

Our silence after his words said that we all agreed. There was nothing logical about it, but somehow we all believed it was the right thing to do. We may have all believed it for different reasons, but ultimately it is the belief itself, and not the reasons for it, that matters most.

We whiled away the hours of the afternoon on the banks of the river, watching the Rio Grande flow by, mostly in silence, mostly with each of us in our own separate worlds. I took a long nap, but had no dreams.

When we finally decided to set out again, evening was upon us. The goal was to drive the Enchanted Circle toward Questa, the only town I know of that misspelled its own name and couldn't be bothered to correct it. We crossed the river and drove the mostly desolate road, save for a couple of easy rider motorcyclists who felt the need to pass us as loudly as possible. I think they were trying to make the point that their choppers were inherently cooler than our white van, as if that were a point that needed to be made.

It was when we turned north on the 522 that things changed. In one of those moments where, if I were writing a screenplay, I would certainly call for a dramatic slow motion effect, we passed a police car—actually a police SUV—coming from the opposite direction, and as we all looked into the immaculate black and white vehicle from our dusty and dirty yet stubbornly white van, our eyes met the eyes of authority, covered as they were with reflective sunglasses. In that long, uninterrupted moment, we knew this was Sheriff Lex, and Sheriff Lex knew it was us.

Andrew instinctively hit the gas. It was the first time I had seen him express both doubt and fear.

—Do you really want to give him even more reason to stop us? asked Joe.

Sheriff Lex had turned around and was now following us in what was possibly the slowest police chase in the history of law enforcement. We drove at the speed limit, as did Sheriff Lex right behind us, at a safe distance, of course, as the law required. Andrew turned off the 522 onto a smaller road.

—I think I can make it to native land, he said. It might give us a chance.

—We haven't done anything wrong, said Maria resolutely.

We headed in the direction of Valdez and Arroyo Seco, toward Taos native land, but as we got closer, it became clear that Sheriff Lex knew what we were trying to do and made his move. The police lights went on, and he pulled past us, hoping to block our way. Yet when he did so, Andrew saw an opportunity and made a quick left onto a side road. Where it went, none of us knew. Sheriff Lex scrambled to turn back to pursue us—I could hear the angry screech of his tires—and with vibrantly flashing lights he continued behind us.

—*There*, said Maria.

—I see it, said Andrew.

Andrew suddenly sped up and drove with great purpose to a small cluster of adobe buildings at the end of the road. He approached and then stopped quickly, turning the van sideways as he did. As Sheriff Lex drove up through the dust of our trail, we scrambled to run through an open, well-weathered wooden gate. Maria was the last in. She closed the gate behind her, with grace and intent, turning to face Sheriff Lex, who now stood on the other side. Maria on one side, Sheriff Lex on the other.

—We declare sanctuary in this church, she said with defiant serenity.

REBELS

1

On the first day, we explored the new world we had created, this site of sanctuary that, at least for the moment, had given us protection and refuge. The small compound was a cluster of adobe-style buildings. By adobe-style I mean they were made of plaster and cement textured to look like dried dampen earth and then painted with earthen-toned colors to mimic the color of the true adobe that they were not made of. There was the main church, which turned out to be rather plain on the inside, with the requisite rows of stern wooden pews, the standard stained glass windows to let colored light into the grey-ish nave, and the bespoke modest altar that hinted a presence of humility rather than an absence of funds. There was a separate building in back of the church, connected by a short, covered walkway, that appeared to be some sort of administrative space, and contained a kitchen, two bathrooms, an office, and some meeting rooms cluttered with boxes that seemed either partially packed or partially unpacked. There was a third structure that was a solitary shrine to the Virgin Mary. The compound was surrounded by a thick, low wall—also faux-adobe—so one could see over the wall when standing upright but not easily climb over it if one were curiously young, playfully old, or middle-aged bored. There were two entrances into the compound, one being the wooden gate through which we had entered, another being a larger wooden gate to the front, wide enough for a vehicle to drive through. The large wooden gate was held shut by a curiously large chain sealed by a curiously small lock. Nothing could have broken that chain, but a mischievous mouse could have broken that lock.

The whole compound seemed abandoned, recently so judging from the thin dust that had built up here and there. The electricity worked and the water flowed, but the phones were disconnected and the grass was untended. The only thing we knew for sure about the place was the name, for just outside the entrance was a wooden sign into which the name had been deeply and decidedly carved. *The Cedars of Lebanon.*

—That's an odd name, said Joe.

—It's an odd church, said Andrew.

—What's so odd about it? asked Jim.

—It's out of place, said Andrew.

—So are we, said Maria.

Andrew paused pensively.

—I mean, it's a Maronite church, said Andrew. Thing is, there's not really a Maronite community here.

—Dude, where is everybody? asked Si.

—We're right here, said Maria, with jocular resolve.

Si looked at Maria with a wisp of exasperation.

—Dude, no, I meant, where is everybody *else*? he said.

—They're not here, replied Maria.

Andrew kept looking at the church and at the sign, now one, now the other.

—It's just odd, he reiterated. I don't know why it's here.

—It's here because we needed it to be here, said Maria.

We had shelter, and we had water, but what we didn't have was food. We still had some leftovers from our lunch, but this would only last us into the next day at best. Maria suggested we fast, not just to conserve food, but to focus our thought and effort. At first we resisted, but as the day wore on and our fast took hold, we became more focused in both thought and effort, and began to separate the necessary acts from the incidental ones. At one point Andrew had offered to leave the compound to get some food for all of us, thinking he might negotiate something with Sheriff Lex, but Maria had a different idea.

—You should go, she said to Andrew.

—Why, are you hungry? asked Andrew.

—No, she said. You should *go*.

Andrew then realized what she was saying. In the next moment, the rest of us did, too.

—We will never forget your kindness, said Maria. But it is not your purpose to fight our battle here. Not in this way, not in this place.

—What is my purpose? asked Andrew.

—That I cannot tell you, said Maria. I can only tell you what it is not.

—You don't want me here? asked Andrew somewhat morosely.

—It's not that, said Maria. It's that in this moment, your absence will do more for us than your presence.

—I don't understand, said Andrew.

—You will when you are gone, said Maria.

—What about Sheriff Lex? asked Jim.

—I can handle him, said Maria.

We all walked toward the gate, the very same gate through which we had entered, and the very same gate through which Andrew would now leave. Sheriff Lex, who was sitting in his police car, noticed us and instinctively got out of his vehicle to approach us, with more caution than I thought necessary.

—If you declare sanctuary, you know you can't leave, said Sheriff Lex.

—We're not leaving, said Maria, facing Sheriff Lex through the wooden gate.

Sheriff Lex looked at her, then at the rest of us, with more suspicion than I thought necessary.

—But he is, said Maria, turning toward Andrew.

—He can't leave either, said Sheriff Lex. He's with you.

—Father Andrew is a man of the cloth, said Maria. We turned to him for help and he was bound by his vows to help us.

Sheriff Lex was confounded.

—Surely there is no crime in helping others in a time of need, continued Maria. Surely there is no crime in offering compassion and kindness. Surely there is no crime in a man of faith practicing the tenets of his faith.

Sheriff Lex searched for a reply but found none.

—Or do you consider it illegal for a priest to practice his religion? asked Maria, clearly demanding an answer.

Sheriff Lex didn't know what to make of this. The man of law whose world was always black and white had to confront the possibility of greyness in the world.

—If he leaves, he cannot come back, said Sheriff Lex.

—He knows, said Maria. And he won't be coming back, will you? asked Maria, turning to Andrew.

—No, I guess I won't, said Andrew, not without resigned hesitation.

Andrew turned to look at the rest of us, standing as we were behind Maria, who was standing beside Andrew, who was standing at the gate.

—This isn't goodbye, said Andrew to us.

—This isn't goodbye, he repeated, directly to Maria.

—Of course it isn't, said Maria, as she placed her hand over her heart and nodded slightly.

Andrew smiled a sad smile and returned the gesture.

—This isn't the end, she said.

Andrew opened the gate, which let out a creak that seemed unusually loud in the silence that now surrounded us. Andrew climbed into the van and we all exchanged one more glance with him. I saw him sigh heavily. Yet as he started the van, his sense of sad resignation transformed into a spirit of determined hope. Without a wave he turned the great white van around and drove off. I had gone through three vehicles since my journey began, and as the white van drove off, I realized for the first time that I had nowhere to go and no way to get there.

Maria had closed the gate and Sheriff Lex stood just on the other side. The two faced each other directly, eye to eye, or more accurately, eye to sunglass. Sheriff Lex stared firmly at her, while Maria just as firmly stared back. They stood motionless like this for quite some time, face to face across the gate, neither backing down. Then, in a moment, Sheriff Lex's lip twitched ever so slightly. We all saw it. Sheriff Lex knew we saw it. Maria knew that he knew. That was enough.

—*Vámanos*, said Maria.

She turned from the gate, and we followed her, leaving Sheriff Lex standing at the gate, staring straight ahead. I don't know how long he stood there, but I imagine it was for a long time, longer than he expected. Longer than he wanted.

Maria was right about Andrew. He was a man motivated by compassion, moved by love. I wanted to be moved like that, to have some spirit that moved through me, a spirit that I trusted completely, the essence of true faith. But Andrew was right in what he told me, that faith is never a source and always a response. My response was not faith but incomprehension, and I could not have faith in what I could not comprehend. I understand the role that mystery plays. The divine essence of anything can never be fully understood or grasped, and what lies between comprehension and divinity is mystery. Mystery churns faith, and faith carries mystery. I knew mystery, so I knew I was capable of faith. When I gazed into the night sky with Maria I knew the stars could not just be accidents, but I also could not explain them in their existence and entirety. There was mystery in the heavens. But I did not have the comprehension to generate faith, so the mystery I felt left me longing for a faith I could not yet possess.

Maria, like Andrew, had this capacity for love that seemed endless. It gave her a sense of surety in her movements, and a sense of knowing things beyond what seemed knowable. I remembered something that Maria had said to me that night under the stars in the clear desert sky. *Love is the continuous effort to understand in the face of endless contradictions.* One could never fully understand God, she said that night. But if one could understand love, then one would understand enough of God to respond with faith. Love is thus the closest thing we have to God.

I knew the stars were beautiful in the night sky. If an astronomer had told me they were merely spherical globes of burning gas whose twinkle was nothing more than the product of residual heat in the earth sky night, I would not have found them any less beautiful. My sense of awe was a genuine sense of awe. Mystery was necessary because it bypassed the rules of reasoned knowledge, built as they are on their own limitations. Mystery bypasses the rules to give us wonder. Ultimately, faith, too, bypasses the rules. Faith can only be understood as faith, and can have no recourse to reason. In that sense, it is a bit like love. If faith continuously flaunts the rules, then faith is continuous revolution. And if love exists, in so far as it persists in the face of contradictions, love is a continuous rebellion. *True faith is an endless revolution. True love is an endless rebellion.*

I knew in that moment why Maria had done the things she had done. I knew in that moment why she sought sanctuary in this place. What I did not understand then, though I do understand it now, is why I followed, why I joined, and why I stayed. This was part of Maria's rebellion, part of her revolution. It was beautiful and it was glorious. The rest of us were there because we knew we wanted to be a part of it, though each of us did not quite understand why, and each of us did not understand for our own different reasons. The only thing we knew is that we could not leave, though we did not understand how we knew that.

When night began to fall, we decided to break our fast and eat what was left of the food. Maria had been right about that, too. The fast had given us a sense of purpose and a sense of determination. On top of that, the food tasted even better than it had when we had eaten it before. Same food, different feast. We ate in silence. After we had finished our meal, we began to discuss what we were going to do. The first matter was where to sleep. We agreed that we would sleep in the church, since the pews had pads on them and the floor could get cold in the high desert night. We told Maria that we could take some of the pads and put them on the desk in the office for her, so she could have a separate place to sleep, but she insisted that a pew was enough for her, as it would be enough for all of us.

—What will we do for food tomorrow? asked Joe.

—Not to worry, said Maria. Something will happen.

—Dude, how do you know? asked Si.

—I don't know, said Maria. But I believe it so.

We heard voices outside the church compound. Then we noticed the multicolored blue and red flashes reflecting off the walls that were unmistakably the lights of the law. There was a small choir loft in the rear of the church, reached by a narrow and steep stairway, with a small window that looked out over the area where Sheriff Lex had parked his vehicle to begin his legal vigil. There now was another police vehicle parked alongside Sheriff Lex, and the two men were talking. After a few minutes, Sheriff Lex started his vehicle and drove away. For some reason he, too, had his police lights flashing, though there was no pursuit, no hurry, and no reason to do so, other than perhaps an unnecessary display of officiousness and authority. We were deep into dusk, yet Sheriff Lex drove off still bespectacled with his dark sunglasses. Perhaps the flashing lights were intended to light his way. The second policeman did not wear sunglasses, and seemed to stare straight ahead with tremendous authority and determination, all heightened by an ominous moustache that seemed thick and wiry and long enough to cover his upper lip. For us, though, there was some comfort in all of this. Sheriff Lex needed relief, he needed rest. His machine-like pursuit of the mechanics of the law had a human element that could not be denied. The human element was an indelible flaw. Sheriff Lex was fallible.

We made our way back down and slowly prepared ourselves for the night. Part of the preparation was to make the church pews into an inn for the weary— not just a place of sanctuary, but also a place of rest. I learned that night that pews are not designed for sleeping. They aren't even designed to be comfortable. I did not fully appreciate the intentional construct of this wonder of sacred furniture until that moment. When I was a child, I would squirm all through the mass, partly because at that age I did not yet know of the open sores of the human soul, the everyday infractions of humanity against itself that made sentiments like grace and forgiveness a necessary vehicle for survival, and partly because the hard wooden pew was unendurably uncomfortable. I looked forward to the part of mass when the kneeler came down, only because the kneeler in my childhood church had a pad on it, which meant that kneeling was a moment of relief from sitting. That was the extent of my childhood theology.

Jesús had found some blankets earlier, when we discovered that at least some of the boxes in the church contained what must have been charitable donations, though whether they had been donated to the church, or whether the church was donating them to others was unclear. It didn't really matter. We had blankets—that's what mattered. We were able to fold up some of the pads from the other pews to make some makeshift pillows, and eventually we settled into our pew beds. You never realize how narrow a church pew is until you try to sleep on one. Over the next few nights we became accustomed to the sound of at least one of us falling off the pew to the ground below. We quickly learned to put the mercifully-padded kneeler down as we slept, as it would at least help to break the fall in case gravity beckoned us from our sanctified slumber.

That night I had trouble sleeping, though whether it was the awkward discomfort of the pew bed, or just the fact that I had become a restless soul at that point in my life, I could not say. I stared at the ceiling, which to my surprise contained images of stars. In this church, it seems, the heavens were always visible and always beautiful, and the stars never disappeared from view. I had my notebook with me, and I wrote only one thing in it that first night, and I remember it well because it is the only thing written on the entire page. I did not feel there was anything else that belonged on that page. The blank space was as much a part of the sentiment as the dark-inked words. What I wrote was this—

The hardest thing to do in life is to believe in something.

2

On the second day, we penned, pondered, plotted, and persisted, though not necessarily in that order. We woke slowly, our anticipation of the new day dulled by the awareness that we had no food to break the fast for breakfast. Our spirits and morale seemed to slumber on even after we had emerged into waken life. Joe was holding his elbow, which turned out to be quite distinguished by a bruise procured in the night by an inelegant fall from pew to floor. We all did our best to create some semblance of a morning ritual in an unfamiliar place. My left arm reached out at times to grasp a phantom cup of coffee. Si opened the refrigerator, half expecting to find something there.

—Dude, he said.

A short while later we heard a car pull up. It was now daylight so we could not see the glimmered reflection of flashing lights, though we assumed it was another vehicle of those who enforce the law. Yet voices were heard in an unfamiliar tone, so we slowly wandered outside to see what was the matter. Out of a dark green car appeared a familiar face. It was Khalil, who saw us and gave us a familiar wave.

—A certain angel told me you might be hungry, he shouted to us.

—Andrew, said Maria, under her breath and inside a faint smile.

Khalil reached into the back seat of his car, and began piling a few things onto the hood—a cooler, a thermos, and a few neatly-packed boxes. My stomach growled, as if suddenly aware of a benevolent food spirit. Sheriff Lex watched Khalil with anticipation, as if he knew what he was trying to do and was just waiting for him to try to do it. And sure enough, when Khalil picked up the thermos and the cooler and began to head toward the gate, Sheriff Lex sprang like a bobcat in uniform to stop him in his tracks.

—What exactly do you think you are doing? asked Sheriff Lex, in a voice imbued with more confrontation than he probably intended.

—Good morning, said Khalil with a cheeriness that at an earlier hour might also be mistaken as confrontational, depending on one's morning demeanor. I am here to visit my friends and provide them with much-needed sustenance.

Sheriff Lex regarded Khalil with measured intensity, as if looking at a person slowly from head to foot and then foot to head would reveal hitherto unseen truths.

—You can't go in there, said Sheriff Lex.

—I'm quite certain I can, said Khalil. It is you who cannot go in there.

Sheriff Lex made a quick adjustment of his hat, as he looked now to the side, now to the ground and now to Khalil. Clearly this was not an attitude that Sheriff Lex found acceptable or appropriate. One did not act defiantly in front of the law. This was an unwritten rule, of course, but to Sheriff Lex, it was unwritten gospel.

—Who are you, and what are doing here? asked Sheriff Lex, this time with an intentional tone of confrontation.

—My name is Khalil and I am from Dar al-Islam, just near Abiquiu, said Khalil. These are my friends, and they are in need of food and other supplies. I have brought them what they need.

Sheriff Lex thought for a moment in silence.

—I don't like it, he said.

—There are many things in this world not to like, said Khalil. And yet they still happen, whether we like them or not.

—I won't allow it, said Sheriff Lex.

—Am I to understand that you are denying nourishment and medical assistance to these people, and that you take full responsibility as an officer of the law for any and all consequences thereof? asked Khalil.

Sheriff Lex made another small adjustment of his hat and then for some reason looked up to the sky. He stepped aside with a frustrated sigh. Khalil was allowed to pass through the gate. He made a few other trips out to the car to grab the rest of the things he had brought for us. On the last trip Sheriff Lex stepped up to the gate, Khalil on the inside, Sheriff Lex on the outside. Sheriff Lex staring with his sunglasses. Khalil staring with his eyes.

—What's a Muslim doing at a church? asked Sheriff Lex with uninnocent suspicion.

A moment passed. We watched, Khalil pondered.

—What's a policeman doing at a church? replied Khalil with unsuspicious innocence, who then turned to us, as we all entered the church together.

It was good to see Khalil—a comfort, one might say. We all felt it, though none of us said it. We set all the boxes and the cooler and the thermos and the utensils on a table in the kitchen. The thermos was opened and the smell of coffee filled the room.

—There is a God, I said.

—Really? said Khalil. Coffee is your standard of proof for divine existence?

It was good to see Khalil indeed.

The food had been nicely packaged and wrapped.

—I hope you brought hummus, said Jim with marked anticipation.

—No, I brought pizza, said Khalil.

The woman with the enigmatic smile had struck again.

—Dude, pizza for breakfast? asked Si, with a sense of hope rather than consternation.

—No, there are some pastries and things in that box there, said Khalil. I also brought some juice, bread and jam, and milk and honey.

—Khalil? queried Maria.

—Yes? replied Khalil.

—Medical supplies? continued Maria.

Khalil looked at her with a smile that hinted of a subtle plot of conspiracy.

—I do have some aspirin in the car, he said. Perhaps you need some?

Maria was right—again. Something had happened. What she believed would happen and what actually happened were one and the same thing. None of us had her certainty, her strength, her depth of faith. We doubted and we feared, especially me. She had no doubt and no fear. Her universe unfolded in some orderly plan. My universe tumbled and faltered and floated unpredictably through space. Or maybe my universe was as well-ordered as hers, only she could see it where I could not. But for now, at least, I had coffee and I had food, and that was order enough for the moment.

After we finished breakfast, there came the moment when we all had to face the day. When we were on the move, there was always something new—a distraction, a spectacle, a crisis, a disturbance, a sight, a sound—anything and everything new had a way of compelling time forward. In our place of sanctuary, the day suddenly seemed impossibly long, a vast chronological space that needed to be filled. Time slowed, and we all struggled in our motions, as if to recover a balance that we had not quite lost but not yet found.

I wondered to myself how many revolutions had occurred in human history that, in spite of their fiery oratory to the contrary, were really fought to alleviate boredom. Perhaps the greatest struggle of the revolutionary is fighting ennui. Every image we have of the great revolutionary shows them in their moment of enchantment, leading the charge in the streets or engaged in spirited battle. But there are many days in every revolution in which nothing happens. The days in which nothing happens are the most important of days, because those days can make or break the revolution itself.

There had to be days Moses just got tired, when the whole exodus thing seemed pointless. Even with the greatest of purposes, walking ten miles through the desert with a large group of people, many of whom were no doubt complaining incessantly about the smallest of inconveniences—the sun is too bright, the manna is too starchy, and so forth—is something that can wear down the hardiest of souls. Moses was a prophet, it is true, but even that offers no comfort. For a prophet is a seer, and a seer sees things. Their expectations are always diminished because they always have an idea of what to expect. There's no dramatic tension in the life of a prophet—no surprise, no unexpected twist. And even when there is superlative drama, such as the parting of the waters, how does one carry on afterward? The day after the parting of the Red Sea must have seemed impossibly dull. It's hard to top a miracle. People want to see more once they see one, but if you are a miracle-worker, then another miracle is just another day's work. After you've raised the dead and healed the sick, you begin to wonder why anyone finds this miraculous. Even Moses had to yawn sometimes, or scribble meaningless shapes in the sand only to erase them. Anyone can be inspired in moments of miraculous drama. Those who remain inspired in the long moments of silence and inaction are the true rebels among us.

Around mid-morning, Khalil asked us to assemble in the kitchen. The kitchen had a table with some chairs, none of which matched, and on the table were some legal tablets and some pens. None of us had any idea what this was about.

—Dude, what's this all about? asked Si.

Khalil then explained that he wanted all of us to write out in words what we thought we were doing there, a personal testament to explain our motives and actions.

—Can't we just be rebels without a cause? asked Joe.

—There's no such thing, said Khalil. A rebel without a cause is just an aimless idiot, so unless your cause is idiocy, that won't do.

—Aren't we just fighting against Sheriff Lex? asked Jim.

Khalil then explained that there are two types of rebellions in the world—those that are defined by what they are fighting against, and those that are defined by what they are fighting for.

—Only the latter type of rebellion can succeed, he said.

He circled the table behind us with his hands folded in front of him, and spoke as he circled.

—Sheriff Lex may not be a rebel, said Khalil. But he does have a cause.

He then stopped circling and put his hands on the table and looked at each of us.

—So write out in your own words not what you are fighting against, but what you are fighting for, he said, and then left the room.

And so we all began to write. A curious thing happened as we wrote our personal manifestoes. One by one, we all realized we had something to say, something to fight for, and one by one, we began to find a separate space to be alone with out rebellious thoughts. Si went off into the church to sit in a pew. Jesús pulled his chair back from the table and used a box for a desk. Maria went outside, Jim stood and wrote on the kitchen counter, Joe went into the office area, and I alone remained at the table. It wasn't that we were afraid of the others seeing our words. It was that we that Khalil's request had drawn us each into a deeply personal space, and the more we traveled inward, the more space we needed outward.

I can't say how much time passed as we bled our introspective ink onto paper. We were all aware that more time had passed than we thought, because we all had noticed the shifted shadows and changed angles of light coming through the windows. At some point, for no particular reason and with no particular plan, we reassembled in the kitchen, which is where Khalil found us, as if he expected us to be there right at that very moment. Where he had been all this time, none of us knew.

—So what do we do now? asked Joe. Do we share these with each other?

—No, said Khalil. I would prefer you not share them at all.

—I don't understand, said Jesús. Then why did we do this?

—So that you know what you are fighting for, said Khalil.

—Shouldn't we make sure that we are all fighting for the same thing? asked Joe.

—If you found out otherwise, would it change the way you feel? asked Khalil.

We looked at each other, and knew that we all knew the answer.

—No, I suppose it wouldn't, said Joe.

Khalil had a whispered laugh to himself.

—And besides, he said. If you were all fighting for the same thing, you wouldn't be who you are.

As the afternoon darkened with age we ate again, gathered as we were in the kitchen. As we ate, Khalil surprised us with a story.

—I know this church, he said.

Khalil was originally from Lebanon, and though he was a Muslim, he had many friends of all faiths in the Lebanese community. The person who founded this church was a Maronite Christian, also from Lebanon, who had come to New Mexico to study astrophysics at the university. He came here to the high desert and at once felt a special presence, surrounded as he was by cedars, the tree that represents the durable spirit of the Lebanese people. The church had been built originally as a Lutheran church, but when the Lutherans ran a bit long on faith and bit short on budget, they put out a call for cash, but people sent kind instead.

—You can't build a church with blankets, said Khalil.

—No, but you can sleep in one, said Maria.

The Lutherans decided to downsize and relocate, and when our aspiring Lebanese astrophysicist heard the news, he decided he would found a church here.

He worked hard, raised money, reached out, did everything he could to make this happen, and happen it eventually did. Quite recently, in fact.

—So what happened? asked Joe.

—Aside from the lack of a Maronite community in the area, continued Khalil, it really all came down to a bad case of allergies.

—Allergies? asked Joe.

—It turns out the cedar trees here aren't really cedar, continued Khalil. They're mountain cedar, which is not cedar at all, but juniper.

Jim, the Texan, immediately understood.

—Mountain cedar kicks up fierce pollen, he said. If you're allergic to it, it's miserable.

—Yes, said Khalil. And so the church was built and founded twice, but never actually used as a church.

—Until now, said Maria. Let's hope the third time is charmed.

So there we were, in The Cedars of Lebanon, surrounded not by cedars and not anywhere near Lebanon, and inside a church that was not a church until Maria declared sanctuary within it.

—All these boxes? asked Jesús. These are acts of charity?

—It looks like people all across New Mexico unloaded everything they had but didn't want, said Jim.

—There's a box of diapers in the other room, said Joe. Who sends a box of diapers to a church?

—People might be inspired by the divine light, observed Khalil. But that doesn't mean they'll always be bright.

As night arrived, there was a moment when Khalil had to make a decision to stay or to go. He knew and we knew that this was not his fight to fight, but at the same time, he felt a kindred spirit to our little rebellion and thought it important to show his solidarity—a one-person spiritual sympathy strike, so to speak. Khalil was a married Muslim man, and Maria knew that this would require an alternative arrangement. Maria offered the office to Khalil, but Khalil insisted that she sleep in the office, and that he would sleep with the rest of us on the pews in the church. Maria did not like being given special treatment, but under the circumstances we all insisted, and she accepted. We made a makeshift bed in the office that was rudimentary but functional.

—I almost forgot, said Khalil. I brought you all a gift.

Khalil walked out to his car, tracked by the suspicious and watchful eye of Sheriff Lex, still in his car, still on his vigil. He took out a large, black plastic bag, and brought it back in. Khalil had brought us pillows, which turned out to be the perfect and most thoughtful gift, given the rough slumber of the night before.

The last question of the day involved the door to the church. The main door had a lock, and the question was whether to lock it or not. None of us had noticed it or thought of it the night before, but now there it was. We all thought of Sheriff Lex. So long as he retained his vigil, we had to retain our vigilance. Then Maria spoke.

—I don't like the idea of a locked church, she said definitively.

So we left the door unlocked. Maria was right. As I fell asleep that night, my head on a soft pillow, I somehow felt more secure. I think we all did. I know we all did.

3

On the third day, a tremendous storm blew through. It came early in the morning, when it was still dark, when we were all still asleep. It woke us with its boisterous arrival. I remember waking to the flash of lightning, waiting, as I have always done since as long as I have had memories, for the roll of thunder that always follows. At first the rolls were gentle, like the resonant purr of a contented cat, but they slowly rose to a growl and then to a roar, as the storm drew near. We could hear the rain on the roof growing freight-train loud. When the storm was finally upon us, directly overhead, the wind was fierce, the rain was torrential, the lightning was frenetic, and the thunder was apocalyptic. In some moments the thunder cracked so loud that the church seemed to shake right from its foundation. The storm lingered far longer than what seemed natural. The storm shook and rattled, uprooted and tore down, upended and over-turned. The earth moved, and all we could do was move with it. Whatever control we thought we had over things, we quickly realized we simply did not have.

The rain was intense and relentless. Puddles formed, water pooled, and the church was gradually surrounded by water. Sure, it was only a few inches deep, but it did give us the feeling of being stranded in the midst of a great flood.

Sheriff Lex looked ghostly as he sat in his truck and stared at the church through his sunglasses. His vigil was a solitary one that morning—only Sheriff Lex alone in his vehicle. The rain cascading over his wind-shield would blur his visage, and then momentarily he would appear again, fading in and out between two shades of opacity. His vehicle sat in what looked like five or six inches of water, like a boat anchored just off our island.

The electricity went out as the storm came in, as if the common spirits of the public utilities demurred to the extravagantly undeniable authority of the gods of thunder. The flashes of lightning were indeed dramat-ic, especially against the dark grey sky and the deep textured clouds. Thunder undeniably humbles even the most arrogant soul. The storm took me back to an earlier time in my life. This is what storms do best— they connect us to what we once were. We remember ourselves as children, a time when hope could easily prevail over disillusionment, when trust seemed like the only acceptable demeanor with which to face the world. Any child remembers a storm flowing in from the distance, the ever-shortening gap between lightning and thunder, the fear of the impending storm giving rise to the courage to overcome that fear. I felt the inner stirrings of a great nostalgia, even though I knew in my heart that nostalgia is one of the more deceptive emotions in the architecture of human frailty.

We ate cold pizza for breakfast. There is something unexpectedly comforting about eating cold pizza in the morning. You can discern a lot about a person and their day if you understand how they have consumed their pizza. If you tell someone you had cold pizza for breakfast, they will assume your day was a good day. If you tell someone you had cold pizza for dinner, they will assume your day was a sad day. If you tell someone you had cold pizza for lunch, they will assume that you were too lazy to heat it up, which says more about you than it does about your day.

There was one slice of pizza left. You can tell you are among good people when the last piece of food just sits there. It means that everyone is thinking about everyone else. It means that everyone is putting others before selves. It means there is still reason to believe that humanity might actually be a thing. It means there is still reason to believe.

—Anyone want the last slice? asked Jim.

No one made a claim.

—Give it to Joe, said Maria.

—Why should I get the last slice of pizza? protested Joe.

—Because you once told me that if you could eat pizza every day of your life you would be happy forever, said Maria.

—You remember that? asked Joe, dumbfoundedly.

—I never forget, said Maria. Unless I want to. Which I don't.

Jim gave the last slice of pizza to Joe, and Joe looked both slightly embarrassed and genuinely grateful for the offering.

It wasn't the pizza that was on my mind and in my heart, however. It was something else, something brought in with the storm. Maria had an empowered serenity about her that I could not fathom. Even in the most violent and brash moments of the storm, she showed not the slightest trace of fear. I watched Maria and wanted to have her depth of conviction. I was always anxious, always worried about things. Even when I ate I thought of hunger, already worried about the next meal—what it would be or where it would come from. I struggled with the uncertainty of not knowing what comes next. For a long time I did not understand Maria's faith. I thought she simply lived in the moment, that she simply did not think of the future.

Only much later did I grasp that this was not the source of her faith. It wasn't that Maria did not concern herself with the future, or that she lived only in the present, or that she simply believed in all good things.

She *did* think of the future, but she had learned to embrace any and all possible futures with poise, dignity, and peace. It was never passivity or acquiescence. No, Maria worked harder than anyone I had ever known to make the world the kind of beautiful place that no one else thought possible. For Maria, the storm didn't disturb the beauty of the world. The storm was part of that beauty.

The source of my doubt, the fount of my hesitation, was the lack of certainty that if I followed the path I had chosen, I would reach the destination of my desire. No matter what action I would take, or what path I would follow, I knew there were so many things beyond my control, so many obstacles, seen and unseen, standing in the way. So many other things had already been set in motion by the actions of others, a tempest of intertwined fates that collided ceaselessly into one another like waves on an unsettled sea. Adrift on that churning sea, most people pray for their lifeboats not to sink. They make wagers with God. *If You save me, I will live differently, I will be a better person, I will change and transform and be the kind of person I always knew I should be.* Such is the faith of most people.

I never made wagers, because I never knew what wager to make. But Maria had a different faith. She never made a wager because she knew there was no game to play. Maria lived in a way where faith and life had become one. There was an ease of being in her that masked the great effort it took to achieve it. Maria knew it was not her place to wonder why she was on this tempestuous sea. She only knew that as long as she was there, she should enjoy the journey for what it is, no matter how difficult or frightening it might be. She knew that even if she could control her boat, she could never control the sea and it made no sense to try. For most people, being cast into such a wide angry sea in such a small frail boat would make them question their faith and curse the heavens. For Maria, it only confirmed her faith, and if she looked to the heavens at all, it was to give thanks for the boat she had and for the chance to ply the ever-restless waters. Maria saw beauty everywhere, even where others could not see it at all. To believe was to see, and never the other way around. This was her faith.

Maria opened the door and a tremendous rush of air blew through, carrying with it the unmistakable and inimitable scent of fresh falling rain. Maria stood in the doorway, letting the eddies of wind move around, past, and through her. She closed her eyes and smiled gently. A tremendous flash of lightning, followed immediately by a deafening roar of thunder, caused all of us to jump, all except for Maria, who was still standing with eyes closed and hair flowing in the arrhythmic whims of the storm's turgid air.

—That was close, said Jim, unsettled.

—Dude, I think it hit a tree, said Si.

The lightning had indeed hit a tree, right next to the church. We looked out the window to see one of the cedars split asunder, its timbered interior now exposed, its leafen branches lying lithely and still on the ground. There was a faint smell of acrid smoke in the air. This tree bore witness to something that was indisputably greater than all of us.

—Maybe it's an omen, said Joe.

—If it is, then it's a good one, observed Maria.

—How can you tell? asked Jim.

—I just can, said Maria.

—But how?

—Do you have any reason to consider it bad? offered Maria.

—Well, no, said Jim.

—Then there it is, said Maria with definitive grace.

All of us were staring through the window at the shattered tree, humbled by the power it took to rend it in two. What had seemed solid and certain only moments ago now seemed fragile and precarious. At the time I remember feeling disturbed by the sight of the now fallen tree, as it reminded me of things I did not want to remember—hints of the ephemeral, hints that all things in their time must come to an end. Only later, when I revisited this moment, after all of these events of which I write had already passed, did I finally understand how Maria could see this act of destruction as a sign of the inherent goodness of things.

—It's a reminder, Maria said.

—Of what? asked Joe.

—Of the things we should not forget, said Maria.

A huge gust of wind blew through the door, and the roaring sound of the relentless rain filled the inside of the church. Jesús walked across the room, as if to close the door, but then did something none of us expected. He walked right through to the outside, right into the pouring rain.

—Jesús! said Joe, his shout muted by exasperation.

—Let him go, said Khalil. He knows what he is doing.

We walked over to the open door. Jesús was standing at the gate, soaked as he was by the rain but in complete acceptance of his circumstances. He didn't even try to wipe away the streams of water flowing down his face. He stared stolidly at Sheriff Lex, and Sheriff Lex, who notices all, or at least claims to, returned the stare in earnest measure. Jesús did not wave a hand or offer any sign of his intent, but simply stood at the gate and stared at Sheriff Lex. Sheriff Lex slowly understood that Jesús wanted something, wanted to say something, and Sheriff Lex methodically got out of his vehicle, wearing his standard issue rain gear, the ever unnecessary sunglasses, and in his right hand, an official police umbrella. He walked over to the gate and faced Jesús.

—You got something to say? asked Sheriff Lex, his voice loud and strained against the sound of the rain.

—I want to make a confession, said Jesús.

Sheriff Lex looked confused.

—I'm not a priest, he said.

—It's a legal confession, said Jesús.

Sheriff Lex adjusted his demeanor and readied himself like a priest about to hear a confession.

—Go on, he said.

—I am in this country illegally, said Jesús.

Sheriff Lex adjusted himself again, his face quizzically contorted.

—Come again? he asked, though clearly he had heard and understood the first time.

—I have crossed into this country without regard for the word of the law, repeated Jesús. I have violated the laws of this land.

—Is this some sort of trick? asked Sheriff Lex, perturbed.

—I'm afraid not, said Jesús.

—What's it to me?

—You are an officer of the law, said Jesús. You have sworn to uphold the law.

Sheriff Lex's countenance went blank, grasping the import of what Jesús was saying in the very same moment when Jesús said it.

—That means that you must now arrest me and take me to the station, concluded Jesús.

Sheriff Lex was in a quandary. He was the only officer of the law present. If he abided by his sworn duty to uphold the law of the land, he would have to arrest Jesús and take him to the police station, where he would be detained. If he did that, however, Sheriff Lex would have to leave his vigil at the church, creating the possibility for the rest of us to escape and to evade the law. No matter what Sheriff Lex chose to do in that moment, he would have to accept that the law, the same law that was so necessary to create order in his well-ordered universe, would be violated. More than that, when it occurred, he would be the one who let it happen. Order would beget disorder. Submission would create transgression. Things would fall apart, decay, unravel. Necessarily so. This was beyond his control. This was beyond the control of the law.

—You get back inside right now, barked Sheriff Lex.

Jesús turned to walk back inside the church, back through the doorway where we all had stood and watched. Sheriff Lex turned to walk back to his vehicle.

—Tricksters and charlatans, he shouted with inelegant gesticulation.

Sheriff Lex returned to his vigil, sitting in his vehicle, the black and white reflecting the endless shades of grey still churning through the restless sky. The rain continued.

Later in the day, our minds slowly turned to hunger and sustenance. It wasn't a deep hunger, more of a little annoyance, an everyday reminder of human mortality. When the rain began to wane and the flood began to recede, Khalil made a simple announcement.

—I need to call someone, he said.

About an hour later, we were in the main room of the church, each of us doing our own mindful tasks, when we heard a melodic sound slowly rise above the diurnal din. At first it was very faint, the kind of sound that makes you pause for just a moment, like a train in the distance. As it grew louder, it became more rhythmic, reminding me of music I had heard sometimes in certain neighborhoods in New York. By the time it was close enough to the church to see the source of the sound, we were all up in the loft, looking out the window. A brightly painted, carnival-colored minivan had pulled into the church lot, music blaring, windows down, and behind the wheel sat a man sporting a bright orange turban. On the minivan was a logo that read *Bhangra Brothers*. Beneath that in slightly smaller letters it said *Check Out This Sikh Beat*. The minivan pulled up next to Sheriff Lex, who was too surprised by the sudden and unexpected arrival to react, and before Sheriff Lex had a chance to say or do anything, the man in the orange turban and flowing white-cotton cloth attire had grabbed a box and walked right through the gate and into the church.

—Hello, Hari, said Khalil, with familiarity and sincerity.

—Hello, Khalil, replied the orange-turbaned visitor, with equal affect.

The visitor turned to all of us.

—I am Harinder, he said. But friends call me Hari.

Hari surveyed the room.

—It feels like a monastery in here, he mused. You all remind me of medieval pundits.

Hari had brought food, supplied, as I would later learn, by the Gurdwara, the nearby Sikh temple that offered ever more spirit to an already spirited landscape.

—There's enough here for all of you, said Hari, putting the food onto the closest pew. I'll be back again tomorrow with more.

As quickly as Hari had arrived, he left, leaving Sheriff Lex to wonder what had just happened and who this mysterious visitor was. We ate our dinner together a short while later, a dinner that consisted of simple but delicious Indian food. Our hunger left us, in more ways than one. We had weathered another storm. I knew there would be more storms to come, but for a moment, I no longer feared them.

4

On the fourth day, the messengers arrived. Chatter scatters across the airwaves, gossip clamors over fences, chitchat channels down hallways, prattle blathers through the valley. The word gets out. Some folks, particularly those whose calling it is to grab that word and turn it into good news or bad, live for this moment. The silence in between stories is for them a temporary death. These are the people who tell us the stories that narrate all worldly action, that give order to events, as if everything on earth were a story that had to be told, that needed to be told. These were the journalists, modern-day messengers of the macabre, the murderous, the mendacious, and the meh. The messengers had appeared in the late morning of the fourth day, arriving in their special vehicles, vans with radio towers that reached high toward the heavens, and doors that opened outward so that they appeared like metal angels that forgot how to fly yet tried to do so anyway.

Sheriff Lex was none too happy about this, and held what appeared to be an emergency conversation with the two other officers who had been there since first light to support his vigil of the law and all of the justice and order it implied. I had no idea what they were saying to one another, but they spoke to each other in ways that looked excessively officious, with facial contortions and head nods and hand waves that suggested far more import and drama than was probably present. Sheriff Lex walked over to the gate, and Maria walked out to meet him.

—What is it, Sheriff Lex? she asked.

—I don't want your people talking to the press, he said.

—My people? replied Maria. I make no claim on anyone.

—Just don't any of you talk to the press, said Sheriff Lex.

—Why not?

—Because people believe the news like it's the gospel truth.

—People believe the news like it's the news. They believe the gospel truth like it's the gospel truth.

—Look, said Sheriff Lex, clearly not in the mood for semantics. I'm just telling you not to speak to the news.

—Are you going to speak to them? asked Maria.

—I'm a public official. I am authorized to speak publicly and officially.

—Will the people believe your words like they are the gospel truth?

—The law is not something you believe in. It just is. The law is the law.

—Unbelievable, said Maria, who turned away and walked back inside.

I watched the news messengers setting up their equipment, each involved in a separate task. Here a cameraman framed a shot, looking for the most dramatic angle. There a reporter rehearsed her presentation, looking for just the right tone to convey just the right amount of drama. This was once my tribe, my people, but as I watched them engage in their various tasks, I felt a distance I had not felt before. I was no longer one of them. Their movements seemed strange to me, their language, foreign.

Maybe an unnarrated world is a better world. Maybe letting stories remain forever untold is the path to peace. Not that the stories aren't there. Just that they're not told. Yet it's the storytellers down through the ages that have been most revered. The bards and poets and prophets whose tongues are laced with hypnotic elegance—these and those like them are blessed, or cursed, with a special gift. They conjure a world so real we believe it to be true. We would swear we were there, though in truth that world was not anywhere.

In the early afternoon, we were talking amongst ourselves—about what I cannot remember—when Khalil quietly stepped away to pray. When he returned to rejoin the conversation, the conversation returned to him.

—How do you know when to pray? asked Joe.

—I have an app on my phone, said Khalil.

—How often do you pray? asked Jim.

—I pray all day most days, said Khalil. But five times a day, every day, I stop all that I am doing and focus only on the prayer.

—Is it the same time every day? asked Joe.

—No, it depends on the position of the sun and the earth, said Khalil.

—And your app tells you this? asked Jim.

—Yes, said Khalil. And it tells me the direction of Mecca, too.

Khalil looked at his phone and pointed in the direction of Mecca.

—Dude, do you think if Jesus were here now, he would be on Facebook and Twitter? pondered Si, clearly hoping for an answer.

—You mean, like, *Just turned water into wine* #Jesus? said Joe.

—People might think that was me, said Jesús.

—*Like me on Facebook* sounds desperate for a Messiah, observed Jim.

—*Like me on Facebook* sounds desperate for anyone, said Khalil.

—Jesus would not be on Facebook or Twitter, said Maria, with her usual certainty.

—Why not? asked Jesús.

—Because His life had meaning, said Maria.

I realized as I listened why I had so little faith in technology. It seemed too ephemeral when what I wanted was permanence. Just as our emotional calibers know to listen not just for what is said, but for *how* it is said, so, too, do we notice not just what is written, but *how* it is written. Moses came down from the mountain with two stone tablets that heralded power, authority, and certainty. What if instead he had scribbled them in haste on the palm of his hand? Had he walked down with a laptop, with the Ten Commandments written as a pdf in a nondescript sans serif font, would anyone have taken notice or cared? Or what if he handed them out as flyers, much like the oafs and waifs who stand on street corners and shove documents into our hands, transferring their written word to us almost as quickly as we transfer it to the trash. If it's handed out on the street, we think, it isn't worth knowing. Perhaps if they were handing out stone tablets, we'd think differently.

Or what of this: *Check out the new guidelines from God* #Moses #Ten Commandments. Or this: *Follow me on Twitter* #God. What if we awoke one morning and found the Ten Commandments spray-painted on the wall of an inner city slum? Would we value them?

Revere them? Would we still think they were sent by God? Would we lampoon, ridicule, and belittle those who thought so? God wouldn't waste his time with the inner city, some would say. Even then, the most likely outcome would be that someone would snap a picture and Instagram it, send it to the cloud so it could be closer to digital heaven, while we all sit around and wait for God to go viral.

I flipped through my notebook. On page after page, I saw the words I had created, created in my image, imagined in my mind, written in my hand. Only a few days ago, I could think of nothing else but telling this story. But watching the messengers practice their craft and rehearse their rituals, and seeing them now as strangers from a foreign world, I thought differently. Would I ever tell this story? Should I ever tell it? Whose story was it? Was it ever mine to tell? I wasn't sure.

I wondered what sort of story I would write, if I ever decided to turn these words, notes, scribblings, and sketches into a coherent narrative. Would anyone believe these things really happened the way they did? Would people find them uninteresting, improbable, impossible? I could probably write ten different versions of these events, ten different ways to interpret the archive in my notebook, and there would be no way of anyone knowing which was closer to the truth than another. Or perhaps I should leave the truth out of it altogether, as the one story that remains untold and unnarrated, out of respect for the wishes of my companions, and instead write a beautiful story that was at least believable enough to pass as some truthful version of all that had come to pass. The truth is often better as fiction.

Later in the day Sheriff Lex came over to the gate, the threshold of sanctuary, with something to say. He walked with authority and stood with assumed power. The messengers clearly noticed and had gathered round to hear the voice of authority speak.

—Alright, all of you can come out now, he said. The charade is over.

Inside, none of us were really paying attention to the outside.

—I said all of you can come out now, repeated Sheriff Lex with insistent volume.

This time we all heard. We looked at each other first with apprehension, then with resolve. Was he speaking to us?

—Wait here, said Maria, who then exited to see the man with assumed authority.

—What is it that you want, Sheriff Lex? asked Maria, with the resigned sigh one often gives to a repeat offender, whether they offend criminally or socially.

—The game is over, said Sheriff Lex, with a poorly hidden smugness.

—I was unaware we were playing a game, said Maria.

—I have been informed by the County Assessor, one César Romero, that this here property has never been officially used as a church, said Sheriff Lex with an air of certainty and finality.

—That sounds officious, said Maria. It also sounds pointless.

—Pointless? asked Sheriff Lex with exasperation. The authority of the state of New Mexico has made it clear that this is not a church. If there's no church then there can be no sanctuary.

—On what grounds is it not church? asked Maria.

—On the grounds of the County Assessor, said Sheriff Lex.

—Who is he to make that call? asked Maria.

—He's the County Assessor.

—You already said that.

—Then why did you ask?

—Because that is not my question.

—What is your question?

—Who is he to make that call?

Sheriff Lex was wading into a swift rhetorical current.

—This man of whom you speak, César Romero, continued Maria. Is he the arbiter and judge of whether God is present here?

—Well, no, said Sheriff Lex. He determines the tax-exempt status of religious institutions. This institution never received tax-exempt status.

—So God does not exist until His tax-exempt status has been approved by César? asked Maria.

—Well, when you put in that way—, began Sheriff Lex.

—Is there some other way to put it? interrupted Maria.

Sheriff Lex stumbled and balked.

—Look, he said. The point is that you can't use it as a sanctuary because this church has never properly become a church.

—But we are using it as a sanctuary, said Maria.

—But you are not the original users.

—Actually we are, apparently.

—I mean, you are not using this structure for its original purpose.

—The original purpose of any church is sanctuary.

—It has to be a church for you to declare sanctuary.

—When we declared sanctuary it became a church.

—Not according to the state.

—Tell César he can have all the authority he wants, but whether or not this is a church, that's a matter of God, not César.

Maria moved slightly closer to the gate, eyes fixed on Sheriff Lex.

—A church is made from the inside, not the outside, she said.

Sheriff Lex changed his demeanor and stiffened with irritated incredulity.

—Don't make me come in there, he said.

—You want to violate a holy site? asked Maria. Right here, in front of these people, in front of these cameras?

—If it's not a church it's not a holy site, said the Sheriff, shedding patience.

—Tell me, if I drive your car, is it no longer a police car?

—You threatening to steal my car?

—Do you feel threatened?

—Nothing threatens me.

—I beg to differ.

—Why is that? asked Sheriff Lex, struggling for rhetorical salvation.

—You already know, said Maria.

And then she was done. Maria turned and came back inside, leaving Sheriff Lex to stew and fume while trying to act as if he were neither stewing nor fuming. Cameras were rolling, after all. Sheriff Lex was struggling, that much was clear. What was Maria to him? An instigator? A demon? A heretic? Even so, what of it? The world needs its instigators and demons and heretics. It is the heretics of the world that point out the different and unseen paths that make us reconsider our own. For Sheriff Lex, the law was a perfectly straight line that cut through an endlessly serpentine universe. For Maria, the endlessly serpentine universe was a refuge from those who sought to draw perfectly straight lines. For Sheriff Lex, temptation had to be removed from the world, leaving only salvation in its place. For Maria, salvation could only exist in the presence of temptation. We needed temptation as much as we needed salvation. Otherwise, she often said, there was no point.

Hari returned, announced once again by his most awesome soundtrack, and stepped out of his sonic bhangra machine to offer food for everyone. He had brought food for us, as he promised he would, but he brought food also for the messengers, who were so happy they stopped messaging momentarily. He even brought food for Sheriff Lex and his partners-in-anti-crime. Sheriff Lex refused the gesture, however, lest he owe a debt to our co-conspirator in mischief and malfeasance. When the other two officers showed an eagerness to partake of the fragrantly spiced feast, Sheriff Lex had a conniption, scolding them for their betrayal of the way of the straight line, for falling under the influence of gustatory concupiscence. The law could have no sinners, only saints.

Hari then walked through the gate and entered the church, carrying the wonderful gift of food with the same aplomb as the previous day. There was a certain amount of defiance in the orange turban that adorned his head. It wasn't just orange, it was flagrantly orange, one that offered no apologies and had no reason to give one anyway. It was an audacious rebellion against the relentless emotional inertia toward a drab, colorless world.

—Dude, you own a restaurant or something? asked Si.

—No, not like that, said Hari. This food is all from the langar.

—The langar? asked Jim.

—It's a sort of communal kitchen at the temple, said Hari. All are welcome, no one is turned away.

—And it's free? asked Joe.

—Yes, said Hari. Always vegetarian, too, and always halal, as it turns out. That way anyone and everyone can join us for a meal, which we gladly share.

—Will you share this meal with us? asked Maria.

—Gladly, said Hari. Though only a bit, as I already ate at the temple.

As we ate, Si was seated at the right hand of Hari.

—Dude, can I call you brother? asked Si.

—Only if I can call you Dude, said Hari.

—Dude, that would be epic, said Si philadelphically. Hari thought for a moment.

—Actually I prefer brah, he said.

—Brah, repeated Si. Righteous.

—Dude, said Hari. Epic.

Later, after Hari had left and while Khalil had re-treated for his evening prayers, all of us settled into our own contemplative space. There was an ambient sacrality in the silence of those moments, a time when moving inward and outward came together in ways that only happen in a sacred space. I went up to the loft of the choir and stared out the window, watching only the jagged, mountainous horizon. The sun was setting, and long after it dipped below the line that separated heaven from earth, it sent out a tremendous orange glow, as if somehow trying to carry on Hari's color revolution as far into the night as it could carry us. Eventually the orange glow dissipated, and I thought for a moment that the color revolution had gone into retreat. But as my eyes adjusted to the darkness, I noticed the first star of the night, radiating a faint blue, as if calling to the other stars to join in, which they soon did. Even the darkness has color, if we know where to look. And how to see.

5

On the fifth day, we witnessed how heresy creates faith, and how faith creates heresy, and how neither can exist without the other. We didn't see that all at once, of course. Things rarely dawn on us as quickly as we would like. But at the end of every day, if we would simply take the time to reflect, we should hope to end each day wiser than we began it. Trouble is, most people rarely take the time to reflect, which is why most people struggle with the eternal scourge of inner blindness.

When the day began, the news messengers were setting up their stations, looking both busy and bored in the process. They were waiting for news to happen, seemingly unaware that news is always happening, just not the type of news they wanted. From time to time, the messengers would glance at the church, looking for signs of motion and commotion—anything that signaled that something out of the ordinary had occurred or was about to. None of them had backed down about their versions of events from the day before, nor did any of us expect them to. There would be different versions of the same story, and people would have to sort through them, not to find the truth necessarily, but to find what they believed to be the truth.

There was now a whole new layer of information to deal with as well. While the professional messengers tried to portray events in a certain way, with a specific angle, other everyday messengers had already created their own narratives and counter-narratives. Blogs were churned out incessantly, verbal sparring and acrimony filled the comment sections of countless websites, and memes were created in our own image. Someone had grabbed a photograph of Sheriff Lex in his sunglasses, looking as officiously authoritarian as he could be, from some of the news footage that had been aired. That image was now spreading into ever expanding circles with a myriad of messages attached to it. Overnight, Sheriff Lex had developed a new life as a meme, and thus represented both law and the mimicry of law, authority and the antithesis of authority, though I am quite sure he was blissfully unaware of it at the time. So much time he had spent the day before carefully crafting his version of events, only to emerge into the new day unaware that others had already recrafted his story in ways he could neither imagine nor control.

It was odd to sit and listen to Khalil read different versions of events from various blogs and other texts, knowing they were written about us by people who genuinely did not know and probably did not want to know anything about us. These were *our* lives and *our* events, yet others coveted them and wanted to make them their own. I knew from my previous work as a journalist, and from the lectures I sat through as a student, that many people in the world believed that original events no longer mattered, that we live in a world of representations and texts—representations of texts and texts of representations. Those who pontificated such ideas usually did so with a sense of giddy bravado, as self-styled rebels who thought they were fomenting subversive tact by ridiculing the security and smugness of the very same society from which they sought accolade and attention. Yet these rebels were not rebels at all. They were fools, dolts, and hypocrites. Dissenters who themselves tolerate no dissent are neither dissenters nor rebels. They are illusionists. They offer only the representation of rebellion, an illusion without substance with illusionary results. You can't trust a text, they say, and tell us so in a text they beg us to trust.

A person who drools with delight when discussing representations of poverty, yet is not moved by poverty itself, is a fool beyond fools. A person who confuses the representation of bread with bread itself is not a wise and learned person, but a person who knows only endless hunger. A person who confuses love with the representation of love is a cynical crank who cannot feel empathy for others and yet denies the work of his own hand in designing the architecture of his own loneliness. There's not a rebel among them.

Around mid-morning Brother Hari made his return, heralded of course by a bhangra chorus that rang out rather gloriously in the high desert. Yet this time when he arrived, messenger crews sprang into action and Sheriff Lex did, too. Sheriff Lex had drawn a line the day before, a line that emanated from his own authority as an officer of the law, the protector of the people. He had stated in front of all the messengers that Hari would no longer be allowed to enter the gate, the gate that Sheriff Lex believed he controlled. With the cameras rolling, the question was on everyone's mind—what would Sheriff Lex do?

Hari, however, was unfazed by any of it. He was neither defiant nor impressed. He was a man sitting on a small island in the middle of a large pond, watching all of the perturbations of the pebbles constantly being thrown in the water, acknowledging them yet unaffected by them. Not indifferent, simply unperturbed. This time he had not come alone. He arrived with his sister, whose name, we would soon learn, was Devindra. Like Hari, Devindra had her own spirited ambience about her. She appeared as a steadfast soul, as someone who, if caught in a stampede of cattle, for instance, would be more likely to run along than to run away.

Sheriff Lex had positioned himself in front of the gate. But Hari did not approach the gatekeeper as Sheriff Lex had expected, and instead Hari engaged in a different act that Sheriff Lex had not anticipated. Hari, along with Devindra, began to remove pre-packaged containers of food, and one by one, as Hari had done the day before, they handed them to the messenger crews. No one was overlooked and all received the same package. The messengers were delighted, and in no time the cameras were put away and microphones set aside in order to have a collective feast. Sheriff Lex was certainly perturbed—the guard was caught off-guard. Hari and Devindra spoke with the messengers in their own kind and calm way, telling entertaining stories and explaining the rhythmic joys of bhangra. No one thought this was anything out of the ordinary, no one except for Sheriff Lex.

When Hari and Devindra finally picked up two large parcels of food and headed toward the gate, Sheriff Lex stood up tall and made his stand.

—Put the food back where you got it, said Sheriff Lex. You're not passing this gate today. I won't allow it. Not today.

Hari stood there across from the gatekeeper, offering only a gentle smile, and without a hint of confrontation. Devindra crossed her arms, not as a sign of defiance, but as a show of strength. Before either of them could speak, the messengers came forward to speak for them. *Let them in, let them pass*, they pleaded, still enjoying their feast. *How can you let those inside go hungry?* they asked. Does the law condone this? said one. If it does it's no law, said another.

—It is the law, said Sheriff Lex. The people inside have committed acts that have violated the law, and the law must be upheld for the safety of all.

Hari looked at Sheriff Lex.

—I'll tell you what, said Hari. I'll leave these bags right here. I've got two more in the car, and I'll just get them and leave them here, too. My friends inside are hungry, and surely that is no crime.

Hari returned to his car to retrieve the other bags and put them neatly next to the others. Devindra didn't move an inch, which made Sheriff Lex move backward, though he probably wasn't aware of it. Sheriff Lex remained in front of the gate and glanced at the bags, then carefully resumed his position of looking straight ahead. The messengers had gathered closer. One had grabbed a camera to film the drama.

—Now it's in your hands, said Hari to Sheriff Lex. It's up to you to decide what is more important, the letter of the law or the letter of humanity.

Hari and Devindra returned to their car. Sheriff Lex stewed for several moments, and just when he opened his mouth to say something to the messengers, the sound of bhangra filled the air, leaving Sheriff Lex silent. The messengers waved as they watched Hari and Devindra drive off, Hari's bright orange turban a defiantly bright reply to the darkness of Sheriff Lex's sunglasses.

When the attention returned to Sheriff Lex, and when the cameras and microphones returned to their places of prominence, Sheriff Lex realized that the people were awaiting his decision in the case of the felonious food. What would Sheriff Lex do? The messengers leaned in. Would Sheriff Lex give the food to the messengers? The messengers leaned in, expectantly. Would Sheriff Lex keep the food for himself? The messengers leaned in, dubiously. Would Sheriff Lex give the food to the people inside? The messengers leaned in, anxiously.

The messengers awaited his judgment.

Sheriff Lex eyed the messengers and measured his words.

—It would be a shame for this food to go to waste, he said. You inside the church, if you want, you can send someone to collect the food.

Sheriff Lex then looked intently at the messengers, as camera lenses were adjusted and microphones were put forth.

—But this does not affect the law, he said through clenched teeth.

Inside we had watched all this transpire through the window in the upstairs choir. Now we had to decide who would go out to get the food. We decided that Si would go, for no specific reason whatsoever.

Si went out and made it to the gate, and once there he hesitated. It was clear that he couldn't go beyond the gate, and it was clear that Sheriff Lex couldn't come inside the gate, so there was the predicament of how to get the food across the sanctuary threshold. Si looked at Sheriff Lex.

—Dude, he said.

Sheriff Lex pulled his sunglasses down on his nose just enough to reveal his eyes, focused intensely as they were on Si.

—Did you just call me Dude? asked Sheriff Lex, with authoritative disbelief.

—Yeah, I guess I did, said Si.

—What gives you the right to call me Dude?

—I call everybody Dude.

—I'm not everybody.

—Then I guess you're somebody.

—That's right.

—Well, everybody is somebody.

Sheriff Lex was so puzzled by how he had been lexically check-mated that he hadn't noticed that a young boy whom no one had seen before had walked up beside him, apparently out of nowhere. The young boy grabbed the food and with dedicated effort hoisted one bag and then the other over the gate to hand them to Si.

—Thanks, Little Dude, he said. You're mighty righteous.

As Si took the bags to bring them inside, the messengers rushed to the wall, thrusting their microphones and cameras forward, and hurling questions one after the other. Who are you? What does your group want? Do you have a message?

Si looked at them across the wall.

—Dudes, I am who I am, he said.

—What does that mean? they all asked.

Si hesitated, reflected, and delivered.

—My Dudes, he said, just remember that you can't spell Stone without the One. Once you understand that, you'll understand everything.

Si brought the bags inside, leaving the messengers to scramble, looking for meaningful intent in what was intentionally meaningless.

—We need to be careful, said Jim. If we repeat that phrase often enough, we might start to believe it's a thing.

—You mean, if we're not careful, we could actually fool ourselves? asked Joe.

—You can't fool yourself, said Maria. No one can.

Maria was right. We can fool others, and we can make fools of ourselves, but we cannot fool ourselves. God knows we try. I think sometimes of all the ways in which the world tries to create its earthly heavens, its terrestrial utopias, and if they all have one thing in common, it is the manic desire to rid the world of heretics and live only among those who believe as every other person believes. The believer cannot tolerate the unbeliever. Yet why is the believer so threatened, so discomfited by the presence of the unbeliever? Is it because this is what God wants, only a world of believers? No, it is in fact because the unbeliever reminds the believer that there are other possibilities, other visions and beliefs, other ways of seeing, that might lead to different ends, or even worse for the believer, to the same end. The believer cannot believe that there can be two paths to the same end. There can only be one true path, says the untrue believer.

But here is the irony, the flaw that unravels every utopia, every ideal community ever built from the beginning and as it will be until the end. The believer who cannot tolerate the presence of the unbeliever does so not because of the certainty of his belief, but precisely because of the lack thereof. The unbeliever calls his bluff, shakes his confidence, reminds him that he cannot fool himself, though he may succeed in fooling others. The irony is that the believer needs the unbeliever, for it is the unbeliever who is his true spiritual guide. Belief that is not tested or challenged is not belief at all, but merely ritual, and mindless ritual at that. The heretics and unbelievers and infidels among us make us uncertain, and for that we should be eternally grateful. Uncertainty is the handmaiden of faith, certainty its destroyer.

When I was young I remember hearing the story of Jesus wandering through the desert, and as if the wandering and fasting and relentless thirst weren't bad enough, along came Satan to tempt him in the very moment when Jesus was most vulnerable. When you are a child in a church, the lessons are kept simple: Satan was very bad to do this, and Jesus was very good to reject him. But when you grow older and experience a bit more of the grit of the world, you begin to realize that Jesus was not really tempted so much as tested. You also realize that the story would make for a very pointless story without Satan in it. Had Jesus wandered around for forty days and met no one and never been tested and met only people that already believed in His divinity, the whole episode would have been a waste of forty days. Jesus would be the same person on the fortieth day that he was on the first, and so there would be no point. But Satan came along to test Him, to show Him alternatives and different pathways, easier routes, and in many ways that is exactly what Jesus needed and perhaps what He wanted. Jesus needed to be tested and He had to let Satan test Him. Jesus is transformed in the process, and He is drawn closer to understanding the things He must do for his mission to succeed. It is the obstacle in the path, the thing that tests us, and not the path itself, that allows us to cultivate our faith. Heretics, sinners, saints, and believers cannot exist without one another. They need one another. The architects of utopia too soon forget this. They forget that for any utopia to succeed, it must be intentionally imperfect. The quest for perfection, the quest for heaven on earth, is the dissolution of every utopian quest. If we could create heaven on earth, we would not need heaven. This is why heaven is always heaven, and never earth.

This is also why Jesus taught love more than He taught anything else. Many thought Him a madman, while the priests thought Him a heretic and the authorities thought him an instigator. And why? Because He thought we should forgive our enemies? Make friends with others, asking only for friendship in return? Jew and Gentile, believer and unbeliever, sinner and saint—all were there for a reason, all were on the same quest, whether they knew it or not. *This was blasphemy*, they said. If He were a madman, He could be dismissed as harmless. No one is threatened by a madman, just as no one is threatened by a fool. But Jesus was neither madman nor fool. There was substance to His words, and once those words were put into practice, the judges with their laws that could not be broken and the priests with their faith that could not be questioned and the officials with their authority that could not be challenged—all had to conspire to remove the obstacle from the path. Clear the path, they said, and so they did, and Jesus was put to death. Satan merely tried to test and challenge Him. It took the arrogance of humanity to condemn Him to death. He taught love where others wanted hate. He taught community where others wanted conformity. For that,

Jesus walked a path of endless obstacles right up to the very end, and would never have had it any other way.

The day was tempted by the charms of the night, to which it gradually gave way, only for the night itself to fall prey to the seductive charms of daybreak, but not before first finding its own solitary peace in the dark desert stillness through which it silently wandered.

6

On the sixth day, we contemplated the sound of the end of the world. At least according to one version of how it will all play out, the main event will be harkened by the blast of a trumpet, to be followed in due course by the blast of six more trumpets. What key these trumpets are in, and whether they all play the same note or offer a more polyphonic experience, perhaps combining to make for the most epic power chord ever, is unclear, especially as the sheet music has yet to be revealed. I imagine these must be rather sizeable trumpets, considering they are supposed to reach everyone on earth simultaneously. I must confess that I have always found the trumpet a mellifluous instrument, and so find it an odd choice for the sonic harbinger of the end of time. A better choice by far would be seven electric guitars, perhaps Les Pauls or a even a few vintage Telecasters, run through a Marshall stack, preferably cranked up to eleven, and with plenty of overdrive and sustain mixed in to ensure the message is delivered divinely loud and heavenly clear. But alas, trumpets were the original plan, and so to avoid confusion among those who expect and anticipate the end of the world—lest they think a concert has broken out rather than the apocalypse—trumpets it shall remain.

I do wonder about those who follow other pathways of faith or who have no path at all. What will they make of an indescribably loud trumpet blast? My guess is that their first reaction would be to call local authorities to make a noise complaint, making the end of time more of an irksome nuisance, at least in its initial moments. There's also no rhythm section for the end of time, not even a kick drum or a bongo ensemble, so clearly, dancing would be out of the question for the apocalypse and would probably be inadvisable in any case.

The main reason I started thinking about all of this was that about mid-morning on the sixth day of our sanctuary, a windowless van pulled up alongside Sheriff Lex, carrying a man and a woman whom I took to be junior police officers. They began to set up what appeared to be a haplessly amateurish sound system. First one speaker then another were assembled and stacked atop each other, eventually forming a well-ordered rectangular pattern, and then a few other things were attached and arranged to complete the ensemble. We all watched this with equal amounts of amusement and consternation, until it finally dawned on us what Sheriff Lex was going to do. He was plotting his end game, and the first step in this strategy was one of the oldest in the old book—to resolve the situation with inordinate levels of noise.

I've never seen this strategy work, yet I have seen authorities around the world reach for it repeatedly as if it were the most useful tactic ever devised. Seriously, has any revolution ever been called off because things just got too loud? Has any protest ever been shut down due to the clever deployment of oppressively loud music? If this tactic had any merit to it, concerts would never happen—crowds would flee at the first note. It's a pity this tactic doesn't work to stop war. Only those who have suffered through a war know how horrifyingly loud is the soundscape of war. If only we had no war because war was simply too loud.

To make things worse, Sheriff Lex had also decided to add a new tool to his law enforcement arsenal—the bullhorn. Yes, the bullhorn, the device that can take any voice and make it sound like it's being recorded on a walkie-talkie stuffed in a cardboard tube and broadcast over AM radio into an arena with brutally reflective concrete walls. A voice through a bullhorn never fails to sound like the teacher in the old Charlie Brown cartoons, only with the teacher cast in the role of an aspiring fascist dictator trying to stir up the masses with the special type of blah blah blah that magically excites the hearts and minds of the obsequious and subservient. Idiots of the world unite.

—Wonder what he'll play for us, pondered Jim.

—I don't think it will be Tejano, said Jesús.

—He'll play what he hates, said Maria.

—It might be more effective if he plays what he likes, said Khalil.

—Dude, we should make an end of the world playlist, said Si.

—I'd avoid anything that has trumpets in it, said Joe.

—I beg to differ, added Maria. I would think that if the angel trumpeters heard some Miles Davis, they might be a bit more in the mood for redemption and forgiveness.

Sheriff Lex had picked up his bullhorn, which seemed absurdly unnecessary given that he was twenty feet away, and began his announcement, surrounded as he was by the news messengers who were quite eager to film this strange spectacle.

—This has gone on long enough, squawked Sheriff Lex. I have shown great patience over the past several days but my patience is reaching its end. I'll give you sixty seconds to give up or else we will commence enhanced auditory procedures.

—Enhanced auditory procedures? asked Joe, bewildered.

—It's sort of like being annoyed to death, said Joe.

—It's a sonic apocalypse, said Maria, shaking her head bemusedly.

We waited out the sixty seconds with a bit of resignation and anticipation, much like the fate of a condemned prisoner, provided the prisoner had been sentenced to ordeal by extraordinary nuisance. I think we were all curious to see what sort of auditory malevolence was about to be unleashed, what sort of playlist Sheriff Lex would think to be so unbearable that we would rather walk out and surrender than stick to our beliefs and principles.

Sixty seconds later, Sheriff Lex lifted the bullhorn to his mouth once again, which let out a loud crackle followed by intense feedback, after which Sheriff Lex briefly lowered the device and glared at it in anger, as if the device should somehow have seen the error of its ways. Then Sheriff Lex resumed his spectacle.

—Your sixty seconds has expired, he shouted, clearly not understanding that the point of a bullhorn is so that you don't have to shout.

—Commence the procedure, he shouted through the bullhorn to the junior officers standing right in front of him.

One of the junior officers, aspiring perhaps for the title of world's most unimpressive dj, pressed the button on his phone to launch the sonic onslaught, except that no one heard it except him. He had forgotten to connect his phone to the sound system, leading to some muffled laughter among the news messengers, and a bit of muted fuming from Sheriff Lex.

—Commence the procedure, shouted Sheriff Lex again, as if the first effort had never happened.

The junior officer again pushed the button, and this time a wall of sound emerged that left us utterly impressed with its volume and utterly perplexed with its sound.

—ABBA? asked Maria. Really?

Yes, the first weapon of choice in the arsenal of Sheriff Lex's end game, the first volley of sonic violence designed to shake us from our refuge, was none other than "Dancing Queen." All of us struggled to understand the thought process by which anyone might have thought this would be the ultimate opener in a playlist of authoritative power. Perhaps since it was about a queen, it represented authority? Yet it's hard to take authority seriously when it is dancing. It's hard to take anyone seriously when they are dancing, unless they happen to be an authoritarian dance instructor. No one is going to stop if they are told to freeze by a police officer, if said officer is simultaneously engaged in a demi-pointe pirouette, no matter how well-executed, or a foxtrot with his or her partner, no matter how elegant or well-timed the routine may be. Watching a police officer do a Buddha float might cause an assailant to freeze, but more out of catatonic astonishment than authoritative obedience. Personally I would have figured Sheriff Lex for an ABBA fan, not openly so, more like a person who shows disdain for it in public company but in the evening with the shades drawn and the lights down dances wildly around, singing every word of every song, badly out of key and madly unaware of it. On top of it all, ABBA are palindromatically-named—the name being the same forward as it is backward—and anything that ends the same way it begins and begins the same way it ends is in a whole separate class of awesomeness.

It wasn't long before all of us were tapping our feet and swaying to the music, not necessarily because we liked the music, but because it seemed the most entertaining way to resist and endure what was now referred to as The Procedure. Maria expectedly danced full of grace, while Jesús had unexpectedly good moves. Jim and Joe had only awkwardness in every effort they made, but they were aware of their awkwardness so their efforts came across as both genuine and genuinely amusing. Khalil did not dance, but from time to time I detected a fluid nodding of the head that appeared to have the sway of rhythmic oscillation. I merely observed and took everything in, as was my usual mode of operation.

The second song was a tune by Justin Bieber, which at first made no sense and seemed horribly disconnected from the surprise opening by ABBA, and led Jim to opine with considerable amusement that perhaps the songs were arranged in alphabetical order. When the third song proved to be from Creed—assuming that Creedance Clearwater Revival was filed under G for Good by Sheriff Lex and was thus left off the doomsday soundtrack—and the fourth from Def Leppard, we all realized that the ludicrous had become the real, even more so since the song that followed Korn turned out to be from Ludacris. Even in his efforts to create sonic mayhem, Sheriff Lex could not sway too far from his sense that for all to be right and just in the world, everything had to be just in the right order. The order of the law and the order of the alphabet were both parts of this larger plan for a well-ordered universe.

As Ludacris was playing—by this point we had made a game of guessing what might come next—Si left our perch in the choir and without mentioning a word of what he was going to do, went downstairs and walked outside. Sheriff Lex looked on with excitement—perhaps his well-ordered intentions were about to deliver the results he had anticipated. He signaled to the amateur dj, the junior officer who, like Sheriff Lex, was wearing earplugs, to stop the music, which he momentarily did.

—Is there something you would like to say? asked Sheriff Lex, with an expectant tone that hinted that he in fact knew what Si would like to say.

The news messengers had been through a rough time with The Procedure, and they were happy for the lull of silence and for the moment of drama. They sprang into action, eyes and lenses focused, ears and microphones opened. Si looked out on everything and seemed in that moment to appreciate the absurdity of it all. He then spoke to Sheriff Lex.

—Dude, can you turn it up a bit? We can hardly hear it in there.

Sheriff Lex bristled at the act of insouciance, made evident by the twitch in his moustache and the quiver in the corner of his mouth. I couldn't see his eyes through his sunglasses, but I could see the muscles of his face tighten around the lenses, so it was clear that Sheriff Lex was glaring and scowling, yet doing his best not to let the news messengers see any of it. The news messengers themselves leapt forward with microphones and cameras at the ready, and a thousand unintelligible questions emerged into a cacophony of verbal disorder. They wanted information, any information, anything to make a story, any story.

Si paused momentarily from his leisurely gait back to the entrance.

—Dudes, long live pumice! he shouted.

This was concluded by a new slogan we didn't yet know we had in our imaginary movement.

—Get Stoned!

With that, Si came back inside and rejoined us in our choir perch.

—Get Stoned? asked Joe, tickled.

—Not bad, said Maria with a smile.

Khalil chortled.

—This is far more fun than it should be, he said.

—Is there any other way for it to be? asked Maria.

Sheriff Lex responded to the incident with outrage and vengeance. He ordered the young officer to turn up the volume—again shouting through his bullhorn—ironically and unwittingly fulfilling Si's request in the process. The music resumed and Metallica blared through strained speakers. Sheriff Lex apparently did not understand that Metallica improves with volume the way that wine improves with age.

When we reached Nirvana, however, something happened that none of us could have predicted, had you asked any of us what was going to happen next. A police car entered the church lot and pulled up behind Sheriff Lex's vehicle. A police officer that none of us had ever seen before approached Sheriff Lex and told him something—what it was we did not know. We watched Sheriff Lex's countenance change, and he looked as if he were going to spit on the ground, but chose instead to remove his hat and pound it against the side of his vehicle until he had sufficiently discharged his inner frustrations onto an inanimate object that could neither feel nor understand his emotion tirade.

—Turn it off, he shouted to the young officer, without realizing there was no way for the young officer to hear him.

—Turn it off! he shouted through the bullhorn, without learning the lesson that there was still no way for the young officer to hear him.

He grabbed the young officer by the arm and as the startled officer turned toward him, Sheriff Lex gave the international signal for cutting things off, the double wave of the hand blade to the neck. At first the young officer looked confused, as if he understood that Sheriff Lex wanted something cut off but didn't know what exactly was to be cut. Then Sheriff Lex pointed to the speakers and made the same gesture again, only this time with additional emphasis and animation. The young officer-turned-unintentional-dj reached for his device and a few moments later, there was blissful silence. Nirvana indeed.

Sheriff Lex was beside himself. Sitting inside, we had no idea what had happened. Later we would learn the cause of Sheriff Lex's angry consternation—a local resident had phoned in a noise complaint, and as it turns out, Sheriff Lex had in fact violated the local noise ordinance. Sheriff Lex had violated the very law he claimed to protect and enforce. There was disorder in the world, and Sheriff Lex had been the cause of that disorder. He was once again in the murky and discomfiting world of grey, the world where black and white are no longer possible, the world where compromise holds more sway than absolute order. It was a world that Sheriff Lex hated and had always tried to avoid. And here he had created his own grey-toned apocalypse.

Yet it's only in the grey world where we can find any hint of true justice and true faith. Maybe one day

Sheriff Lex would see that, or at least come to terms with it. We humans are highly imperfect creatures, living as we do in a world that gives us many difficult questions and few easy answers. The beauty of the world coexists with hideousness. Indescribable kindness coexists with unspeakable cruelty. Order with disorder, justice with injustice, triumph with defeat, joy with despair. It is only folly and arrogance that lead us to think we can find a way out of this, to resolve this, to control this. It is sheer madness to think that we know what God wants, what side He has chosen, what path He prefers. The law is no different. There are a thousand reasons why a poor man might steal a piece of bread. What the law can't understand is that the real crime is his hunger.

We sat there in reassuring silence for quite some time. After so much noise, the silence was a sonic refuge. Clouds moved in and there was neither sun nor shade, and the afternoon moved toward evening without any discernible moment when one fell into the other. Though none of us said a thing, we all had the feeling that something was about to change. An unexpected wind blew through and I could see the moon. I wanted it to mean something. It had to.

7

On the seventh day, the world became still and quiet. Not the entire world, mind you, just ours. After the previous day's carnavalesque events, the morning felt exceptionally gentle and quiet. None of us felt any rush to speak, and we started going about our various things with dedicated mindfulness. We all became aware of the silence and agreed it was exactly the right way to decorate the day.

—Silence to sunset? asked Maria when we were all in the kitchen.

—You mean, a vow of silence? asked Joe.

—No need for a vow, said Maria.

—A mindful day is a good day, said Khalil.

—What are we supposed to be mindful of? asked Jesús.

—The things that come to mind, said Maria.

—I don't understand, said Jesús.

—By sunset you will, said Maria.

We had already gotten into the habit of being silent during the times when Khalil prayed. At first we thought we were just being respectful, but as each day wore on we realized that Khalil's prayers were giving us an empathetic lift to reflect on our own inner lives. We could pray, we could think, we could meditate, we could daydream, we could saunter, we could read, we could write, or we could just be still. The point was to become aware of the time that passed and to give it meaning, or better, to understand the meaning it already had.

There is a depth to silence that you cannot understand until you find it. I remember a fellow journalist back in New York who had signed up for a ten-day retreat, a spiritual cleansing, as she called it, which she felt was exactly what she needed after a particularly exhausting string of stories that had taken an emotional and physical toll on her. Part of the cleansing involved staying in silence for the entire ten days. To my co-worker, that sounded positively blissful, a chance to turn everything off and just be for a few days. She left on a Monday and on Tuesday was back at work. When I asked what happened she appeared distressed and agitated and didn't want to talk about it. Only later did she confess that the silence was the one thing she could not bear. Most people, when left alone with themselves, don't like the company they keep.

None of us had bothered to look outside as morning opened, but we all became aware of the sounds of birds singing in the trees. We had not heard that sound in several days, as the news messengers had brought with them considerable noise, including a continuous and persistent hum from the electronic equipment and power generators. We walked up to the choir and looked out the window and discovered that the news messengers were gone, or at least had relocated to a distance. At the edge of the church compound, where the entrance met the open road, we could see the unmistakable yellow tape that marked a police line. Both the news messengers and the spectators that had gathered to see the spectacle they hoped to see were now pushed back behind the line. It's an imaginary line, really, one backed up by the power of law, because in reality, it's just tape. On the inner side of the barrier of authority were now only police—Sheriff Lex and his vehicle, and two other police cars, each with two officers. There were nearly as many of them as there were of us. Thankfully they had the yellow tape of authority to keep the peace.

There was incessant online chatter about everything we had done, as well as some speculation about what we would do. Some wanted peace, some wanted conflict, some wanted the police to let us go, some wanted the police to never let us go, and some wanted Waco. There was considerable speculation on the meaning of *pumice*, as Si had mischievously shouted just to stir things up. Someone had even created a website that claimed to outline the central beliefs of the movement—which of course didn't exist—and conveniently had a link where one could make monetary contributions to support the movement and further its non-existent agenda. Later, long after all of these events had come to pass, I learned that the founder of the website pocketed a handsome sum of money from those who wanted to believe, leaving many people, including myself, in disbelief.

The website claimed that pumice, or Pumice, was a secret society of religious devotees. No one seemed to question why a secret society would have a public website explaining that they were a secret society. Speculation was rampant as to who might be on the list of members. Some said the Pope himself was among the select. An artist claimed to have found evidence of a pumice-like material in Da Vinci's illustrative magnum opus, The Last Supper. Talking heads and pontificating pundits were eager to weigh in on all of this, perhaps because the only people who knew anything remotely resembling the truth, which would be us, were intentionally silent.

I was reading through all of the endless links and stories on Khalil's phone, shaking my head in some moments, and offering a slightly sighed laugh in others. Maria, who was busy writing things in her notebook—the sound of her pen scribbling intensely on paper was pleasantly palpable in the silent air—was amused by this, as she knew very well what was circulating out there. Even if she didn't know for certain, she could guess with exquisite accuracy. She had a gift of intuition, a sense of things. But for me, it was disturbing to think that there were so many people in the world who wanted to say things that shouldn't be said, and so many other people who wanted to hear things that shouldn't be heard. The deceiver needed to deceive, and the deceived needed their deceiver. For every person who wants to seduce, there is always someone else who wants to be seduced.

Jim spent the quietude reading. He had rummaged through a few boxes and found what looked to him like a good book. I don't remember what book it was but I could tell from the way he was reading that it was most certainly a good novel. People read different kinds of books in different ways. People reading a good book on history or politics will focus their eyes and purse their lips, often running their fingers gently down the page as if it were the smooth nape of their lover's eager neck. People reading a bad book on the same will furrow their brow and slightly raise one side of their mouth, as one does to show disdain and disbelief toward an incompetent thief caught in the act. People reading bad fiction, on the other hand, such as the kind filled with secret codes, cretinous conspiracies, or some other such insipid nonsense, often become lithe and melancholy, lamenting the lost moments of life they can never reclaim, fretting over the seemingly limitless capacity of humankind to be duped by the enfeebled words of hacks, lackeys, and scriveners. People who read good fiction, however, no longer move among us. They exist in a different world than ours, a world where waking life and deep-sleep dreams coexist and intermingle. No one knows when or how that moment occurs. They enter their separate, fictional world unaware that they have crossed over. For a time they are lost to us. Jim had entered that world, for he appeared radiant and transfigured, and for the whole duration of his otherworldly existence, a world that was his alone to experience, peace was upon him.

Joe spent his day in the world of imagery. There were images all around the church—in the rooms of the compound, some on walls, some leaning against walls, some in boxes, some leaning against boxes. Joe was intrigued by these images, images that were to him familiarly Catholic and yet not so. The style of the Maronite images rendered the familiar unfamiliar, and yes, the doves were there as he might have expected, but the rooster and the peacock? Why were they there? Joe wandered from image to image in the style of the slow rhythmic dance of the art aficionado, moving from image to image, painting to painting, sculpture to sculpture, stopping at each for nearly the same amount of time—never too short a time so as to appear uninterested, never too long a time so as to appear confused. Joe moved with a different purpose that day, and began to see things he had never seen before, things that perhaps no one else had seen either. Anyone can look at art, but very few can see it. In the quiet of the afternoon, Joe discovered the difference between looking and seeing, and in that moment, peace was upon him.

Jesús sat down in front of a window and looked out on the world. At first I thought he was looking out the window as he thought of what he might do with his silent day, but then I realized that looking out the window was precisely the thing he wanted to do. Jesús was going to watch the day go by. And really, how many of us can say we have ever watched an entire day for the thing that it is? Jesús watched the light change from moment to moment. He listened to the sound of the wind, even when it was a gentle whisper. He watched the sunlight reflect off the grass, the glass, the leaves, the stones, the water—all in different ways, all in different colors. He watched the birds fly among the trees, and he watched the ants move along the earth. He watched the blue sky change from one hue to another, and the white clouds change from one shape to the next. Jesús seemed lost in thought, perhaps in a daydream. The world made him dream and he dreamed of the world, and in discovering the endless beauty that exists in any day and every day, peace was upon him.

Si immersed himself into the deep waters of music. Some might say this violates the premise of a quiet day, but the premise of a quiet day is that the silence goes from the inside out. There can be no pretense of controlling or obstructing the sonic flow of the world from the outside in. Even the most isolated hermit must hear the world as it is—the buzz of the bee, the muffled ruffle of the mouse, the hallowed cry of the hawk. The point of inward silence is not to stifle sound, but rather to be in the presence of it, to feel its temptation and to remain steadfast in the grasp of its affective allure. Si had found some CDs of religious music, and was listening to the music on a fax-machine era CD player in the office, through his headphones. I could not hear what he heard, but I could watch him as he heard it. To watch a person listening to music is to understand the emotional gravity of music. Every religion in the world knows this emotional gravity, which is why every religion in the world has had to come to terms with music. Some religions have tried to harness it, seeing the ecstatic impulse as something that moves us closer to God, while others have tried to suppress it, seeing the ecstatic impulse as something that moves us further away from God. Si moved to the emotional timbres of the music in his ears, letting them move through his mind and body, struggling to understand how the ordering of sounds can translate into feelings that have no object other than themselves. Spiritual music was not Si's preference, but on that day it was, and Si heard things he had never heard before. As he journeyed through the quiet afternoon, Si finally understood the difference between hearing the world and listening to it, and when he did, peace was upon him.

Khalil spent the quiet of the day in spiritual reflection and devotion. He was inclined to that path anyway, so he was following his inclinations further and deeper than perhaps he otherwise would have done on any other day. I watched Khalil at prayer. I had never really paid attention to the intricacies of prayers, and what impressed me most was to watch Khalil go through the various motions—the standing, the bowing, the sitting, the prostrating—and give each movement and each gesture the sort of meaning one normally gives such things when they are still new. Khalil performed a ritual as an anti-ritual, consciously avoiding mindless repetition, constantly embracing mindful action. His every movement was meditative, his every word contemplative. I could see his mouth move, uttering the words of his prayers in silence, each word imbued with meaning but bereft of sound. Khalil prayed alone but seemed in communion with all things and all people. In solitude, or together with a million others, Khalil was the same man. There are few who walk this earth who can say the same. Khalil finished his prayers, and stood contemplatively for a moment. He looked upwards and smiled the way one smiles when one sees an old friend, and in his prayers and in his thoughts, peace was upon him.

Maria spent the quiet of the afternoon sketching in her notebook. I could see her from time to time, engaged in long periods of inaction, her eyes struggling to envision the image she already had perfectly in her mind, her hands struggling to recreate that image faithfully on paper. There are always things lost in the translation, as any artist knows, but there are many other things found there as well, things that the visionary did not know were there initially. I could tell when she felt the image on the paper had come close to the image in her mind for she would evince a furtive smile, and the furious motions of her pencil would recede to a gentle scrawl. There was a struggle at play here, as Maria worked to make her sketch match her imagination, but over time, her imagination reconciled with her sketch, and accepted the sketch for what the imagination thought it had really been all along. In the moment of her imaginative reconciliation, her aesthetic intuition took form as material creation, something was now there that was not there before, and seeing that it was there, and seeing that it was good, peace was upon her.

We retired to sleep early that evening. It was dark out, but perhaps not yet night. Maria turned the last light out, and in that transitional moment when the eyes adjust to the darkness, struggling to recover a world that has momentarily disappeared, there was a voice that broke the silence.

—Maria? asked the voice.

—Yes, Jesús? replied Maria.

—You were right, he said.

—About what?

—I understand now.

I could not see Maria in the darkness, at least not clearly, but knew somehow she had the same furtive smile I had seen earlier.

—I know, she said.

We fell to sleep, each hoping that the silence of the night would bring to us the same enchantments as the silence of the day.

8

On the eighth day, we saw how easy it is for darkness to steal a victory over light. That's certainly true for the great cosmic battle between the forces of light and the forces of darkness, but in our case, the battle was a bit more parochial, though I'd like to think in some small way it still carried the drama of its more cosmic counterpart. We were awakened in the morning by a rather loud pop, one of those sounds you notice because it doesn't remind you of any other sound. We looked around, and the morning light that hinted of the day it would soon become showed us nothing at first to make us think something was amiss or awry. It was only when we went to the kitchen and turned on the light switch that we realized the problem.

—Electricity's out, said Jim without reason for concern.

—Is it out everywhere? asked Joe.

—Don't know, replied Jim.

We went round the rooms, flicking switches and checking things. Nothing was working. Khalil checked his phone.

—There's no report of a power outage, he said.

—Do we know where the breakers are? asked Joe.

—I'll find them, said Jesús, leaving to find them.

Jesús returned a short while later with his report.

—Nothing is thrown, he said.

Maria entered the kitchen where we all were sitting in the opaque, indirect light that struggled to reach us through the windows of the other rooms.

—It's Sheriff Lex, she said.

Maria turned the light switch up then down.

—He's cut the power.

There was a palpable sense of gravity in her words. Something far beyond what those words could carry had been brought into the room. She knew it, and when she said it, we all knew it, too. There was certainly a sense of finality, of some sort of ending that simply had to be. Not in the sense of impending death or a sudden awareness of mortality—nothing like that. We became deeply aware that things were going to come to an end in one way or another, but we were also equally aware that, even if we didn't know what it would be or what it would look like, there would without fail be another beginning after the end. Indeed, sometimes the end *is* the beginning.

I also remember thinking that this was such an uninteresting way to bring this odd and peculiar standoff to an end. The water had not been cut off, so at least we had that. But now that Hari could no longer bring us food—we told him not to risk crossing the yellow police tape of authority—we were running dangerously low on provisions. We were in no imminent danger of starvation or thirst, but we knew we couldn't hold out forever. Unlike an action film where the clock starts ticking—oxygen is running out, a bomb is about to explode, a gunfight erupts and everything ends in a definitive hail of bullets—this seemed more like death by slow inconvenience, and even then, without the death. Electricity was not essential to life. I knew that because I had survived many an outage while I lived in New York, some of them brought on by forces of nature, some of them brought on by the dubious electrical wiring of my apartment.

—Check the phones, said Khalil.

None of us had thought to recharge our phones, as electricity is just one of those things you assume will always be there. When it disappears, things that sit in the background move to the foreground, afterthoughts become imminent thoughts. The batteries in our phones were all very low, and now, with no way to recharge them, we only thought of why we had let them become so low. Foolish of us not to imagine a different future, a different possibility of the way things would unfold. Our battery indicators were all in the red, reminding us of the pressing need to do what we could no longer do, to breathe electric life into their dying cells.

—Turn off the phones, said Khalil.

Joe walked over to the office and picked up the phone. The landline didn't work when we arrived and it certainly wouldn't work now, but Jim apparently felt the need to be unnecessarily thorough. Or maybe it was his way of preparing for something.

—Nothing, he said.

Jim pondered for a few seconds, looking down and askance at nothing in particular, then walked straight out the door to the gate. Sheriff Lex approached calmly with what I remembered being a slightly higher level of smugness than he normally carried about.

—Sheriff Lex? asked Jim.

—Yep? came the reply.

—There's no electricity.

—Yep.

—This your doing?

—Yep.

—Any chance of getting it back?

—Nope.

—So this is your move?

—Yep.

—Your endgame?

—Yep.

—Think you'll win?

—Yep.

—Funny.

—How's that?

—None of us do.

Jim came back inside.

—You were right to say that, said Maria with gentle sincerity. We will prevail.

—Do you really think so? asked Jim, doubting his own words.

—There's no other way this ends, said Maria.

Maria had more faith in Jim's words than Jim did. Jim had boasted to Sheriff Lex as a show of strength, but in his heart he clearly feared his words might be a bluff that Sheriff Lex could call at any moment.

—What if he calls our bluff? asked Jim, to us and to himself.

—There's no bluff to call, said Maria, without a trace of doubt.

For me, though, there was still a hint of uncertainty, of anxiety. The day before, in watching the others find their place and find their space, I could not find mine. Watching others find peace did not bring me peace, only a desire to have a peace that I did not yet have. I had wandered around the church the day before, searching for something in the silence, something inspirational, something aesthetic, something meaningful, something that would show me the path that others had already found. But that revelation never came. I was still a restless soul. Not even a weary pilgrim with so many more miles to go. A pilgrim who could not find the path. A pilgrim in search of a pilgrimage.

In the evening, as the light evanesced into a periwinkle dusk that in turn conceded to a twinkly night sky of constellational candelabras, Maria had us gather in the church. She lit a single, solitary candle, around which we all gathered.

—Let us each tell a story, she said.

—What kind of story? asked Joe.

—Something from the heart, said Maria.

—About ourselves? asked Jesús.

—There is far more in the heart than just the self, said Maria. Otherwise there would be no love in the world.

—Dudes, who wants to go first? asked Si, intimating in his question that he did not want to be the first.

We sat there, all of us in a circle facing the candle. The flame flickered from time to time, casting fleeting shadows across the room and across our faces. Lines appeared and disappeared on our faces, silhouettes fluttered on walls like spirits who had come to listen. The candle then settled into a perfect stillness. There was deep silence and no wind.

—I'll go first, said Jim into the still silence.

Jim told a story of his mother. More specifically, the story of how his mother died from cancer, and the slow, agonizing process of how she made the difficult journey from life into death. He described cancer as if it were a separate entity, something inherently ugly, something soulless, relentless, indifferent. Something that thrived on death, something could not live without it. For the first time in his life, said Jim, he had come across something that could only be evil.

—It made me question a world I had otherwise seen as inherently good, he said.

—The doctors did what they could do until there was nothing left they could do, he continued. People told me it was God's will, that God had a plan we simply could not discern. But my mother lived a good life, and then died such an ugly death. The world seemed so unkind, so unfair, so intentionally cruel. She kept her faith until the very end, but when she passed, for the first time in my life I doubted the very existence of God. It's why I left to wander. It's why I wander still.

Jim finished his story, and again there was silence and stillness.

—Dudes, said Si into the silence. I'll tell you a story, but only if you promise not to laugh.

—Why would we laugh? replied Khalil.

—Because it's about a kitten, said Si, staring at the still flame burning in the middle of our circle.

—All living things are creations of Allah, said Khalil. Not just us.

—This happened many years ago, said Si. I've never told this story to anyone.

I heard Si tell the story of a kitten, a stray kitten that wandered like a mendicant, who one day for no other discernible reason than chance crossed paths with a group of young boys with too much time on their hands and too little love in their hearts.

—They were my age, said Si. I knew them.

Si wandered into their path, too, also by chance, and found them in a circle, in an open lot, the kind where children would play because they could imagine it to be any place they wanted it to be. When Si came upon them, they were animated, with raised voices, worked up in a brash racket. Only when Si approached did he see what they were doing. In the middle of the circle was the stray kitten, meowing frantically, wanting to roar but still too young and too small to do so. She wanted only to escape. But the young boys had sticks, and they kept poking the helpless kitten. When Si arrived, they had already drawn blood.

—I begged for them to stop, he said. But the more I begged, the more determined they became. One of them raised his stick high above his head and crashed it down on the kitten with all his might. The kitten let out a sound I will never forget. It was not a natural sound. It was the sound of pure pain and suffering. The boy had broken its back legs. The kitten crawled frantically on its front legs, but the boy had already raised his stick again. I jumped into the circle and kneeled over the kitten, taking the full brunt of the stick on my back. The other boys flailed on my back, too, until one of them told me to move aside. They wanted to finish their mission, but I wouldn't move. Their frenzy decayed into a lull, then they left, frustrated and angry.

Si stopped his story for a moment, for his voice had waivered.

—I carried the kitten home, he continued. I asked my parents to take her to a vet, but we didn't have the money. I took the kitten to my room. I did everything I could to help her, to save her, but she was dying. She knew it, and so did I. She kept looking at me with this expression on her face. She would never understand why or how these things were done to her. She looked to me as if she needed an answer, but I had none to offer. Her whole, short life on this earth had been one of pain and suffering. All of it. I could not understand this. I could not accept this. It was beyond me. I still see her expression, everywhere I look, every day of my life. I wanted to have an answer. I didn't then, and I still don't now. I'll never stop trying, but sometimes, I feel weary.

Si finished his story, and there was stillness and silence.

After some time, Khalil told a story of why he left Lebanon, of how he lost Lebanon and Lebanon lost him.

—People fell in love with themselves, he said. They fell in love with their identity. The more they loved themselves, the more they hated others. The more they turned to their religion, the more they turned away from God. The whole country went blind.

—Do you think you'll ever go home? asked Joe, after some moments.

—I am home, said Khalil pensively.

A brief pause.

—You know, he added. I make my *mujaddara* with Hatch chilies. Now I can't eat it any other way.

Joe told a story of dislocation, too. He told of his life growing up on a reservation, of the day he felt his roots come loose.

—One day I looked out across the land and had this itch to see everything that was not where I was, he said. I wanted to leave and see the great wide world. My friends and family disowned me, thought I was abandoning my roots. Only my mother understood. She knew I wasn't abandoning anyone or anything. She understood that you never know the meaning of home until you leave your own. You can't find meaning in things until they first lose their meaning.

Jesús spoke into the silence about a man he had seen many years ago on the streets of Santa Cruz in El Salvador.

—This man was very ill, he said. I didn't know his disease, but he was shaking uncontrollably, his whole body. He could not stop. He couldn't hold anything. He couldn't feed himself. He couldn't speak. He couldn't even beg. He lived on the street. He knew no one and had no family, or perhaps his family would not have him. People would sometimes put money beside him, now knowing what else to do. But mostly they would walk around him. I thought to myself, Was this man simply waiting to die? What was the purpose of this man's life? What sort of world was this? I could not understand. I still see this man's face. But I still cannot understand.

Maria spoke last. She reached for her notebook and pulled out a folded piece of paper. On the paper was a sketch of a young girl, with an expression on her face that I would struggle to describe—perhaps raw hope.

—This is what I made on the day Khalil asked us to write out what we were fighting for, she said. This picture is my story. It is everything I want to share tonight.

—Do you think one day you will tell the story of all that has happened here, during this time together? asked Jim.

—I don't know, said Maria. If I did, I'd have to write it as a novel. Nothing else would do. I certainly couldn't write it in first person. That would be too arrogant. I'd have to invent someone, a narrator, perhaps, to tell the story, to see myself through someone else's eyes. That's if I told the story at all. Which of course I won't.

There we were. Each of us lepers in search of a healer. Each of us healers in search of a leper. A world of lepers and healers, the sick and the weary, the tired and the hungry. A world of so much suffering, so much pain. Yet we all pushed onward on our own way, never giving up, even in the face of a world that every day gives us an endless list of reasons to do exactly that.

The night turned to silence, save for a few rebel crickets. The flame surrendered to darkness, save for a stubborn ember at the end of the wick. I don't remember the story I told that evening, or maybe I do and just don't think it something I need to share. But as I fell to sleep that night I remember thinking about Maria's words. If Maria ever did tell our story, what role would I play in it?

9

On the ninth day, the end was near. The news messengers were long gone, off to create other stories, to spin other tales. Whatever curious crowds had come to gather were now curiously gone, as the yellow-tape police line made it all but impossible to catch a glimpse of the church. Even if you could, it wasn't like we were outside building barricades. Building barricades makes for good drama, of course, but it usually makes for a bad rebellion. The best rebellions are the quietest ones.

Sheriff Lex had put his endgame into play, and an endgame it certainly was. The only question was whether we were to go out on his terms or ours, and none of us had any intention to go out on any other terms than our own. We had just enough food left for the day, and even if we had had more, it probably would not have been fit to eat after another day.

We had water still, and that kept us going and kept us clean, but without food there was no way we could continue much longer—one day at best. So yes, the end was near, but when exactly would it happen, and how? None of us knew. No one in the world knew. Sheriff Lex thought he knew, but he didn't.

—We should spend the day cleaning, said Maria.

Her statement came out of nowhere. There was no conversation it was a part of, no context that hinted or intimated this course of action.

—Why should we clean? asked Jim. This place was a mess when we arrived, and we will be out of here soon enough. There's no point.

—It isn't functional, clarified Maria. It's ritual.

—Why do we need a ritual? asked Joe.

—We don't need a ritual, said Maria.

—We don't? followed Jim.

—To need a ritual is to depend on the ritual, said Maria. To depend on a ritual is to develop a habit.

—Dude, are you saying it's wrong to have habits? asked Si.

—No, said Maria. Habits are fine. But they are done mindlessly. Rituals must always be mindful acts. Otherwise they are merely habits.

—So how do we mindfully clean? asked Jesús.

—Cleaning is a habit, said Maria. Cleansing is a ritual. We will cleanse this place and when we do, we shall cleanse ourselves.

—Why do we need to cleanse ourselves? asked Joe.

—It's not about us, said Maria. It's about the Spirit that lives here. We came here seeking refuge and sanctuary, and we found it. We have been safe here.

—So how does cleansing help that? asked Jim.

—It doesn't, said Maria. It's a way of showing gratitude to the Spirit that has kept us safe.

—It's a sacred space, added Khalil, perfectly in tune with Maria. We should offer it the respect it deserves.

I will confess that as I write this, I now understand Maria's words. They are as clear to me as the slow flowing water of a high desert stream. But then, at that time and in that moment, I struggled. I, too, had habits, and I thought of my habits as rituals, and my rituals as habits. They were ways of ordering the day, ways of marking the space. They put me at ease. They offered harmony where there would otherwise be noise. They offered comfort where there would otherwise be uncertainty. Yet here was Maria telling me that if I needed them, they were habits, and if they were habits, they could not be rituals. Rituals were something different, something special.

I hadn't had a cup of coffee since the electricity had been cut off. I thought of making a cup of cold coffee, using tap water and instant coffee, but as I contemplated doing so, I felt pathetic and desperate. Coffee was a habit, something I leaned on in certain moments of the day, especially in the morning, and without it, I let my irritable moods loose, as vengeance on a day that had really done me no harm. I stood there in a darkened kitchen, with a spoon, a mug, a sugar packet, and a jar of instant coffee, and realized I was not in control of this rhythmic pattern. Rather, that pattern was in control of me. It wasn't me who had let loose my irritable moods when my life patterns were disrupted. It was they who let themselves loose. I was too weak to stop them. Yet on that day, after listening to Maria, I put everything away, and decided there would be no coffee, not on that day, not on this day, and not on any other day—not until coffee became something I wanted and not something I needed. It's the difference between a man who feels he has to pray at noon versus a man who wants to pray at noon. From the outside, no one would see a difference. But inside, everything is different. The man who needs to pray is looking to find order. The man who wants to pray is looking to find God. The former is looking for comfort. The latter, for meaning.

I remember years ago, before all of these events happened, when I was still working as a journalist, I had an idea to write an article on Pavlov's dog. People always refer to Pavlov's dog every time they become aware of an unconscious habit. But with my journalistic curiosity, I wondered—who exactly was Pavlov's dog? Did she or he have a name? It turns out that this wasn't the easiest information to come by. Why we should know Pavlov so well but hardly know anything of his dog somehow seemed wrong to me, since it is the dog, and not the scientist, to which we refer when we invoke the connection. Pavlov in fact had more than one dog, lots of dogs, in seems—about three dozen or so. So why is it, I wondered, that we refer to Pavlov's dog, and not to Pavlov's dogs? We had incorrect and incomplete information, yet even with this new information, no one I interviewed felt right referring to Pavlov's dogs. It had to be Pavlov's dog. What was incorrect sounded correct, and what was correct sounded incorrect. I eventually found the names of all of Pavlov's dogs, and came to the conclusion that the whole affair reveals as much about Pavlov as it does about his dogs.

One of his dogs he named Chinggis Khan. Chinggis Khan? This was either a great insult to the Mongol leader or a great tribute to the dog. Another was given the highly un-Russian name of Jack. There had to be a story behind that, too, but I couldn't find one. The best names on the list, however, at least as far as I was concerned, were Rijiy I and Rijiy II. It was as if Pavlov had just given up. He couldn't think of another name for his dogs so he opted for numbers. I decided to write the article from the perspective of Pavlov's dogs, who no doubt had their own questions about Pavlov, this strange man obsessed with watching them eat. *Why is it that every time this guy wants to feed us, he has to ring that Godforsaken bell? What an idiot!* Pavlov, like all of us, had a day just as full of odd habits as did his dogs. Whether the story is told by the dogs or told by Pavlov, it turns out to be the same story.

My editor decided not to publish the article, on the grounds that readers might be upset if they were reminded of just how much their lives were filled with unconscious, unnecessary habits. He also didn't feel comfortable with the possibility that dogs could have a perspective, let alone tell stories. On the other hand, I also remember that my editor always drank a lot of coffee. He also smoked furiously, didn't like dogs, and looked suspiciously like Freud. People sometimes told him his face rings a bell. Every time someone told him that, he always reacted the same, angry way.

In the kitchen, in the cupboard below the sink, we found all the cleaning materials we would need. And of course we found them there—it's the most habitual place to store them. No one ever looks for bread under the sink. There was a broom in the closet, which Maria took to quite fondly. I think it was something about the sweeping motion that she liked—it was like a graceful, rhythmic dance. The rest of us fell to our roles quite naturally. I was always struck by how well we found our tasks in everything we did. We never planned anything and yet there was always a plan.

We each set to work in separate rooms. Only Khalil and Maria were working on things that involved the whole compound. Maria was sweeping each and every room, and Khalil was cleaning each and every window in each and every room, including the windows of the church itself. I do remember looking out one of the windows and watching Sheriff Lex, who was of course watching us. I couldn't help but think how puzzled he must have been, watching Khalil clean the windows. It's not the kind of thing one would expect to see, and Sheriff Lex preferred a world where expectations remained firmly within the boundaries of what a person could normally expect.

All of us remembered the words of Maria, that this was meant to be a mindful ritual, not a mindless task. As I cleaned, I felt the church in ways I had not done before. I ran my hands over the surfaces. I touched things and became aware of textures. I felt things and became aware of patterns. I remembered things that I thought I had long ago forgotten. I felt like a blind man reading a world that was entirely cast in braille. There was meaning in everything. I felt for the first time in a very long time that peace was something I could find, one day. I was very aware that I was still a restless soul. I wasn't there yet, but I felt a hint of something stirring, like a promise to myself that there would be a time when I could find my way home.

I looked at each of my companions as they went about their own rituals. What was going through their hearts and minds, I did not know. But like me, there was a tenderness, a gentleness, and even a hint of grace in each of their movements. Maria swept with slow, purposeful motion, as if each sweep of the broom was its own little ritual, as if each motion brought new meaning into the world. Si was cleaning the kitchen floors, down on his hands and knees, his hands pushing a towel in small, uniform circles, his eyes focused as if he were seeing images in the floor that no one else could see. Jim was washing the mirror above the sink in the restroom, polishing the surface with every pass of his hand, staring both into the mirror at his own image and far beyond the mirror, to a place that only Jim knew. Joe was gathering up the carpets and rugs, feeling each one, almost caressing, seeing that each carpet and each thread was different in its own way—no two were worn the same way, no two bore the same tears, stains, frays, or tangles. Jesús was dusting all of the places that never get dusted, searching for the places that are overlooked and forgotten, finding the places that no one finds, thinking only of the things that no one thinks of—the awkward corners, the hidden undersides, the narrow gaps, the odd shapes, and the difficult contours. Khalil cleansed every window until he was sure the window was no longer there, until he saw his reflection, which made him reflect as he stared through the window until his reflection was no longer there.

—Now that's a big spider, exclaimed Jesús, breaking through the spell of our ritualistic day.

We all came over to see the spider, which was indeed very big. Jesús must have stirred it up as he was dusting, and now, there it was, in the middle of the floor, surrounded by all of us. We all crouched down to have a closer look at it. The spider noticed us, and seemed to lean on its back legs, as if to stand, or perhaps to fight.

—You have to admire that, said Maria.

—Admire what? asked Jim.

—The way the spider stands her ground.

—How do you know it's a she? asked Joe.

—I don't, said Maria. But I know how she feels.

—She's actually quite beautiful, said Khalil.

—Want me to take care of it? asked Jesús.

—How do you mean? asked Maria.

—You know, get rid of it. I mean her.

—You mean, kill her? continued Maria. On what grounds?

—It, I mean she, could be poisonous, said Jesús.

—*Could* isn't a reason, said Maria.

Maria regarded the spider, and the spider in turn regarded her.

—Even if she were poisonous, she said. She's not threatening anyone.

—Dude, I can take her outside, offered Si.

Si went to the kitchen and returned with a glass and a plate. He gently set the glass on top of the spider, then slid the glass onto the plate. Si stood, and brought the spider, now in her temporary refuge, close to his face. He stared at the spider, marveling at her subtle colors, her appearance, her existence. Si looked into her world, as she looked out on ours. They had a moment, then Si walked outside, set the plate down and lifted the glass. The spider hesitated, unsure of her new environment, then scurried off into the grass.

—She'll find her place, said Maria, quite sure.

—Now we just need to find ours, said Jim.

We returned to our various acts, our cleansing rituals of the day, and easily returned to the same entranced, enchanted mood we had been in before our encounter with the spider. It is difficult to describe the emotional ambience of a ritual done with intent and meaning, this liminal space far beyond habit. A place where ritual is only ritual. We were cleaning without cleaning. There was effort without effort. One action flowed into another, and each action we found only in the moment of finding it.

The rhythmic sweeping of Maria's broom had stopped. The silence called attention to itself. She had moved on to a new project, that of trying to make some sort of ordered sense of all the half-opened and helter-skelter boxes that seemed to be in every room. The way they appeared made it impossible to guess if someone had been unpacking to stay or packing to leave. There was no tangible pattern and no discernible order in the contents of the boxes or in their placement, and so Maria devoted herself to the process of trying to recreate an imagined order, of taking things back to their moment of origin, to discern the original intent of what we now had before us. If any of us had any hope of doing that, it would be Maria. She was the one who could see things no one else could see, to see things before anyone else could see them.

About an hour after that—it may have been longer or shorter, as my sense of time passing on that day was exquisitely distorted—Maria walked into the church, at a place where we could all see and hear her, and made an announcement.

—I know how everything will end, she said with power and poise.

—You do? said Jim, intrigued and surprised.

—When did that happen? asked Jesús.

—Just now, said Maria.

—Are you going to tell us? asked Joe.

—I can't, said Maria. Not now. Not yet.

Maria stood there for a moment, resonant with resolve.

—I need a phone, she said.

We scrambled for our phones to see if any power remained in them.

—Mine's dead, said Joe.

—Mine, too, said Jim.

—Dude, I've got nothing, said Si.

—I have something, said Khalil. It's deep in the red, but there's probably enough for one phone call.

—That's all I need, said Maria.

Maria took the phone from Khalil and looked at it intently.

—I need for all of you to trust me, said Maria.

We looked at one another and it was clear that we all trusted Maria. None of us could imagine any other way for things to be.

Maria then took the phone and retreated to the office and closed the door behind her. She came out a few minutes later.

—Is it set? asked Khalil.

—I don't know, said Maria. Your phone died before I could finish.

—Who did you call? asked Joe.

—I'd rather not say, said Maria.

—What's going to happen? asked Jim.

—You'll find out tomorrow, said Maria.

—Are we leaving? asked Jesús.

—You'll find out tomorrow, said Maria.

—Dude, should I be worried? asked Si.

—You'll find out tomorrow, said Maria.

Maria stood still for a moment, looking slightly downward, deeply retreating in her own thoughts.

—Tomorrow, she said.

She smiled slightly as she left the room.

10

On the last day, the world came to an end. Not the whole world, of course. Only the world we had created, there, in our place of refuge and sanctuary. This was the closest thing I had had to a home for a long time, and I'll admit at the time I was both sad and nervous to feel it was coming to an end. But end it did, though I must say that the way it ended was yet another of Maria's exquisite miracles. None of us had any idea of the way the day would unfold at the start of the day, but by the end of the day, it had all been simply glorious. I can think of no other word and no other way to describe it.

In the morning, after we were all awake, Maria called us to the kitchen. There was one piece of bread left, one piece of *naan* to be specific, left over from the last time Hari had brought us food. We had water, and Maria had poured seven glasses. With the *naan*, Maria broke the bread into eight pieces, and gave each of us one piece. She was standing at the table, while we all sat, bread in hand, water on the table.

—And the eighth piece? asked Joe.

—It's an offering, replied Maria.

—To whom? followed Joe.

—To Whomever.

Maria walked over to the window and opened it wide. It appeared that she whispered some sort of blessing, though what she said is forever lost except to Those who received her offering, which she threw out the window with the same agile grace with which she moved through life. Sitting around the table with her, with each other, we slowly came to the moment of acceptance, when fear begins to dissipate, and when sadness lingers and momentarily saturates the soul. Yet we appreciate that sadness for what it is—the sacred residue of love. A life without love offers the alluring promise of a life without sadness, yet a life without love is the saddest sadness of all.

These were my companions. It was only in the tempest of sadness that engulfed me as we sat to eat our bread together, our last meal in this place of refuge, that I fully understood for the first time that I loved these people. I learned I had the capacity to love. I had doubted that for so long. I felt the stirrings of a heart that could love, and a soul that one day could find peace. The enemy of love is not hate but forgetfulness, so as we sat at the table, I promised myself I would remember this moment and these people for the rest of my life, for in so many ways they made me what I am. Eternal remembrance is an act of love, and any act of love is its own rebellion, and so at that table, at that moment, in the company of my companions, I found my purpose. I launched my own rebellion from within. I didn't have all the answers—I didn't then and I still don't now—but out of this moment of ending I discovered a beginning, and a beginning was the best place I had been in a very long time.

Maria cleaned the table and also the glasses. We all offered to help but this was her ritual to perform—she had made that clear. When she was done, she called us all into the church. She joined us there carrying a box, one of the many boxes that were lying around the compound and one of the boxes she had gone through in the cleansing rituals of the day before.

—I found these yesterday, she said.

Maria reached into the box and pulled out what at first looked like a nondescript pile of highly unfashionable clothes. But as she unraveled them and placed them on the pew behind her, it became clear what they were.

—Costumes? I asked.

—Yes, said Maria. Costumes for the Nativity.

—And what are going to do with them? asked Joe.

—We are going to wear them, said Maria, her voice gentle yet insistent.

—Wear them for what? asked Jim.

—You'll see, said Maria.

Maria was smiling a smile that only true faith can bring. The rest of us, if we were smiling, were smiling a smile that only incredulity can bring. Yet each of us took a costume and each of us retreated to a separate place to put on the costume we had taken. When we were finished and had regrouped in the church, Maria had us line up side by side. As we stood there, Maria then walked around the compound, opening every door and every window, even walking out to the gate with the big chain and the small lock to pull it open as widely as she could. The small lock didn't hold and the two sides of the gate opened wide with a rusty creak that sounded mournful and joyful at the same time. Lastly Maria walked over to the wooden gate through which we had first entered this holy place ten days ago. She pushed the gate open as wide as she could. The entire place was now open to the world.

Sheriff Lex had noticed all this movement, and had come nearer with a walk that suggested caution, curiosity, and confusion.

—You coming out? asked Sheriff Lex, now moving closer.

—Not yet, replied Maria.

—But you'll be surrendering today? asked Sheriff Lex.

—Surrendering? asked Maria. How do you mean?

—Surrendering to the law, said Sheriff Lex, with a certain insistence on the last part of the phrase.

—Then no, said Maria. We will be coming out to-day, yes, and we will certainly surrender, just not in the way you imagine.

Maria returned to the church. There was a beau-tifully cool breeze blowing through the entire com-pound, now that it was completely open to the world. Maria went to change into her costume, and then, looking at the sun to guess what time it was—none of us really knew for sure—she turned to us, and placed her hand over her heart.

—It is time, she said.

She led us to the open yard in front of the church and had us line up side by side, facing the same direc-tion. Maria was dressed as Jesus, Jesús was dressed as Mary, Si, Jim, and Joe were the three magi, and I was dressed as a shepherd. There were only six costumes, and Khalil was the only one without one.

—Sorry about that, said Maria.

—I'm a Lebanese Muslim man standing outside a church in the high desert of New Mexico, said Khalil. What costume could I possibly need?

A sense of anticipation suffused the scene. There was a thick silence that surrounded us, and as I recall, there was not even the sound of birdsong. The gentle breeze softly rustled both grass and leaf, but beyond that, there was a stillness that I would almost describe as dramatic.

—What's going to happen? asked Jesús.

—Wait for it, said Maria.

—What if it doesn't happen? asked Jim.

—Why think about things that might not happen? countered Maria. Only when they don't happen should we think about them.

—I don't understand, said Jim.

—I can't explain, said Maria.

We stared into the indefinite distance, looking beyond Sheriff Lex, mostly because that was what Maria was doing. She was searching for something, looking for a sign, though only she knew what it was that we should be looking for. After what seemed like a long while of scanning the horizon—though I am sure I am remembering it as longer than it actually was—there came one of those moments when you know that something has changed, though you don't know exactly what it is that has changed.

A faint dust cloud appeared on the horizon, almost imperceptible at first, little more than a wisp—something you might see out of the corner of your eye, except that I was seeing it straight ahead. I though at first it might be an illusion, something other than what it appeared to be. But no, a dust cloud was certainly there, and it was slowly but relentlessly becoming perceptibly bigger, until it threatened to turn into an actual dust storm, one of those things that insurance people like to call an Act of God. The plumes of dust gently rose to the sky—later people would say the skies darkened but I don't remember it quite like that—and slowly I could hear the din of distant voices, the volume of which rose quickly from murmur to clamor as surely as the dust rose toward the heavens.

Sheriff Lex had now turned round to face this. Though I could not see his face, I could only imagine it held an expression of profound disbelief.

—On any other day, I would be afraid, said Joe.

Traipsing through the trees, flowing through the flowers, rallying over the rocks, sauntering over the stones, vaunting through the valley, gallivanting over the grass, marauding through the meadow, meandering down the mountain, running through the river, careening by the creek—by all means necessary and by all routes possible came running a veritable procession of humanity, a cacaphonic caravan of compassion, if you will (and you must), dressed in what I can only call a carnivalia of costumes. How can I describe the wonder that I saw? There's really no need to describe every single thing, even if I could, for I have no aspiration to describe every little aspect and facet of a scene, as if to convince you that you were there when clearly you weren't. A few descriptive snippets will suffice. If you feel you need more, use your imagination.

There were throngs of Marys, crowds of Jesuses, some carrying crosses, some wearing thorny crowns, one wearing what looked like a regular crown, and more than one wearing a Guy Fawkes mask. There were men dressed as Tibetan monks, and there were actual Tibetan monks, too, chanting calmly as costumed chaos flowed around them. There were too many saffron robes to count, and a respectable showing of pink ones as well. There was a whirling dervish who seems to have waited his whole life for this one moment, such was his radial glee, and there were at least a dozen Hindu gurus, blessing everyone and everything they came across, including a white rabbit that leisurely hopped through the crowd as if this whole thing were standard fare in the life of a white rabbit. I saw people dressed as Jedi knights yielding light sabers, except for one who was carrying a child dressed as Yoda. One woman defiantly stood wielding a yoga mat, which she twirled gallantly as if it were a gentler sort of light saber. I saw a man dressed in white robes with a white flowing beard, walking slowly as he leaned on a sacred staff. Not sure what religion he was but he did his best to look holy. There were Hare Krishnas, because of course there would be Hare Krishnas, and elsewhere there was an a cappella group wearing fedora hats and singing show tunes and calling themselves the Harry Krishnas. There were witch doctors and also witches, none of whom needed a doctor, and there more than a few Doctor Whos and Hortons hearing Whos. There were priests and pirates, a man wearing a leisure suit in what I could only hope was an act of sartorial irony, four women dressed as different stages in the life of

Elvis, one man dressed as an oversized leprechaun skipping about and throwing cereal on everyone and babbling incessantly about hearts, moons, stars, and clovers, and at least one person on stilts dressed as Abraham Lincoln and, if my sense of smell served me right, smoking what locals in those parts like to call the mountain herb. There were fairy princesses with magic wands, Tinkerbells of every shape and size, and a gentle troupe of ecstatically elegant Elsas who were clearly eager to let it go. There was a Martin Luther and also a Martin Luther King, Jr., who had a brief but awkward encounter before embracing one another, and one dashing gentleman who may or may not have been Patrick Stewart.

The flood of humanity descended upon us, flowing through the gates and entering the grounds of The Cedars of Lebanon. Sheriff Lex was surrounded by this sea of people, which he tried in vain to part as he stood atop his vehicle, wielding once again the bullhorn of authority, to no avail of course, since no one could hear him and even if they could, they wouldn't listen. He was far too preoccupied with losing control of the situation to notice the moment when the seven of us slipped into the costumed crowd and followed the flow right out of the church, straight out into the great wide open, and back to the source from which all these people came. Everyone went their separate ways, and in no time the silence had returned, leaving behind

only an empty church and a solitary Sheriff Lex standing atop his vehicle, bullhorn in one hand, hat in the
other. I have no idea how long he stood there, but my
guess, or my hope, is that it was a mighty long while.

We had hitched a ride with a group of the revelers,
in a minivan that desperately needed to be cleaned,
much like the man who drove it. Maria told them
precisely where to drop us. To this day I do not understand how so many cars and busses and vans and
people could assemble like that without giving any
hint away until the moment when it all began. I suppose there are some things best left unquestioned, and
if they are questioned, left unanswered. We didn't talk
much at first, but then the people in the van began to
realize who we were.

—You're *them*, said one of them, in the tone one
might use when meeting a superhero, whether an actual superhero or an actor who plays one.

They exchanged excited but whispered chatter.
One of them had a question for us.

—The stories, I have to know…are they true? she
asked, clearly hoping they were.

—What you believe of them, replied Maria full of
grace. That much will always be true.

This answer pleased them all greatly, for they took
it as the confirmation that it wasn't. The stories did not
have to be true for their faith to be so.

They dropped us at a point that would be difficult to find, with or without a map. Two dirt roads

came together in an unnecessary intersection, which for some reason had a yield sign placed so that you didn't know which way it faced. Not that it mattered, as the sign had also been properly defaced in the tell-tale manner of bored suburban youth. A sticker that read Love Animals Don't Eat Them had been placed over the word Yield, and over the sticker someone had scrawled Bacon Lives.

Hari was waiting for us at the intersection, in his Bhangra Brothers van. He got out to greet us.

—You made it, he said, clearly happy to be able to say that.

—Nothing else we could do, said Jim.

—Brah, said Si.

—Dude, said Hari.

We all walked toward Hari's car, but then Maria stopped me. She turned to speak with me face to face.

—We need to go, she said.

She paused, looked down and then looked directly into my eyes.

—You need to stay, she said.

I was unprepared for this moment. The others had stopped. They sensed what was happening.

—You are all my brothers, I said to them, surprised by the emotion that those words unleashed in me.

—And you will always be my sister, I said to Maria.

—No, said Maria. I am more than that. One day, when you find your peace, you will know what I am to you.

—I want to go with you, I said.

—You can't, she said. Not yet. You have a story to write.

—What if I get it wrong? What if I don't remember everything?

—No matter how you write it, it will be the right story.

Maria still looked into my eyes, and I into hers. I felt like a child and wept gently.

—Andrew will be here soon, she said. He will take you where you need to go.

—He's the one you called, wasn't he? I asked.

—Yes. It was he.

We stood there facing each other. I did not want that moment ever to end.

—Will I ever see you again? I asked.

—You need to learn to have more faith, she said with a gentle smile.

—In you?

—In everything.

She kissed me gently on the forehead and walked over to get into the van with the others. They drove off, kicking up dust that lingered and drifted in the arid air. The winds carried the dust up into the heavens, and just as effortlessly let it rain down from the sky. Slowly I was bathed in red ashen dust and black dusty ash. I had to close my eyes to shield them, and with my eyes closed I stood and felt the dry rain of dust and ash cover me. When I opened my eyes, it was as if the world had been created anew. Flowers opened, birds sang and called, creatures of all kinds scurried across the warm desert sand. Light illuminated the land and the world was filled with color. I took a deep breath and everything became still and quiet. Something had changed. In the distance I could see the mountains.

Made in the USA
Middletown, DE
11 August 2018